# FIREBREAK

### Spark: Book 2

## T.D. WILSON

authorHOUSE®

*AuthorHouse™*
*1663 Liberty Drive*
*Bloomington, IN 47403*
*www.authorhouse.com*
*Phone: 1 (800) 839-8640*

*Published by AuthorHouse   09/29/2018*

*ISBN: 978-1-5462-6210-7 (sc)*
*ISBN: 978-1-5462-6209-1 (e)*

*Library of Congress Control Number: 2018911611*

*Print information available on the last page.*

For Nahum

# CONTENTS

# *ACKNOWLEDGEMENTS*

I would like to thank my family for being so strong and supportive through this entire process, and for always believing in me that I could make my dreams come true. Thank you to Elizabeth Plake and Faith Sehon, for reading the rough drafts and telling me the honest truth, and to my wonderful husband - you are my rock.

# *PROLOGUE*

Kermit, TX

It was late October, and Jess Sheffield couldn't even pretend to be interested in her book. She sat on the porch swing in the late afternoon, dangling her feet. She was fifteen years old, with sandy-brown hair and freckles from the west Texas sun. Inside the house, her father, Arden, typed away at his laptop. The faint tapping sound of the keyboard had been going on nearly constantly all day… well, all year.

Jess looked out at the gray, dead grass and dirt that stretched to the distant horizon. It all looked lonely and desolate. A gravel road led right up to their yard, which held the only green that could be found for miles; a month after they moved into this house, Arden planted a small vegetable garden where he grew tomatoes, cabbage, kale, rhubarb, and squash. He built a white-painted arbor hung with bougainvillea and philodendron, and two mesquite trees grew by the fence. It did look pretty, even if it accentuated how dead everything else around it was. Overhead, the sky was pale blue, almost white with dust and haze.

The typing noise inside stopped and Arden's chair scraped back. Jess looked back over her shoulder and saw him get up and wander to the tiny kitchen for more coffee. It was twenty minutes past his promised break time. He poured his coffee, then paced the floor while glancing periodically back at the screen.

"Dad?" Jess said through the window screen. "Are we leaving soon?"

"Hmm?" he grunted, then looked up, bleary-eyed. "Oh, yeah. Are you ready?"

"I've *been* ready," she replied, annoyed. "And I'm starving. Can we go, please?"

"Alright, alright... I just wanted to finish that one thought."

"Sure, Dad."

Jess sighed. He always "just wanted to finish that one thought." But to her relief, he set down the coffee, then jammed on his boots and took his hat off the rack. He stepped out onto the porch and blinked in the sunlight, stretching his back. He was a tall man, with a barrel chest and broad shoulders. His arms and neck were well-tanned from his work outside in the garden, and his beard was streaked with silver.

"Well, let's get going then," he said with a sigh.

He descended the steps and crossed the yard to the truck, a 1967 Ford pickup, and Jess followed. She climbed in, but as Arden opened his door, he paused to look back at the horizon.

"Huh," he said thoughtfully.

"What's wrong?" Jess asked.

"Looks like a thunderhead," he noted.

Jess stood on the passenger's seat to see over the roof of the truck. To the east, the sky had grown dark. Clouds had gathered, swirling into a shape like a snowy mountaintop; thick, gray haze showed underneath where the dust had been kicked up by the wind. Directly overhead though, the sky was still clear, and the sun was beginning to set behind them.

"Will it rain?" Jess asked.

"Wasn't supposed to," Arden said. "Forecast said sunny days til Friday."

"Hmm."

Arden shrugged, then got in the truck.

"Maybe it'll blow over," he said.

The engine started up and they eased out onto the gravel road. A hot breeze blew in through the open windows. It was Wednesday, and Jess and her dad always went to Jimmy's Diner for dinner on Wednesdays. A thirty-minute drive lay ahead of them to town; the single-lane gravel driveway fed them onto a long stretch of highway, and Jess put on her sunglasses as they cruised.

"How was your book?" Arden asked her, breaking the silence.

"Alright, I guess."

"Did you finish it?"

"No, I still have like three chapters left, I think."

"And? What do you think about it?"

"I don't know," Jess said with a shrug. "It's just not that interesting."

"It's *Jane Eyre*," Arden said incredulously. "It's a classic. Girls love *Jane Eyre*."

"Well, not me," she replied, crossing her arms.

"You didn't like Jane Austen, or *Island of the Blue Dolphins*, or *The Great Gatsby*... these are important books, Jess. You have to appreciate them, at least, right?"

"Sure, I just don't like them. They make us read the most boring books at school. I want to read something with - I don't know, just a little more going on. Something exciting."

Arden gave an exaggerated gasp of shock. "You're killing me. You're hurting my soul, you really are."

Jess grinned as Arden slapped a hand over his chest and winced, feigning a wound. Outside, the storm drew nearer. The clouds swirled deep purple and blue. The shadow cast by the truck almost met the darkness that gathered beneath them.

"Wow," Jess remarked, leaning forward to peer at the sky overhead. "That looks really bad."

Arden glanced away from the road and nodded.

"Yeah, it does."

"Should... should we go back home? Wait it out?"

"No, I think it'll blow over," Arden mused.

He seemed relaxed, as he always did. Arden never got excited; Jess wasn't sure his pulse could ever get above eighty-five. She decided not to worry and sat back, watching plumes of dust chase each other across the road. Wind buffeted the truck from the side and the vehicle jerked, but Arden quickly righted their course. The clouds continued to advance and soon the sunset faded, plunging them into a sepia darkness. Arden switched the headlights on, and that's when the cannon sounded.

At least, Jess thought it sounded like a cannon. A great boom shook the windows of the truck, reverberating in her ears.

"What was *that*?" Jess cried. "I didn't see any lightning."

"Me neither," Arden said, eyes slightly widened. He gritted his teeth as he gripped the steering wheel, keeping the truck on the road.

The wind picked up speed, whistling loudly; there was no rain, only dust churning in the air so thick that Jess could barely see twenty yards ahead. She had seen dust storms before, but this... this was something different. And through the mud-colored fog, Jess saw a figure. He wore a scarlet coat and tall riding boots; long, black hair blew around his face. Gold buttons shone on his coat that was open and flapping in the wind, revealing a white shirt soaked with blood. She saw all this though she glimpsed him only briefly as he staggered down the edge of the road before they passed him.

"Dad, stop!" she shrieked.

Arden slammed on the brakes, and the truck screeched to a stop. Jess was rocked forward and braced her hands on the dash.

"Are you okay?" Arden asked breathlessly.

"I think so," Jess answered. Her heart pounded, but she didn't think she was hurt.

"What the hell was that?" Arden inquired, craning his neck.

Cold air blasted them as he opened the door. He immediately sprang from the truck, plunging into the windstorm, his hat still on the dash. Jess watched him through the back windshield running to the man, whose chin was held high though his cheeks puffed with effort. Seeing Arden coming, he raised his arms, then stumbled and fell forward.

"Jess, get over here!" Arden's voice reached her, small over the wind's howl.

She opened the door and climbed out; her knees felt weak as soon as her boots met the asphalt. She was wearing shorts and a t-shirt, dressed for a sweltering Texas afternoon, but the air was cold. Freezing cold. She took a deep breath and ran, clumsily and arduously, to where Arden knelt forty yards away. The man lay face-down in the road, one arm under his body. Arden took him by the shoulders and turned him over as Jess arrived and she stopped dead. She had never seen so much blood.

"Looks like a stab wound," Arden said, shouting over the wind. "It went clean through to the other side."

His long black hair stuck to his face and neck with sweat, and his cheeks and lips were gray. He looked young, maybe a few years older than Jess. *Not a man,* she thought. *A boy.* His eyes were closed, but his lips moved.

"What's he saying?" Jess asked. The boy's voice was barely audible.

"Don't know," Arden answered. "It's not English, that's for sure. Not Spanish or French either."

Jess looked around, hugging herself against the cold. The dust churned around them and she realized the wind was blowing in circles. She squinted up at the sky, expecting to see a funnel cloud or a twister somewhere, and she felt very small and exposed. There was nothing around for miles.

"How'd he get here?" she wondered aloud. "Where'd he come from?"

Arden gazed around silently, his eyes narrowed against the dust.

"Maybe we'll see a wrecked vehicle on the way," he replied. "Come on; let's get him in the truck."

"What?"

"He's hurt bad, Jess," Arden said firmly. "And he's just a kid. We gotta get him to hospital. Call 911."

He removed the boy's coat, then took off his own shirt and tore it in half. One half he wadded up, then pressed it into the wound. Then without another word, he lifted him up in his strong arms and carried him to the truck. Jess began to follow, pulling her phone from her back pocket and dialing, then she paused. The boy's red coat still lay on the road. She picked it up as she put the phone to her ear, then jogged after Arden. The coat was surprisingly soft, like mink, yet incredibly heavy as if it had lead weights in the pockets.

Arden reached the truck and paused as she opened the door, then laid the boy in the back of the cab.

"I can't get a signal," Jess reported, static sounding in her ear.

"Damn," Arden muttered, then he handed her the other half of his shirt. "Ride in the back with him. Hold this over the wound, press it tight, and make sure he's not jostled too much."

Jess obediently climbed up and squeezed herself in next to him. His lips were still moving, but she couldn't hear what was said. His blood had already soaked the bandage that Arden had improvised; it oozed between her fingers, dark and sticky, but she kept her hand in place. The boy's coat was draped over the passenger's seat now, its gold buttons catching her eye. She wondered if the buttons were what made the coat so heavy, but who wore solid gold buttons on their coat? There also appeared to be tiny, sparkling rubies and emeralds lining the fringe of the collar. Whoever this boy was, he was clearly wealthy… maybe the eccentric kind of wealthy, judging by the rest of his odd wardrobe: his shirt was a strange, stiff cotton, and his boots came up to his knees. But why was he here, out in the middle of nowhere?

The truck jolted as it hit a pothole, and the boy's eyes fluttered open. Jess gaped, her blood running cold. His eyes were solid red; they lacked any pupil. Stranger still, they glistened with a silvery sheen, like the scales of a fish. Then they closed again as his head sagged against the window. Jess' heart hammered in her chest, and she wondered if she'd only imagined it.

A mile down the road, the truck left the shadow of the storm clouds. The wind ceased, and the golden sunset flooded over them. Jess looked over her shoulder, out the back windshield. The thunderhead began to dissipate as the dust settled. Within a minute, the sky was clear behind them.

They reached the Winkler County Hospital and Arden screeched to a stop in the emergency bay. The boy's skin was white and clammy now; his breath was barely detectable. Arden jumped out and opened the back door of the truck; by that point, emergency technicians were already running out to meet them. Jess climbed down as they rushed in and she was told it was okay to let go of the bandage. They pulled the boy out of the truck and loaded him onto a gurney, then wheeled him inside.

"Come on, Jess," Arden told her, wrapping an arm around her shoulders and pulling her along.

They followed the gurney inside until it disappeared through the wide double doors. Jess stood in the middle of the waiting room, staring long after the doors had closed. She felt dazed. *Did all of that really just happen?*

Arden answered some questions at triage, and one of the dozens of people in scrubs showed her a bathroom where she could wash her hands. When she finished and returned to the waiting room, Arden stood there wearing one of his gardening shirts from the truck.

"Ready to go?" he asked.

"Now?" she said with surprise.

"They got everything they need from us. We can go."

"Okay," Jess said tentatively, and followed him outside.

When they got to the truck, she opened the passenger's side door and saw that the boy's coat was gone.

"Where'd his coat go?" she asked Arden.

"I checked it in at the desk," he answered. "It belongs to him; we can't keep it."

*Of course not,* Jess thought. She didn't know why this bothered her.

They got in the truck and turned out of the emergency bay, then out onto the road. Jess watched out the window as the orange and pink sunset began to fade into darkness. Arden switched on the headlights again and drove them ten minutes down the road to Jimmy's Diner, then pulled into the parking lot. Halloween decorations hung in the windows, and cotton cobwebs covered the shrubs along the sidewalk. Arden turned off the engine, then rubbed his eyes. He took a deep breath then looked at Jess. His forehead was shiny with sweat.

"Are you okay?"

She nodded. "I think so."

"That was something else," he said, shaking his head. "I'm sure it's a lot to process. Nobody should ever see something like that."

Jess nodded silently.

"We don't have to eat here," Arden told her, putting a gentle hand on her shoulder. "We can go home, if that's what you want. I'd understand if you're not hungry anymore, or just need some time -"

"No, we can go in," she said, finding a cheerful tone. "I'm hungry."

He gave her a long look. "Okay," he said.

They went inside and found their usual table. Suzie, a plump, middle-aged waitress with bright orange hair came over wearing a broad smile.

"Evening, Arden," she said in her sing-song voice. "Howdy, Jess. What can I get for y'all?"

"Just some coffee for now," Arden answered. "Make sure it's hot."

Jess really didn't feel hungry at all; in fact, she felt nauseated. But, she had insisted they come here, so she gathered up some resolve and forced a smile.

"Grilled cheese sandwich, and fries," she said. "And a Coke."

"Alrighty, I'll put those in," Suzie said airily and sashayed away.

They sat in silence for several seconds. Arden watched the sunset through the big window, his chin in his hand. Jess folded her hands to hide their quivering.

"Dad," she said suddenly.

"Yes?"

She hesitated. She knew she was going to sound crazy, but the mystery weighed on her mind.

"Where do you think the boy came from?"

"I don't know," he answered. "I supposed he might have been robbed and left out in the desert. Or, maybe he ran away - who knows? Either way, it's a terrible thing that happened to him."

"Will he make it?"

"It was a pretty bad injury," he said sadly. "If we got him there in time, he might have a chance, but it'll be a tough fight."

Jess appreciated that he never sugar-coated things. Like her mother's illness; he told her the facts straight, no matter how badly they hurt.

"Dad, I saw his eyes."

He gave her a quizzical look.

"He opened his eyes, and there was something wrong with them... they were red, completely red."

"Like, bloodshot? Honey, that's not unusual. Think of what the poor boy might have gone through -"

"No, they were red. Really red. He didn't have any pupils, and they were covered in something shiny, like scales."

Arden furrowed his brow. Now she was beginning to hate how utterly calm he was.

"Jess, you might have *thought* you saw one thing, but whatever it was, there's probably a rational explanation."

"Like what, Dad? And did you see his clothes? Who dresses like that?"

"I don't know, Jess," Arden said gently. "Why is this bothering you so much?"

She fell silent, unable to give an answer. The questions chased themselves around in her mind, and she couldn't let them go. But before she could say anything else, Arden's cell phone buzzed in his shirt pocket. He pulled it out, and placed it to his ear.

"Hello?"

Suzie came back with their drinks and Jess mouthed a thank-you. She sipped her soda, refreshing her dry mouth. Normally, Arden would be adding loads of sugar to his coffee, but it sat on the table, forgotten. Jess looked up, and saw a thin worry line form between his eyebrows as he listened.

"Are you serious?" he said into the phone.

There was a longer pause as he leaned forward.

"Is that a good idea?" he said quietly. He waited, then nodded. "Okay, we'll be right there."

Then he hung up.

"Is something wrong?" Jess asked, dying to know.

"He woke up," Arden answered. "And he's asking for you."

"What?"

"That was Dr. Boenig. He said the kid's awake. He can't remember his name or what caused his injury, but he's lucid and asking for you by name."

"How would he know my name?" Jess asked, shocked.

"That's what I want to know," Arden said seriously. "He could have heard me say it. I called you over when we picked him up, remember?"

"Okay, but why is he asking for me?"

"They want us to come back so they can find out. They've already called Sheriff Owens and he's going to meet us there."

He slid a five dollar bill under the pepper shaker, then eased out of the booth. Jess followed him out to the truck, and they drove in silence back to the hospital. Sheriff Owens' cruiser was parked in the first space and Deputy Velasquez stood in the second spot. He flagged them down as they arrived, beckoning for Arden to pull in there. They got out, and the deputy shook Arden's hand.

"Sorry about this, Arden," Deputy Velasquez said.

"It's quite alright, we want to help. What's going on?"

"Well, they were rolling him in for surgery when he woke up and started freaking out. Nobody could understand what he was saying, and he was getting hostile."

Arden nodded solemnly.

"Poor kid," he said. "What happened?"

Deputy Velasquez hesitated, then scratched his ear.

"Well, then he looked straight at Doc and started rambling, and Doc tried to calm him down in German."

"Oh?" Arden said, surprised. "So the boy speaks German?"

"The *Doc* spoke German," the deputy clarified. "The kid answered him, and I heard Spanish."

"I don't understand," Arden said slowly. "So he speaks Spanish, too?"

The deputy looked uncomfortable.

"*I* heard him speaking Spanish, but the Doc - who, y'know, barely stepped off the boat - heard German, and the new triage nurse from El Paso *also* heard Spanish, but everyone else heard English."

"I still don't understand," Arden interjected. "Will you get to the point?"

Deputy Velasquez looked away, shifting his weight back and forth in agitation.

"I don't know how else to say this Arden," he said. "We all heard him speaking, but in a different language. All we could agree on was that he asked for your girl here specifically. He was freaking out and wouldn't let anybody touch him, so we didn't have any choice but to call you."

"Alright. Well, take us to him."

The deputy led them through a series of hallways to the doorway of a small room where the sheriff and Dr. Boenig stood waiting for them. He was a fit-looking man in his fifties, with crow's feet around his eyes and well-groomed, graying hair.

There was a window beside the door; through the blinds, Jess could see the boy lying on a cot with an IV tube in his arm. He lay perfectly still; if it weren't for his chest rising ever so slightly and the occasional movement of his eyes under their lids, Jess would have thought he was dead. His skin looked very pale and blue veins showed in his neck and sinewy arms; his chest was bare, and the wound looked inflamed around the stitches that held it together. He had a muscular but compact build, like a runner's, and was also clearly young; Jess doubted that he was even twenty years old. His eyebrows were dark; he had a straight, narrow nose and sharp jawline. His jet-black hair flowed off the pillow beside his head.

"Okay, so before you go in, there's some things you need to know," Dr. Boenig addressed Jess and Arden in his German accent. "He is very… unusual. Arden, did you get a good look at his injury when you brought him in?"

"It looked like he was stabbed with something," Arden answered.

"A very large blade," the doctor nodded. "I measured the wound: the opening was six inches long. The blade entered in through his sternum and went straight through him, out the other side. Oh - I'm sorry, Jess."

"It's okay, I'm alright," she said, disturbed. The image of the boy's bloodied shirt was crystal-clear in her mind.

"Do you want to go wait somewhere else?"

"No, I'm fine," she replied, now with some annoyance.

The doctor looked at Arden, who gave him a nod to continue.

"We were taking him in to surgery when he woke up and started raving. After sedating him, I checked the wound again and it had apparently shrunk by half. He's got stitches now because there was no longer any need for surgery, but it's not enough. His mental state is getting worse, and I fear it's going to keep deteriorating if we can't figure out the problem."

"You mean it's healed? In only an hour?"

Dr. Boenig gave a resigned shrug. "Only mostly, but... yes."

"How is that possible?"

"It's not," Dr. Boenig said, lowering his voice. He leaned closer to Arden, shutting Jess out of the conversation. Jess understood the body language and turned back to the window, though she kept her ears open as Dr. Boenig spoke.

"I really have no idea what this kid is. He burns through the anaesthetic faster than we can administer it. I've never seen anything like it in my thirty years of medicine."

"What, is he on steroids or some other kind of drugs?"

"We've taken blood samples, so we'll find out," Dr. Boenig replied. "I'm on pins and needles waiting for those to come back. And then there's his eyes."

Jess held her breath, listening.

"What about his eyes?" Arden asked.

"They're, um, well, you'll see for yourself," the doctor whispered. "They're not contacts, I can tell you that much. He can see, though *how* is a bigger question."

"What are you talking about, Erik?" Arden said.

"You'll see what I mean," Dr. Boenig replied. "Can Jess handle it?"

"Yeah, she'll be fine," Arden said, giving her a sideways glance.

"What am I supposed to say?" Jess asked.

"Just keep him calm, and try to get him to agree to treatment. We can't keep him sedated, so the best we can hope for is that he'll stay still long enough for us to get near him. Think you can do that?"

"Yeah, I think so," Jess said with uncertainty. *Why on earth would he listen to me?* she thought.

Sheriff Owens, an older man with a pot belly, balding head, and gray beard, opened the door for Jess to enter. The room was cold, or maybe it was her fear that was making her shiver. Arden stood by the door with arms folded while Jess took one step forward, and then another toward the bed; the boy didn't move.

As she drew nearer, the boy's head rolled to the side, and his fingers twitched. His chest rose and fell more deliberately now, and his eyes fluttered open. As Jess held her breath, he craned his neck and those strange, iridescent red eyes fixed on her. Goosebumps rose on her arms. He blinked once, and his dark eyebrows met as his expression became anxious. His lips parted and he spoke rapidly in a language that Jess had never heard before.

"I'm sorry," Jess said, her voice hoarse at first. "I don't understand."

Dr. Boenig's voice suddenly came over the intercom.

"I'm sorry, he's speaking German," he said. "Would you like me to translate?"

"Jess," the boy said clearly. "I remember you."

"No, he's not," Arden said, mystified. "I hear English."

The boy spoke with a strange accent that Jess couldn't place. Maybe he was European?

"Do you remember anything else?" she asked.

"You saved me," he said earnestly.

"No, I didn't. My father did."

The boy looked past her at Arden, who gave a small wave. His eyes were wide with wonder.

"Thank you," the boy said.

"Why did you ask me to come?" Jess asked.

"I was afraid," he answered, lifting his head with obvious effort. "I don't know where I am. They hurt me."

"Who did?"

"Them. Out there."

"They're doctors and they just want to help you."

His head fell back, his muscles tensed, and he sucked in the air with quick, shallow breaths. Jess remembered what the doctor had said about the anaesthetics wearing off quickly. He began muttering in another language that Jess didn't understand, and she looked questioningly at Arden.

"I think that's Russian," Arden said, his brow furrowed.

*Who is this boy, and how does he know so many languages?* Jess wondered. *And how can we hear different ones at the same time?*

"Will you let them help you?" she said, interrupting him. She moved to the bedside, but didn't dare touch him. The boy's fists clenched tightly as he groaned in pain. Jess herself was tense, out of sympathy.

"Hey, look at me," she told him gently. "They're not going to hurt you; they just want to help. Will you let them take care of you?"

He nodded, his bizarre eyes locked on hers. The door opened, and Dr. Boenig and a couple of other nurses entered, wearing gloves and masks. Jess stayed nervously by the boy's side as Dr. Boenig leaned in to check the stitches.

"*Da konnte eine Infektion seine,*" he said through his mask. "*Lass mich dir etwas dafur geben.*"

The boy suddenly moved; quick as lightning, he seized Dr. Boenig by the collar of his scrubs. Jess let out a gasp of surprise and the doctor paled.

"Hey, calm down!" one of the male nurses said, grabbing both the boy's hands to pry them away. The boy was apparently very strong, because the nurse struggled. Arden rushed forward, and the sheriff and deputy charged in.

"Wait, stop!" Dr. Boenig told them. "It's okay!"

The boy was staring, unblinking, into the doctor's eyes. Sweat beaded on his forehead and neck. Jess thought he must be delirious.

"Please, where am I?" the boy asked.

"*Sie sind* Kermit," the doctor answered in a forced, calm tone.

The boy shook his head, his hands still locked on the doctor's scrubs.

"The kid doesn't understand your German, Doc," the male nurse snapped. "He's speaking English."

"Kermit, Texas," the doctor repeated lightheartedly, now in English. "That's alright, nobody knows where it is. You've been hurt bad, and we're here to help you. Do you remember your name, son?"

The boy hesitated, then shook his head again.

"No, I don't," he said with worry. "There's nothing... it's gone. It's all gone."

"I don't understand what's going on here," the doctor said, facing the others with wide eyes. "He really is speaking German."

"What are you smoking, Doc?" the male nurse replied with exasperation. "No, he isn't!"

"It's okay, nobody here wants to hurt you," Arden interjected, stepping forward. He put on a kind smile and used the same low, gentle voice that he spoke to Jess with when she had nightmares as a child. "We're just going to take care of this wound, so you can get better. Okay?"

The boy began muttering under his breath, but to Jess' relief, he released the doctor's shirt. His head dropped back onto the pillow and he lay shivering as his breath came in quick, shallow gasps. Nobody moved for several seconds; the boy remained still, and the doctor finally let out a shaky sigh of relief. The boy seemed to go to sleep, and the room was quiet.

"He's feverish," Dr. Boenig observed. "Let's get to work. Jess, you can go wait outside now."

Jess nodded stiffly, then hurried to Arden who wrapped his arms around her tightly.

"Good job," he whispered softly in her ear.

He ushered her outside and together they watched the doctors work through the window. Dr. Boenig injected something from a syringe into the skin around the wound. Jess turned away, shaken.

"Are you alright?" Arden asked, embracing her again.

"Yeah," she answered quickly, wiping her eyes. "It was just... that was kind of scary."

"That's alright, I'm more than a little disturbed myself," he said after clearing his throat.

"Y'all can go now," Sheriff Owens' grizzled voice said. Arden released Jess to shake the sheriff's hand. The older man smelled like tobacco. "Thanks for bringin' him in. I think we can take it from here. If we need you for anything else, we'll give you a call."

"So tragic what happened to him," Arden said, shaking his head.

"It's pretty common for victims of violence to experience some kind of trauma-induced amnesia. Given time, maybe some of it will come back to him and we can find out what really happened, then bring whoever's responsible to justice."

"I hope so," Arden said. "Come on, Jess. Let's go home."

Jess and her father left the hospital together and began the long drive home. It was well past dark now, and thousands of stars hung in the sky that stretched from horizon to horizon. After half an hour of driving in contemplative silence, they passed the section of road which Jess guessed was the spot where they found the boy. She looked out the window at the surrounding desert, and thought she saw something shiny glint in the headlights, then it was gone. When they reached the house, Jess climbed down from the truck and walked up the steps to the house. She kicked off her boots, and began to climb the stairs.

"Are you hungry, Jess?" Arden asked, stopping her. "I can fix you something."

"No, I'm okay," she said. "I'm just tired. It's late, and I've got school tomorrow."

"Alright. Well, sleep well, and let me know if you need anything."

She nodded, then went up the stairs. She undressed, then showered and brushed her teeth. After slipping on her pajamas, she lay down in her bed and stared into the darkness. When morning came, she was still lying awake.

# CHAPTER 1

Austin, Texas

Lucas Tavera sat in History class, his elbow on the desk and his chin in his hand. On the screen at the front of the class, a documentary about Reconstruction after the Civil War played, but few of the students paid attention to it. Directly in front of Lucas, a boy slept with his head on his desk. Beside him on his right, a boy and a girl exchanged notes and less-than-quiet giggles. Lucas did his best to tune them out and focus instead on taking down the information he was supposed to get from the documentary.

Not that he needed to. He could get everything he needed to know for the paper due on Friday with little more than a thought. Even as he sat there, his eyes on the screen, the nanomachines at the back of his mind were constantly working. They never stopped their busy activity - always learning and storing away information. But, as he learned during his first week back at school, there was very little satisfaction in taking a shortcut.

The documentary narrator named a few semi-important dates, and Lucas jotted them down. He was aware of a boy to his left doing the same thing. The boy was blond, lanky, and had a thin, pointed face. Nate Wissen had been Lucas' best friend at one point, and now... well, Lucas didn't really know what they were. He had been at school for nearly a month now and Nate hadn't said a word to him. Lucas understood that the past year had been difficult for them both, yet he had specifically come back to his old school, rather than the middle school closer to his new house, because he had hoped that things could pick up where they left off. So far, there was no evidence that was working out. At best, Nate ignored him and at worst, shot him angry glares from across the room.

A gentle, bee-like humming resounded in his ears, and he gripped the corners of his desk. His consciousness was brushed by a strong, magnetic kind of force. He squeezed his eyes shut, waiting for it to pass. *Romana.* Ever since his first encounter with her, he felt her presence imposing on his mind constantly. She never said anything, only contacted his thoughts with her cold, emotionless touch. As if he needed a reminder that she was still out there, doing who-knew-what. Sometimes, he thought he caught a glimpse of her auburn hair in the crowded hallways at school, just over the tops of the other students' heads, or briefly on the street, but he could never be sure. In his dreams, he saw her wide, green eyes staring out from the darkness, the moonlight glinting in them like ice.

The documentary ended; the lights came back on, and the chills he felt faded away. Lucas stole another sideways glance at Nate, who kept his eyes down as he scribbled down to the bottom of the page in his notebook. The teacher, Mr. Cole, began moving down the rows, passing out slips of paper as he went.

"Pop quiz!" he announced. "Time to see if y'all were paying attention."

A series of groans erupted from the students who were still awake. As Mr. Cole neared Lucas, he nudged the desk of the sleeping student who jolted upright and looked around, bleary-eyed. When Lucas received his paper, he quickly skimmed the five questions written on it. With the magnetic hum in his mind subsiding, he immediately began to dredge through his many thousands of memory files, locating the proper ones for the information needed. Then he halted the process, and, with some effort, shut down the supercomputer part of his brain. He banished it to the deep recesses of his mind, having resolved weeks ago that if he was going to come back to school, he was going to do it right: without cheating. Instead, he looked to the memory of what he had just watched in the documentary - which was held in the nearer, shallower parts - and got to work.

As he answered the last question, he saw, to his relief, that he wasn't the first one finished; other students were already walking their quizzes up to the turn-in tray. Sliding out of his desk, he walked up to the front of the room, which was growing crowded. He found himself in line behind Lily Hofstetter, a redhead who had lived on his street last year. Her hair was in one long braid down her back, and he could faintly smell her shampoo. She placed her quiz in the tray, then glanced up. She seemed to recognize him, then quickly lowered her eyes and tried to edge around him. Feeling stung, Lucas stepped aside to let her pass and turned in his paper, then returned to his own desk. At that point, the bell rang, and everyone began gathering up their things. Lucas dejectedly picked up his notebook and pencil and headed for the door.

"Lucas, wait," Mr. Cole said, and Lucas paused. "Come here for a sec."

Nate, who was the last one out, shoved past him on the way to the door without looking up. Lucas gritted his teeth, but let it go and approached Mr. Cole's desk.

"Yes, sir?" Lucas said. "Is there a problem with my quiz?"

Mr. Cole sat back in his chair, his fingers meeting to make a steeple. He smiled in a bemused way.

"I haven't looked at it yet, but I'm sure it's fine," he answered. "I just wanted to ask you how you were adjusting to life back at school. How are you doing?"

"Oh, yeah, I'm good," Lucas answered, one hand in his pocket. "Everything's been great."

"Are you enjoying your classes?"

"Yes, sir."

"How's the workload?"

"It's pretty easy."

"Seems like it," Mr. Cole agreed with a wink. "I hope you're considering pre-AP classes for next year, when you get to high school."

"Yes, sir. I'm planning on it."

Mr. Cole nodded appreciatively, then scribbled on a sticky note, signed it, then handed it to Lucas.

"Well, I won't take up anymore of your time," he said. "Here's a pass to your next class, so they don't bother you in the hallway. And Lucas, if you need anything, or just need to talk, my door is always open, alright?"

Lucas put the note in his pocket. Mr. Cole was smiling, but still giving him an intense, appraising look.

"Thank you," Lucas said. "I'll keep that in mind."

Mr. Cole gave him the nod that said he was dismissed, so he backed out of the room and headed up the hallway to Algebra. He was grateful that the bell had not yet rung; he still had one minute to get to class. Music played over the intercom, and the last of the stragglers were hurrying left and right. He made it just in time, slipping in the door just as the bell rang loudly, and found his seat.

Class went by quickly; Lucas listened to the lecture, then worked the assigned problems from the board. He performed all the calculations in his head, then wrote out the work on a piece of paper; the calculator on his desk was really just for show. He didn't consider this cheating; he did all the work himself, after all, and just let the computer in his head do what the calculator would have done for him anyway, had he chosen to use it. When he finished, he turned the assignment in. The teacher announced to anyone who wasn't finished that the rest was homework.

At lunch, Lucas ate alone at one end of a long table. The other end was occupied by a group of boys who all played some kind of magic-based game on their phones. This was the only time of the day that phones were allowed out, so many of the kids sat in groups playing games or texting their friends across the cafeteria. It was also the only time that Lucas felt like he was actually a part of the action, even if the other students didn't knowingly include him. Though none of them spoke to him or gossiped with him in person, as the students texted or shared photos, Lucas could see it all. His mind picked up each electromagnetic signal that passed through the air. He could read texts, view all the pictures posted online and follow conversations, all from the untraceable watchtower of his supercomputer-brain. To the casual observer, Lucas was sitting quietly, eating cheese pizza. No one could imagine the kaleidoscope of activity that went on in his head. Today, he followed a debate over one of the latest fall movies:

*Did you see* The Haunted Cathedral? *Scariest movie ever!!!*

*No way,* Devil's Playground *was way scarier.*

*Are you kidding?? That ghost would totally beat that monster in a fight.*

*That monster was the scariest thing I've ever seen!*

*Yeah, but you're a wuss and everything scares you.*

Lucas pulled away from the conversation when he noticed Nate sitting two tables over. He stared at something intently, his fists clenched. Curious, Lucas followed his gaze. On the other side of the cafeteria, by the trash cans, Val Espinoza, Darren Jones, and Howard Mays stood around a smaller boy who also sat alone. He was Ty Bridwell, a dark-haired boy who had also been Lucas' friend once, but they hadn't spoken since the day Lucas was taken to the CIA's secret bunker. Val and his gang had also returned to school this year; they dropped out last September, so they all had to repeat eighth grade. Lucas felt his blood boil at the sight of them. One year ago, those bullies had chased him into a warehouse where an accident changed his life forever. It gave him his powers, but also nearly killed him while they ran away and left him there. Their actions were unforgivable, but there was nothing he could do about it… not without giving himself away. Lucas glared at them, watching as Val leaned over Ty's shoulder, picking at his food. Darren, a boy with short, black hair and a hoodie despite the eighty-degree weather outside, chuckled as Val took a bite out of the smaller boy's corn dog. Howard was a boy with a thick neck and stained t-shirt; he reached over and picked up his carton of juice and swigged it, then poured the rest over the Ty's French fries. The three bigger boys laughed raucously, while the students nearby looked on uncomfortably.

Lucas gritted his teeth. His hands grew hot, and his pulse began to race. He knew that he could take them on easily; nothing they could do would hurt him. He was sorely tempted to fry them where they stood with his lightning, but he didn't. He couldn't. Instead, he got up and walked his paper plate to the trash cans by the door. He passed by Nate, who narrowed his eyes and shook his head. Lucas pretended not to see him as he disposed of his trash, then left the cafeteria.

He was already at the door of his next class when the bell rang. By the time the school day ended, he was flustered and ready to get home. He walked to the corner with his notebook and waited for the bus that he took across town. When it arrived, his brain automatically connected to the bus's onboard wifi. He chose a seat by the window so that he could watch the Austin city life happening around him on the hour-long ride back home. He enjoyed observing the people on the other side of the window going about their lives, and this late in the afternoon, the city was busy. Pedestrians filled the sidewalks and traffic was at its heaviest. Stickers depicting cutesy vampires and witches coated shop windows, and skeletons danced in doorways. Cooler fall weather was approaching, so some people wore jackets and boots, while others stuck to their shorts and t-shirts; that was the conundrum of Texas weather.

The bus crawled through block after block, but Lucas didn't mind because he wasn't just people-watching, he was also searching.

*Where is she?*

He still hadn't been able to shake the impression that Romana had left in his mind. He knew she was out there somewhere, and the haunting echo of her mental presence was his constant reminder. The remainder of his mental capacity was spent combing the internet for any sign of her, or the Rising - the group that owned both of them. That was the deal Lucas had made with the CIA that allowed him to go back to school: any information he found was passed directly to them, but there hadn't been much to go on. She contacted him with ease, seemingly whenever and wherever she felt like it just to grate on his nerves, but he couldn't reach out to her. How was she doing that? Whatever her powers were, she was much stronger and more skilled than he was. She could simultaneously plague his thoughts and block him from seeing anything of hers.

The bus stopped a block from Lucas' house. A black Cadillac sedan sat parked under a tree at the corner, and Lucas paused. Two men sat in the front seats, wearing sunglasses. He turned long enough for them to see his face, then continued walking. The leaves were beginning to change on the trees, and a gentle wind rustled the branches. The grassy lawn, however, was still vibrant green due to persistent watering, ensuring that his house looked quite picturesque. He crossed the front walk, then climbed the steps to the porch. The curtains were drawn, and through the large front window he could see his mother sitting in the big easy chair with a glass of water.

Pushing open the front door, Lucas saw that she was talking and laughing with a tall, broad-shouldered man in his forties, with neatly combed blond hair. He smiled easily, but his icy blue eyes assessed everything sharply and quickly. His name was Agent Seth Kowalski. He leaned on the back of the easy chair with a bottle of water in one hand, and was dressed in track pants, an athletic shirt and running shoes. Behind him, a younger man in a suit stood by the stair landing, his arms folded.

"Good afternoon," Kowalski said as Lucas walked in.

"Hi, Lucas," his mother, Leah, said and her smile brightened.

"Hi, Mom," Lucas answered. She got up from the easy chair and came over, giving him a kiss on the cheek. Her dark hair was pulled up in a ponytail; she wore a sleeveless top that exposed her tanned arms. A long scar showed on one of her wrists, and one more on her freckled face, near her mouth.

"How was school?" Kowalski asked.

"Fine," Lucas replied. He nodded at the man by the stairs. "Who's that?"

"That's Agent Kellerman," Kowalski replied. "Agent Figgs had the night off."

Lucas gave the man a brief nod hello, and the man responded in kind. He looked young and uneasy. He nervously shifted his weight from one foot to the other.

"Will you be ready in five?" Kowalski asked.

"Yeah, I'll go change now," Lucas answered.

He climbed the stairs to his room, the loft on the second floor, which was closed off by a curtain. Inside, dozens of naked bulbs were strung up around the room. Besides those, the walls were bare. A card table in a corner was stacked with dismantled hard drives that Lucas had scavenged from the trash weeks ago. On his desk, a laptop lay open with its keyboard removed; he had spent the last few nights piecing it back together. He changed out of his school clothes into a t-shirt and shorts, then laced up his running shoes and headed back downstairs where Kowalski was waiting. Maria, Lucas' grandmother, emerged from the kitchen.

"*Buenos tardes, mijo,*" she smiled, drying her hands on a towel. "How was school?"

"Fine," he said, giving her a quick hug. She kissed him on the cheek. "Are you hungry?"

"No, *abuelita*. Besides, we're about to run."

"Well, you should eat something then," she insisted.

"I'm okay, really," he said with a smile.

"Alright, I'll have dinner waiting when you get back."

Lucas headed to the living room and stopped at the front door, waiting.

"Alright, back in a minute, Leah," Kowalski said, his eyes smiling, and her cheeks reddened. Lucas caught the look that was exchanged between them and quickly tried to forget it. Lately, Leah was the happiest he had ever seen her, but that didn't make him any less uncomfortable to see them together.

"Hurry up," he complained.

"Hey, you better be nice to the old man," Kowalski said, punching him lightly in the shoulder. "Cause you know I'm gonna kick your ass later."

"Not this time," Lucas replied with a grin.

Lucas opened the door and they stepped outside. The sun was only just beginning to set behind the treetops as they set off at a jog down the sidewalk. This was part of Lucas' daily training, and the easiest part by far.

"Really, though, how was school?" Kowalski asked when they were a hundred yards from the house. Kowalski was already puffing, but kept a steady pace.

"Sucked," Lucas answered.

"And Nate?"

"Still not talking to me."

"Well, you can't blame him. Anyone would be traumatized by what he saw."

"Yes I can," Lucas snapped. "I was the one that nearly died! I guess... I just thought it would bring us closer, you know? I thought, 'finally, here's one person I can actually talk to about all this shit I've been through. Someone who gets me.'"

Kowalski was quiet.

"Someone besides you, I mean," Lucas corrected himself. They rounded the corner, then stopped at an intersection, waiting for the light. Kowalski took a deep breath and winced as he massaged the side of his torso, just below his ribs.

"No, I understand," he said with a grunt. "It's not the same as having someone your own age to talk to."

"Who's not an android out to kill me," Lucas added.

"Yeah, well, I wasn't counting Romana anyway," Kowalski said. The light changed and they jogged across the intersection. "Just give him some time. It's only been a few months, after all."

"What if he never comes around?"

"What about Ty? Can't you talk to him?"

"I haven't spoken to him since the warehouse. I think he's avoiding me."

"Hmmm... Well, you can't keep feeling sorry for yourself, Lucas," Kowalski replied. "Friends come and go, and loyalties change, but you just gotta keep moving forward. No sense in worrying about the things you can't control."

Lucas set his jaw and nodded. They reached the park and turned right, following the paved path past a playground where children shrieked and laughed as they chased each other in a game of tag, then along the river. Here, they stopped and Kowalski stepped away to stretch, panting. Lucas was warm and sweating, but far from out of breath.

"Speaking of Romana," Kowalski said, stretching his quadricep. "Anything new?"

"If there was, I would have told you," Lucas answered.

"You still feel her, though?"

"Always."

"We may not know where she is yet, but thanks to that intel you decoded yesterday, the New York team took down the Rising cell that had been planning to bomb Citi Field," Kowalski told him.

"I know, I saw the report. It was all online."

"I know you know, Computer-Brain," Kowalski said. He was still smiling proudly though, and Lucas' cheeks flushed. "You could at least pretend to be surprised, just to give me the pleasure of telling you in person."

"Sure, I'm surprised, okay?" Lucas said with a laugh. "Thanks for the gratitude. It feels good to be so useful. Where would you guys be without me?"

"Alright, enough with the sarcasm," Kowalski muttered. "Now, do your laps, and I'll time you."

"I can time myself -"

"I *know* you can time yourself," Kowalski interjected, feigning frustration. "Jesus, you can be such a smartass. Now run!"

Lucas took off at a sprint, laughing the whole way.

When they returned to the house, Leah was waiting for them with glasses of cold water, and Maria sang in the kitchen as she cooked. Lucas drank gratefully, but didn't rest long. Leah led the way to the garage and flipped on the lights. A month ago, Kowalski converted the garage into a gym, complete with mats, sand-filled punching bags, and air conditioning. Initially, he had built it to provide a safe space for training Lucas, where he taught him basic fighting techniques he could use if he found himself facing down Romana again. Then Leah began using it, coming alone to hit the bags. Lucas caught her practicing moves she copied after watching him train, so he asked Kowalski to give her private lessons. Now they trained together, and, after several weeks, Lucas noticed a change in his mother. Her timidity was gone, replaced by a fearless calm that he had never seen before. Then, shortly after that, Kowalski began staying late in the evenings, chatting with Leah over coffee.

"Let's warm up," Kowalski told them.

Leah wrapped her hands, then approached the body bag with focused intensity. After assuming a fighting stance, she began throwing jabs and punches the way Kowalski had shown her yesterday, while Lucas and Kowalski paced around each other in the center of the mat.

"Ready to lose again?" Kowalski said with a grin.

"I was going to ask you the same question," Lucas replied.

Kowalski stepped back with his right leg, while Lucas stepped forward with his left, his hands up. He studied Kowalski's movements, waiting for an opening. Kowalski lunged, shooting his fist out in a punch. Stepping out to the side, Lucas deflected the punch and jabbed his own into Kowalski's ribs, and Kowalski responded by retracting his elbow, slamming it into the back of Lucas' head. He dropped to his knees, seeing stars.

"Damn it," he muttered, going down to all fours to wait until the world stopped spinning.

"You should have kept that other hand up," Kowalski chuckled.

"Yeah, thanks," Lucas grumbled.

Leah stopped punching the bag.

"Are you okay?" she asked.

"I'm fine," he said, waving a hand. He struggled back to his feet, then took up his stance again.

Kowalski's smile vanished and his blue eyes flashed as he observed Lucas with cold calculation. His knees bent and his hands came up. Lucas glared back at him, energy flooding his veins. He suppressed the lightning that wanted to gather in his chest and focused instead on channeling his anger into movement. When Kowalski lunged again, he was ready. He dodged the first punch, then blocked the second that came straight for his face. He brought his knee up into Kowalski's chest, only for it to be met by the sharp point of an elbow. Then Kowalski barreled into him; his head dropped and his shoulder rammed Lucas' gut as he tackled him. Kowalski was bigger and much heavier, so instead of resisting, Lucas hooked his legs around Kowalski's waist and let his weight take them both to the ground. They grappled, Lucas hanging on until he saw an opportunity to free his legs and use them to kick, bucking Kowalski over his head. Kowalski landed on his back with a heavy thud, then immediately rolled. Lucas, too, was on his feet in an instant, back in a defensive stance. The next thing he knew, something was flying at his head. He reacted on instinct, throwing up a force field. A racquetball hit the shimmering field and ricocheted, bouncing harmlessly against the wall.

"Excellent job," Kowalski said, beginning a slow clap.

The field vanished, and Lucas bent over with his hands on his knees, gasping for air.

"Stand up straight," Kowalski told him. "You'll never catch your breath that way."

"That was dirty," Lucas said, straightening up.

"It was a test, and you passed," Kowalski replied. "Your reaction time was perfect. The game could change in a fraction of a second out there, and good reflexes could save your life."

"So, what, you're going to start throwing things at me now?"

"Yep," Kowalski said, slapping him on the back.

"That's not fair."

"The battle's not going to be fair."

"Mom, are you hearing this?" Lucas said incredulously.

Leah paused hitting the bag and gave him a wink.

"You're doing great, honey," she said.

"More of that later," Kowalski said. "Right now, we switch. Leah!"

Leah stopped hitting the bag and walked over. Still shaking his head, Lucas wrapped his hands and wrists with tape, then approached the bag. Kowalski and Leah began pacing around each other, preparing to spar. Kowalski gave her a stealthy wink, but Lucas saw it and his face reddened. He rotated around the bag so his back was to them, and tried to tune out his mother's girlish giggle. Once he started hitting the bag, though, he was laser-focused. His muscles burned, and his knuckles soon went numb. He recalled his fight with Romana, the way she moved so easily to avoid his attacks. She knew what to do, and did it so effortlessly; before he could even think, she'd had him. He had very nearly died, because he hadn't been ready. He couldn't imagine what he could have done differently, but he was determined never to be that vulnerable again.

As he threw punch after punch, then an elbow attack, and then a kick, his heart rate began to climb. Heat began to gather in his chest and spread down into his hands. That incessant hum in his head grated on his nerves, a stark reminder that he had failed once already. He had lost, and if Kowalski hadn't been there, that defeat would have cost him his life and probably his mother's, too. Romana was out there, somewhere, taunting him... like she was *intentionally* toeing the line, staying out of his reach, but just barely.

Electrical current began to tickle his skin, and he stopped hitting the bag. He stepped back and clenched his fists, willing his heart to slow. The anger that had been building to a tipping point slowly... so slowly... began to fade away.

"Are you okay?" Kowalski asked, stepping over.

"Yeah," Lucas replied, letting out a slow breath. Kowalski reached to put his hand on Lucas' shoulder, but he moved away and pretended to stretch.

At that moment, the kitchen door opened and Agent Kellerman stepped out, his eyes wide.

"Sir, they're calling for him," he said nervously.

"What is it?" Kowalski asked, his hands on his hips.

"Codeword: Firebolt," the young agent said.

Kowalski immediately turned to Lucas.

"Come on," he said sharply. "You're on."

"What's going on?" Lucas asked.

"That means the office has located a bomb, and it's tested positive for the presence of nanomachines."

Lucas' blood ran cold. *The Rising.* His mind immediately opened up, scanning through the millions of electronic signals that flooded the air. Voices and images flooded his mind, and the supercomputer part of his mind worked at lightspeed to sort them out. He soon overheard communication among officers of the Austin PD, calling for a blockade to be put up around a mile-long section of the lakeshore, and an evacuation of the surrounding city blocks.

"It's at Town Lake?" Lucas said.

"Yes, the bomb squad is already on the way," Agent Kellerman answered.

"They're going to need help," Kowalski replied. "Lucas, come on, we have to go now."

Lucas and Leah followed Kowalski through the kitchen and into the living room. Two agents were already there with a large duffel bag that they set on the couch. Leah sat down in a nearby chair, her hands folded anxiously, while Kowalski unzipped it and removed what looked like a stack of folded black fabric.

"Go put this on," he said, handing it to Lucas. "And hurry."

He obeyed, taking the steps two at a time up to his room. He undressed, then unfolded the black fabric. It was a bodysuit made out of a material that was thick and strong, yet very soft. It was long sleeved, and came up to his neck and down to his ankles when he put it on. There was also a set of gloves with padded knuckles and rubber grips on the palm and fingertips. He headed back downstairs, feeling strange in the suit. His mother looked up, her face inscrutable.

"It was specially made for you by R&D," Kowalski said. "The inner layer is heat-resistant, while the outer layer is woven with micro-coils of ruthenium alloy. It should conduct the current you generate away from you while mitigating any burns you might cause to yourself."

"Oh, that's nice, I guess," Lucas said, running his hands over the material.

Kowalski also removed a Kevlar vest that was Lucas' size, marked with *CIA* on the back and a white lightning bolt on the left shoulder, and Lucas put it on.

"I know you heal, but I still don't want you to get shot," Kowalski said.

"Awww, you do care," Lucas said sarcastically.

"And last, but not least," Kowalski said. "Made at your request."

He held out a balaclava. It was black, and light as a feather.

"A mask," Lucas said.

"That's right. Can't have your face plastered all over the evening news. It comes with these," he said, handing Lucas a pair of goggles. "You said you were having trouble focusing; well, these can filter out or amplify various wavelengths of the EM spectrum, so that should help. And they're wireless."

"Cool," Lucas said excitedly, putting them on. His mind connected to the goggles' wireless, and he looked around. As he ran through some mental commands, the goggles showed him the bright, kaleidoscopic glow of the standing lamp and the overhead lights in the kitchen. He could see these anyway, without the goggles, but at his instruction, they reduced the intensity until it was merely a gentle, candle-like flicker. Then he switched to infrared: his mother, Kowalski, Kellerman, and the other agents glowed red-orange, while the furniture and walls were various shades of pink and purple.

"Good?" Kowalski asked.

"Good," Lucas answered, taking the goggles back off.

"Alright, let's go,"

Lucas laced on a pair of boots, and Kowalski changed into his own tactical gear. Leah stood up and threw her arms around Lucas' neck, embracing him tightly.

"Be careful," she said, her voice tight.

"I will, Mom."

In less than four minutes, they were on the road. It was dusk; street lamps were lit and the city skyline illuminated the sky so brightly that no stars were visible. Lucas sent his mind ahead, taking over the security cameras on the patios of the nearby hotels to survey the scene. The bomb, Lucas guessed, was in the backpack that sat at the top of a set of stairs behind the Town Lake Holiday Inn. The cops had cleared an area of lakeshore the length of a football field; even boats were ordered to turn back.

"What's your job?" Kowalski asked from the seat next to him.

"I know what my job is," Lucas said, rolling his eyes.

"I need to hear you say it."

Lucas sighed.

"I defuse the bomb, then bring it to you," he recited.

"And where are the nanomachines?"

"They're still on the bomb. I haven't moved them. It's my job only to escort them and the device away from danger."

"That's right," Kowalski said. "And if Romana turns up?"

"I still defuse the bomb, then bring it to you."

"Do you fight her?"

Lucas gritted his teeth.

"No."

"If she attacks you directly, do you defend yourself?"

"No, I let you and the cops do that."

"What do you do?"

"I defuse the bomb and bring it to you," Lucas said, annoyed. "Do you want me to say it in Spanish?"

"Nah, we're good," Kowalski said, giving his shoulder a light squeeze.

The car pulled up to the barricades that surrounded the area, and Lucas slipped his mask and goggles over his head. Breathing with his face completely covered was going to take some getting used to. He switched on the infrared vision, and saw roughly a hundred glowing officers stationed around the perimeter. The hotel lobby and floors above appeared empty, but along the bridge, dozens of curious spectators were gathering to get a look at the action. On the stairs of the hotel, a person in a bulky suit like an astronaut's was slowly approaching the backpack. Kowalski immediately jumped on the radio.

"Somebody tell that guy to get back!" he shouted. "No one goes near the device without my go-ahead! We have a specialist arriving on the scene!"

"Specialist?" Lucas asked.

"You're the only one who can go near the thing without dying, so I'd say that makes you a specialist," Kowalski replied hurriedly. "Now don't say anything to these people unless I tell you to. Got it?"

"Got it."

Kowalski stepped out of the car, and Lucas followed. It was a long walk from the edge of the barricades to the area where the majority of the police force were gathered. The whole way, Lucas felt like the world was watching him. He felt paranoid that anyone who looked at him would recognize him immediately, by his height, gait, or voice. The sirens flashing and voices from bullhorns ordering the crowds to evacuate were overwhelming. He ordered the goggles to filter out the flashing lights, but there was little he could do about the noise. He tried to focus on simply keeping up with Kowalski's long strides as he made a beeline for the edge of the blast shields, where several cops and the person in the astronaut suit stood waiting.

"This is your specialist?" said one cop, raising an eyebrow at Lucas.

"Yes, Captain Martinez," Kowalski replied. "This is Firebolt. And he is the only person I would trust to approach that device. Will you oblige us?"

Captain Martinez shook his head with disbelief.

"Sorry, but he looks like a kid," he said. "What's he going to do anyway that we haven't already done? We've assessed the situation, and there's no timer on it or nothin'. We were just going to pack it up, remove it from the scene so we can all go home, alright?"

"No timer?" Lucas asked, perplexed. "Or radio receiver? Or mobile phone?"

The captain narrowed his eyes.

"None of that," he said. "Believe it or not, we're actually pretty good at our jobs."

Kowalski sucked air through his teeth, and Lucas looked at him. Those were all the types of triggers he had been trained in. If this bomb was different, he didn't know how he was going to defuse it.

"There has to be *something* to trigger the bomb remotely," Lucas said, closing his eyes and extending his consciousness outward to the device. If there were any wireless, electromagnetic signal surrounding the device, he would feel it. The bomb was absolutely alive with energy, charging the air and raising the hairs on the back of his neck, but he couldn't tell what specifically was producing it. He was afraid to focus too hard and set the device off accidentally while poking around with his mind.

"Let me get closer," he said, opening his eyes. "I need to see it."

"Who the hell is this kid?" the captain asked Kowalski.

"That's classified," he replied calmly. "You are ordered now to let him pass. This is officially a federal matter."

The other officers looked at the captain nervously.

"If you think I'm going to step aside and let a kid die, you're out of your goddamn mind," he snapped.

"Believe me, that won't be a problem," Kowalski responded. "Now, step aside."

The captain threw up his hands in frustration, and the officers parted the blast shields to allow Lucas room to slide between them. He glanced back at Kowalski, who had removed his phone from his pocket and held it close to his face, then gave him a silent nod. Lucas walked out into the clearing, then slowly up the steps. His mind was open, feeling for any change in the electromagnetic signals that flowed through the surrounding space. The backpack sat at the top of the steps, leaning against the railing. It was a non-assuming brown corduroy, with light blue trim and a hole worn in the front zipper pocket, but - invisible to everyone else - rays of energy flickered and fired outward like sunbursts. As Lucas climbed the steps, he felt the air become charged, sparking across his skin like static. Something tugged at the center of his chest, constricting his ribs. His blood pounded in his head. When he was less than five feet away, he doubled over, overcome with the urge to vomit. He called Kowalski's phone.

*Kowalski*, he said, hearing himself on speakerphone. *There are definitely nanomachines here.*

*We know, that's why we brought you*, Kowalski answered. *Can you disable it?*

*I'll try.*

*You gonna make it, kid?*

*Yeah, yeah... I'm good.*

The nanomachines' effect on his body was powerful, filling his brain with a high-pitched screech; he felt like each of his cells was being tugged with a magnet. The last time he had felt this sensation, he was in the warehouse where his accident happened, one year ago. The nanomachines felt almost sentient; they were talking to him all at once in a cacophony that threatened to shatter his concentration. He knelt down and unzipped the backpack. A black box covered in wires lay inside, with four glass cylinders strapped to two of its sides; each contained a liquid that glowed bright, electric blue. Lucas knew that if this bomb went off, anyone who survived the blast would be infected with aerosolized, hungry nanomachines; he had seen the devastating effects of this contamination firsthand. If a person was unlucky enough to escape the slow and painful death, he faced something much, much worse.

This was the Rising's game, and Lucas was the only one who could stop it. But how?

When Brick was infected that day in the warehouse, there was only one thing that kept him from dying...

*Firebolt, what's going on?* Kowalski said.

Lucas found a sensor near the top-left corner of the box, but he didn't recognize it; he took a snapshot with his mind, then began an internet search for any information that would help him. While that went on, he removed his gloves and carefully unstrapped the first cylinder. Sensing his presence, the blue liquid shifted like living mercury, pressing itself against the sides of the glass in contact with his fingers. Lucas' skull felt like it was about to burst with the high-pitched cry of the nanomachines. He closed his fist, squeezing the cylinder tightly. The glass cracked, cutting his skin and releasing the nanomachines trapped inside. They flowed across his open, bleeding hand, then began to disappear as they were absorbed into his flesh, through the open cuts and his pores.

*Firebolt, report!* said Kowalski's voice in his head.

*I'm taking care of the nanomachines,* he answered, seizing the next cylinder. The injuries from the broken glass had already healed, but he was about to open them up again. His skin burned horribly as the nanomachines oriented themselves underneath.

*What!? You need to bring the device to me. What are you doing?*

*Putting them where they won't be able to hurt anyone else. The only place that's safe. If I can't defuse the bomb, then at least the nanomachines will be out of the picture.*

There was only one cylinder left. He unstrapped it from the side of the box, then paused. A tickle ran down the back of his skull. In his periphery, he saw something like a dragonfly shoot out over the roof of the hotel, then hover just above the treetops. His mind registered an electronic signature; it was not a living thing, but robotic.

*A drone,* he realized.

Lucas panicked and raised his hand. Lightning blasted from it, vaporizing the drone mid-air. A thunderous noise echoed over the surface of the water, and the cops ducked behind their blastshields. The air sparked, raising the hairs on the back of his neck. Within a fraction of a second, the bomb exploded.

Time slowed as the hum in his mind swelled to a crescendo. Romana's voice spoke softly, as if her lips were right next to his ears:

*You should have stayed home.*

Terrified, Lucas eyes squeezed shut as he threw up his hands, expecting an onslaught of heat and pain, but none came. Cracking open his eyes, he was surprised to see a shimmering, dome-shaped force field about five feet tall, and inside it, a white-hot, raging fireball. Lucas gasped with shock at the sudden drain on his power, and the dome warped, dancing with the awesome power trapped inside it. He knew that he was the only thing preventing this wave of fire from escaping, so he steeled himself, focusing all his strength on maintaining the telekinetic sphere of energy. He couldn't waver, or he risked releasing the explosion. It glowed like the sun with brilliant white light, refracted by the prism-like wall of the force field.

*Lucas! Whatever you do, don't stop!* Kowalski shouted over the phone.

*You don't have to tell me that,* Lucas growled. The strain was unbearable; a stabbing pain had begun in the center of his forehead and spread across his skull.

*I can't hold this forever,* he told Kowalski.

Then he spotted a patch of blue on the ground near his foot. As he caught the blast of the bomb, he had dropped the last cylinder of nanomachines. The electric blue liquid seeped out onto the stone steps through a crack in the glass.

*The whole block's been evacuated of civilians,* Kowalski answered. *Once all the personnel are clear, you can release the bomb.*

*Hurry!*

Lucas' head felt like it was being drilled with an icepick. Sweat soaked his mask, making it difficult to breathe. He wasn't sure he could hold it any longer, and the nanomachines forming a puddle six inches from his shoe worried him. It was like watching a viper slowly escape its cage, but near a preschool playground. Anxiety weighed in his chest, and the magnetic pull they exerted on his cells was painful to resist. He had to do something, but he was just as trapped as the bomb's explosion.

*We're clear! Release it now!*

Lucas dropped his arms. A wall of fire erupted, and the force of the blast lifted him off his feet. His goggles cracked, and the mask melted onto his face. Before he could even register the pain, his brain shut down.

# CHAPTER 2

———◆———

*J*ess rode the bus home from school, her head down as she scrolled through her phone. She had been distracted all day, thinking about the boy. Hunched down in the seat with her feet up, she searched the internet for people with bizarre, red eyes similar to his. All she could find were pictures of fictional monsters and symptoms of conjunctivitis. This made her frustrated. His eyes weren't bloodshot or inflamed, they were *red*. How was that possible?

Filled with determination, she broadened her search to include animals with red eyes and found a wide variety of reptiles, fish, and birds, but they all had red irises and round or slitted black pupils - none like the ones she had seen. She looked out the window, her head resting against the seat. Maybe he was a victim of some kind of genetic experiment. That was possible, right? Sure, it only happened in comic books or movies, but she knew what she had seen. He was a real-life example of something impossible.

The bus pulled to a stop at the end of the long, gravel road that led to her house, and she picked up her backpack and stepped off. Her boots crunched on the dry dirt, and hot wind whipped her hair as the bus rolled away. Squinting against the dust, she looked back up the road from where she had come. Two miles north was the spot where she and Arden had found the boy, and she recalled the shiny object that she had seen out in the desert last night. Maybe there *was* something out there, some clues to be found that might tell her who he is, or where he came from.

She slung her backpack over her shoulder and jogged down the gravel road, then across the yard to the house. Arden's truck was gone, and the house was empty; she supposed he must have gone to town. She dropped her backpack on the floor by the kitchen table, then filled up a water bottle. After tying up her hair, she was ready to go hiking across the desert.

Setting out across the yard, she decided to walk parallel with the highway, a silver ribbon about five hundred yards to her right. The ground was flat, broken only by the occasional brown, scrubby plant no higher than her knee. She walked for ten minutes, then twenty. The sun beat mercilessly down on her neck, but she was committed. There had to be something out here… some kind of a sign. The ground was completely flat for hundreds of acres, but a range of mountains rose up far in the distance. They were blue in the low-hanging haze. Sweat dripped off her nose, and she wiped her forehead with the back of her forearm. The heat made her legs sluggish, like wading through water, and the bright sunlight burned her eyes; she squeezed them tightly shut, waiting for the white spots to go away.

When she opened them again, she realized the light was reflected at her from something shiny and partly buried in the dirt. A tin can, perhaps, or broken glass. Or maybe not. Heart pounding, she picked up the pace, almost to a jog once more. Ten yards ahead, something definitely glittered on the ground. She ran until she was standing directly over it, then gaped.

It was a sword. A ruby the size of a lime sat at the end of its wire-wrapped hilt, gleaming in the sun.

Jess startled, almost afraid to touch it. She wondered if at any second it would simply fade away like a mirage. Eventually, curiosity overcame her fear and she bent down. With shaking fingers, she brushed the dust away to uncover the rest of the sword. It had a sheath that looked like it was plated with mother-of-pearl. Taking it with both hands and wrapping her fingers around the hilt, she pulled the blade part of the way out. Strange symbols were scratched into the surface of the hammered steel.

Clutching the sword close, she spun around, scanning the desert. Where did it come from? Who could have left it here? There was nothing around for miles, except her own house. And who carried a *sword* anyway? Maybe it was part of somebody's collection - someone wealthy and eccentric.

Jess gasped, remembering that she had thought the same thing about the boy's extravagant coat. It had small rubies set in the collar, and was rich and fancy like this sword. It had to be *his* sword, and he must have lost it out here when he was injured. She had to get home and show Arden.

Cradling the sword in her arms, she began the hurried walk back to her house. By the time she reached the steps of the porch, her arms ached; the sword and sheath were very heavy. She staggered inside and laid it across the table, panting and sweating. Arden was still not home, so she got herself a cold drink of water and paced the floor to cool down. After a few minutes, she sat down at the table with her hands folded, staring at the sword and willing it to give answers. It lay there, silent but seemingly alive. The ambient light glittered off it, almost as if it glowed on its own.

Finally, she heard the truck's engine outside. It grew louder, then died as the truck pulled into the yard. The brief silence was followed by Arden's heavy boots on the porch. Jess jumped up, alive with excitement, and positioned herself in front of the sword to hide it; she wanted to see the look on Arden's face when she revealed her find.

The screen door opened and Arden kicked off his boots, then ducked inside. He was carrying a sack of groceries in one hand.

"Dad!" Jess said. "You'll never guess what I found!"

He looked up at her, but didn't seem to see her. His eyes were distant, like they always were when he was lost in thought.

"Oh, hi, Jess," he said absently. "I got a call today about that boy."

Jess' excitement faltered as she read the troubled look on his face. Her stomach sank.

"What's wrong?" she asked, dreading the answer. "Is he okay?"

"His injuries are all healed," Arden answered. "But Dr. Boenig said his blood tests came back, and they don't really know what to make of it. Seems his DNA is unusual. Dr. Boenig is calling him an 'unidentified life form.' The sheriff called the government to report it, and Doc called me because they'll probably come here to ask us some questions."

"Wait, what?" Jess said with incredulity. "I don't understand. What does that mean?"

"They don't know what he is."

"Isn't he human?"

"I don't know, Jess. I'm just as confused as you are," he said with a frown. "Something's wrong - he shouldn't have told me all of that over the phone."

"Why not? We brought him in."

"Doesn't matter; we're not relatives. It goes against doctor-patient confidentiality."

"*Unidentified life form*," Jess repeated. "Doesn't that mean, like, alien?"

Arden shook his head. "Jess, don't be silly," he said. "Of course not. We can't know what he actually is yet, and the implications there would be enormous. But obviously there is a rational explanation."

Jess was stunned and breathless.

"But Sheriff Owens called the government," she said, her voice rising. "So are they going to take him away?"

"Probably so. He had no identification and no one has come to claim him. They'll want to make sure he isn't dangerous."

"Can we go see him before they do?"

"Why?"

"Because, he's probably still scared. It just doesn't seem right to leave him there alone without saying goodbye. I just… I just want to make sure he's going to be okay."

"Alright," Arden sighed. "Let's go, then."

He stepped toward the table with the sack of groceries, then paused when he saw the sword.

"What's that?" he asked, and Jess looked. Her excitement flooded back.

"Oh, I found it near where we first saw him. I think it's his!"

"A sword?"

"Yes! Isn't it incredible?"

Arden put down the bag, then gingerly touched the handle of the sword with one finger.

"Are you sure it belonged to him?" he asked. "What if someone just lost it?"

"Dad, come on," Jess said. "Remember the clothes he was wearing?"

"They were odd," he nodded.

"Let's bring it; maybe it'll help trigger some memories."

"I don't think they're going to let us just walk into the hospital with a sword, Jess," he said flatly.

"We can try, can't we?"

"No, we can't. We're going to take it to the sheriff's station."

He picked it up; it looked so balanced in his strong hands. He walked out to the truck with it resting on his shoulder. Jess followed, after hurriedly grabbing a few snacks from the pantry. Arden put the sword in the back seat and covered it up with a tarp, then they got in and began the drive back to town.

"Do you really think he might be an alien?" Jess asked. "Is it possible that aliens are real?"

Arden rubbed his bearded chin.

"Jess, there's no such things as aliens," he said. "Don't jump to unreasonable conclusions. He could be from here, just… I don't know, something different."

"But what about the language thing? How does everyone hear a different one?"

"I don't know," Arden answered heavily. "I really don't."

Jess nodded; her mind was already racing with questions, but for the rest of the drive she sat in tense silence. On the edge of town stood two signs in peeling blue paint; the first read, *Kermit FFA Welcomes You!* and the second, *This is Rockcrusher Country.* The main avenue led them past a dozen or so dusty, boarded-up buildings that were all roughly the same shade of brown, like they were trying to disappear into the landscape. Besides the gravel mill, only a few businesses on Main Street were still open: a liquor store, an automotive repair shop, an antiques dealer, K-Town Towing Service, and the Prairie Gas 'n' Sip. All the other establishments bore *For Lease* signs in the dirty windows, and weeds reclaimed the parking lots.

Arden turned the corner, then pulled into the front lot of the sheriff's station. He got out and carried the sword inside, still covered in the tarp; Jess sat by herself in the truck for twenty long minutes, during which time she rolled down the window and began another internet search on her phone. She began by looking up weather reports from yesterday. The forecast had been for a clear day, and the national weather service confirmed that the storm was unusual. The storm, they said, had come out of nowhere, became a cyclone spanning three miles across, then lasted for only ten minutes before dissipating completely. Jess could barely breathe. She remembered, because she was there. She had seen it with her own eyes, just like she had seen the boy. He was real. Could all the rest be true? Could he really be an an alien from outer space?

She continued to look for more information about the storm, refining her search to other strange weather phenomena. She found videos of cloudless rain, ten-second tornadoes, and cyclones that came up out of nowhere and lasted for only seconds before disappearing. These were what interested her, but the more she clicked, the farther the legitimate news sources were left behind. Her screen was filled with links to sites that claimed the storms were cover-ups for alien visits from outer space. They were the usual tin-foil-hat types, with names like TheyAreAmongUs.com. She considered going back and starting over, but the description caught her eye: "What The Government Won't Tell You. Your Daily Insight Into US Government Cover-Ups."

She clicked the link, expecting nothing but nonsense. Most of the articles and videos looked like they'd been edited by a ten-year-old, but she found one that looked particularly interesting. The title read ominously, "This video will be removed from the internet within 24 hours..." The timestamp said it was uploaded just last night and was filmed in Austin, only six hours away. Curious, Jess clicked "play," and saw the outside patio of a building surrounded by police barricades. It was dark, but a single spotlight illuminated a small figure dressed in black, kneeling beside a bundle on the ground that was hard to make out. Suddenly, the figure stood and raised its arm. Light filled the screen, completely whiting it out for a brief second.

Jess was confused. *What just happened?* When the white light dimmed, the figure was still standing, its arms outstretched toward a shining orb, maybe five or six feet tall. The orb looked like it contained a spinning ball of fire. Then the camera shook, and the video went black.

She squinted with interest as the video replayed the scene in slow motion. Just before the screen became completely white, the figure raised its arm. Twisting tendrils of light leapt from the figure's hand; they looked like neurons from pictures in Jess' biology textbook. *No, it looks like lightning*, Jess thought. The bright, snaky branches climbed slowly as the millisecond counter on the video rose. Then the light evaporated, and the figure thrust both hands out toward - what was that? Fire? An explosion? It billowed out before becoming trapped by that weird orb. The orb gave off no light of its own; it was transparent, but also refracted the light from the fire like a prism. Orange and red shards of light illuminated the whole thing with tiny sunbursts of rainbows. The effect was actually quite pretty, and Jess marveled.

She replayed the entire video two more times. It could have been faked, she reasoned. But then again, what if it wasn't? She scrolled down and found a comment section that she glanced over to see what other visitors to the site had to say. The first commenter claimed the video was faked, the second said emphatically that it *had* to be real and had typed an entire paragraph listing reasons why, all having to do with lighting and lens flares and other technical jargon. Then, as Jess scrolled further, she found hundreds of comments below, every one of them stating in all-caps or with excessive punctuation that the video was faked.

*Of course it was,* Jess thought, shaking her head. She was about to exit the site, but paused. She scrolled through the comments section again. After the first two posts, all of the other comments on the site had been posted at the exact same time, a few minutes after noon. She clicked on the name of one commenter. The account had been created the same day. Same went for the next commenter. And the one after that.

*That's strange,* she thought. But maybe it was a coincidence. Or maybe all of it was wrong, and she was getting sucked into the crazy. She told herself she had to stay rational, like Arden said. He was always rational about everything.

The truck door opened and she jumped in surprise. Arden slid back into the driver's seat. "They said they'll hold it until the feds get here," he said.

Jess nodded, tucking her phone back into her pocket. They drove up the road to the hospital, and Arden strolled right up the receptionist's desk.

"Hi, we're here to visit the John Doe that was brought in yesterday," he said.

"Name?" the receptionist said dully.

"Arden Sheffield, and my daughter, Jess."

"One moment please."

She pressed a button on the phone on her desk. A moment or two later, Dr. Boenig hurried around the corner.

"Oh, you're here!" he sputtered. "I was about to call you!"

"You were?" Arden replied. "What's going on?"

"We've got to get that boy out of here," the doctor urged. "Come with me - hurry!"

Arden and Jess exchanged a look of surprise, then followed the doctor. He led them to an elevator which took them one floor up. He then guided them down a long hallway that appeared to be empty. Jess saw police officers at the end, apparently guarding a door. Dr. Boenig stopped in front of the door, then pointed at a wide window that provided a view of the room.

"Look in there," he said, his eyes wide.

Arden peered in; Jess put her hands up to the glass to look. Inside, the boy lay on a cot. He wore a hospital gown, and a dozen wires were attached to his forehead and fed under the collar that relayed information to an ECG and several other monitors. He had a respirator tube in his nose, and an IV stuck in his hand. His chest barely moved as he breathed.

"Is he alright?" Jess asked anxiously.

"Oh, yes, he's perfectly fine," Dr. Boenig said with a nervous chuckle. "He is completely healthy, as far as we can tell. But then, again, we have no idea how his biology works, so who knows? His stitches were removed early this morning, and his wound is completely healed. We're just keeping him sedated for the safety of our staff, and so he doesn't hurt himself."

"Okay, calm down, Erik," Arden said seriously.

That was when Jess noticed the leather restraints around both his wrists and ankles.

"Why would he hurt himself?" she asked.

Dr. Boenig wrung his hands.

"He has… reacted badly to his new environment."

"Has he hurt anyone?" Arden asked.

"He took a swipe at one of the orderlies after waking up in the middle of the night. He missed, thank goodness, but we've increased the dosage. We're using acemoprazine because ordinary general anaesthetic just doesn't cut it."

Arden opened his mouth in shock. "Horse tranquilizer? Is that safe?"

"Look, I don't know what else to do," Dr. Boenig said defensively. "I can't put my staff in danger."

"Do we even know that he *is* dangerous?" Arden demanded. "This is wrong - everything about this. Aren't you worried about getting sued once this kid's family turns up?"

Dr. Boenig's lip trembled.

"I'm more worried about the *creature* in that room," he said, his eyes wide.

"Creature!?" Arden exclaimed. "Erik, listen to yourself!"

"Look, we know that he's very strong, stronger than anyone his size should be, and he's healed from a mortal injury overnight. And that's actually why I was going to call you. We need to take a blood sample to make sure you two weren't exposed to anything when you brought him in."

"Anything like what?" Arden said, lowering his brows.

"Like *anything*. He's an unidentified life form. Who knows what types of viruses or pathogens he could be carrying that you would have no natural defense against?"

"Erik," Arden interjected. "You can't seriously think he's an alien from outer space…"

"I don't know *what* to think," the doctor said with exasperation. "This boy defies everything that I thought I knew. My more *religious* staff are getting anxious. They refuse to come to work. *Das ist verruckt.*"

Jess worriedly looked at her dad. Arden stood silently, his face inscrutable. Then he shook his head.

"Alright, whatever you want," he said. "Then we'd like to talk to him."

Dr. Boenig licked his lips anxiously and nodded. Jess was worried now, wondering what had spooked the doctor so badly, and what her father might do.

"Come with me," the doctor said.

He took them into the room next door and had them each sit in a chair. He and a nurse together drew six vials of blood that were placed on a tray and carried off.

"I'll be back soon with the results," Dr. Boenig said. He left, closing the door behind him.

They waited. Arden rested his arm on the back of Jess' chair, while she studied the small room. It was painted pale pink, with a small window in the wall opposite the door. Their chairs sat against the wall; there was a cot in the middle of the room, then cabinets and a sink to her left. The sun was setting outside, casting golden light through the vertical blinds. The longer she sat, the more stiff she became. Arden paced the floor; the silence was palpable, and Jess didn't dare break it. She watched the sunlight disappear completely before Dr. Boenig knocked on the door again, then entered.

"You're both clean," he announced.

"Thank the good Lord," Arden said sarcastically.

"I have some suits you'll need to put on, and then you can go in to see him. He won't be able to talk to you, because of the sedative, but he'll know you're there."

A couple of orderlies carried in two sets of protective suits that looked like surgical attire, complete with gloves, shoe covers, and helmets. Jess tied up her hair in a bun, then a female orderly helped her put the suit on. She had seen many medical dramas, and part of her was thrilled; she wondered if she looked like a real surgeon. The more reasonable part of her was terrified.

The police officers stepped aside to let them through a room like a small atrium, but filled with sinks and bottles of antiseptic. Then there was a plastic sheet that parted, and they were finally in the room.

The beep from the ECG machine was unnerving. The boy lay like a corpse; his skin was gray, with dark circles under his closed eyes. He looked gaunt, in contrast with the lean, muscular appearance he'd had before. His long, dark hair was matted and stuck to his neck.

Arden approached the bed first. He stepped right up to the side of it and stood over the boy. Jess thought he looked tense; his back was stiff, and his breath fogged the face shield of his helmet.

"I'm sorry, Jess," Arden said. "I wish it didn't have to be this way."

"Are they going to hurt him?" she asked.

There was that worry line again. He looked down at the sleeping boy, then back up at Jess. "We should go," he said, turning to leave.

The boy's eyes suddenly opened. Red, pupil-less eyes stared at the ceiling, and he let out a small cough.

"Who's there?" he said, barely louder than a whisper.

Jess and Arden exchanged a look. The boy lifted his head slightly. Jess couldn't be certain if his eyes were really looking at them.

"Hello," Arden said. "How are you feeling?"

"Better," the boy answered, though he certainly didn't look it.

"Do you remember me?"

The boy nodded. "You brought me to this place."

"Anything else?"

"You saved me. Thank you."

"You're welcome," Arden said, his voice catching in his throat.

The boy continued to stare. His eyes shimmered under the incandescent bulbs. Arden walked closer, his stride slow and easy. The boy turned his head, followed his progress until Arden was directly by his bedside.

"Have you recalled anything since we last spoke?" Arden asked. "Your name, for instance?"

He shook his head almost imperceptibly.

"Well, we'll have to call you something," Arden said cheerily. "How's Martin sound?"

"Martin?" the boy's accent came through as he pronounced it, emphasizing the last syllable instead of the first.

"It was my grandfather's name. Do you like it?"

"Yes, sir."

Arden gave Jess a sideways glance, and she knew what they both found funny; he hated to be called 'sir,' and now an unidentified life form was addressing him with it.

"Then, Martin it is."

"Thank you," the boy replied. His head turned to Jess, who still stood nervously at the far side of the room.

"Jess," he said. "I remember you."

Jess cheeks reddened. She was glad, but wasn't sure why.

"Hi," she said. "It's... it's good to see you again."

"English is not your native tongue is it?" Arden asked.

The boy blinked his rosy eyes.

"English?"

"It's the language you're speaking now," Arden said. "You have an accent that I can't place. What's your first language?"

Martin's expression changed. He looked pained, and Arden noticed it.

"Are you alright?" Arden asked. "Do you need something?"

The boy didn't seem to hear him. His gaze was fixed on Jess, while it seemed to take more effort to speak.

"I missed you," he said. "I'm so afraid."

Martin stopped, his breath catching. His eyes widened, and he flexed his hands against the restraints.

"What's wrong?" Arden asked again.

"This hurts," he gasped. "I can't breathe."

"What's happening?" Jess asked, panicked.

"Please, let me go," Martin pleaded, his pitch rising. "You can't do this to me - please!"

He struggled against the restraints, fighting to lift his head. The door opened and four men in protective suits entered. Three went to Martin's bedside, checking the machines; one had a syringe in his hand. The fourth began to usher Arden and Jess out of the room.

"It's time for you to go now," he said sharply.

"I thought he wouldn't be able to move or talk," Arden said. "He *was* sedated, right?"

"It's alright, we can take it from here," the man insisted. "Please, exit the room."

Jess kept watching the boy. She was frozen, unable to look away as Arden wrapped his arm around her shoulders and guided her back toward the door. Martin was yelling now, and his wrists and ankles rubbed raw under the leather straps.

"Please, Jess! Don't go!" he cried. "I am begging you. Help me, please!"

Jess's heart ached and tears stung her eyes, but she was already behind the plastic sheet. A mist sprayed down from the ceiling, and a woman began taking the suit off of her. Then she and Arden were back in the room next door, and a few tears of worry leaked down her cheeks.

"Dad, can't we do something?" she asked.

Arden hugged her tightly, his own face flushed with emotion.

"I don't know," he said in her ear. "I really don't... I'm sorry."

Suddenly there was a loud yell from the other room, and everyone startled. Arden was the first to move. He opened the door into the hall and hurried out, pulling Jess behind him. They rushed to the wide window; Dr. Boenig was already there, watching anxiously with his arms folded.

Martin had apparently broken free of one of his restraints, and was battling the man that was attempting to tie him back down. The IV stand lay on the ground. Martin grabbed the orderly by the collar of his scrubs, and the man strained to peel Martin's hand away. Jess couldn't believe that, even in his weakened state, this boy could be so much stronger than the male orderly - and he was using only one hand. The second man picked up the IV stand and fiddled with a syringe, nearly dropping it. Suddenly Martin's face contorted, and he let out another yell. He tossed the man away and with his free arm, he reached behind his back as if to scratch it. His expression changed from anger to confusion, then two great wings with snowy feathers erupted from Martin's back and spread wide, more than twenty feet across. They collided with the men on either side of him, tossing them backward like ragdolls. The men slammed into the walls on opposite sides of the room, denting the sheetrock, then dropped limply to the ground.

"What the hell?" Arden exclaimed. Jess could not believe her eyes; she barely dared to breathe.

"Like a goddamned angel," one of the cops said breathlessly, his eyes bugging out of their sockets.

The wings opened upward again with a loud rushing sound, launching Martin from the bed, but they had no room to fully expand. One hit the window directly in front of Arden's face with incredible force, cracking the glass. The other two men in the room crawled on the floor, dodging the wings as they folded, then stretched out as Martin struggled to stand up. He looked just as confused and amazed as everyone else. The sudden change in balance caused him to stumble and fall to his knees again and again. The wings opened rapidly outward again, slamming into the glass window and cracking it a second time, then vanished into thin air.

Jess, Arden, and everyone else in the hallway gaped, speechless. No one could believe what they had just seen. The two men lying on the ground behind Martin were beginning to recover, shaking their heads and blinking in what could only be surprise. The other two that hadn't been knocked out by his wings were back on their feet, but seemed hesitant to move any closer. Martin was on all fours, trembling, his tattered hospital gown hanging off of him in rags. His back arched as he heaved, then he vomited onto the linoleum floor.

Dr. Boenig pressed a button in the wall.

"Alright, grab him - get him back in the bed *now*," he ordered over the intercom.

The four men rushed at Martin and tackled him, pinning his arms to his sides. His head lolled as they lifted him up and carried him to the bed, and he did not struggle. He simply stared blankly up at the ceiling with his rosy red eyes. Two other people in protective suits hurried into the room; among the six of them working quickly, they had Martin strapped back down to the bed and hooked up to the sedative in less than a minute.

Dr. Boenig let out a shaky sigh of relief.

"*Meine Gott*, what are we dealing with?" he said with incredulity.

"It's an angel," one of the cops said. "Can't you use your eyes?"

Jess watched two of the cops crossing themselves as they kept a wary eye on the boy in the room, who was already back asleep. She began to wonder, too, whether this boy was an alien after all, or something else entirely.

"You can go now, my friend," Dr. Boenig told Arden, mopping his brow with a handkerchief. "The CIA will be here tomorrow to take over, and once they do, I'm going to take a much-needed vacation."

"Are they going to be able to handle this?" Arden said with disbelief.

"Better than I can, I hope. They claim they have a specialist on hand... someone who can handle these 'unique cases.'"

He made air quotes as he said the last part. Arden shook his head.

"Whoever that is, he better be pretty damn special," he said.

# CHAPTER 3

━━━━◆━━━━

*I*ntense hunger woke Lucas. He opened his eyes to a blue room, with a lamp glaring down on him. He was lying on something hard, like a bench. A thin blanket was draped over him, pulled up to his chin. Seeing spots, he blinked against the bright light, then turned his head to look around. He was apparently alone. The room was small, and painted sky blue. There was a chair in one corner, and a camera suspended from the ceiling; Lucas' mind traced the camera to a room up the hall full of monitors. Over his head hung two clear bags; one for an IV drip, the other a blood transfusion. The long, thin tubes were connected to his body by needles in the back of his hand.

He began to panic, until he sensed Kowalski's phone in the hall.

"Hello?" he called out, attempting to sit up, but dizziness made him stop short.

The door opened and Kowalski stepped inside, carrying a stack of clothes.

"Whoa, go easy," he warned, standing over him. Lucas realized that he was lying on a wide metal table.

"What happened?" he asked, his mouth dry. "Where am I?"

"After that bomb went off, we brought you back here to our field office to recover."

"How long was I out?"

Kowalski had brought him his own pair of jeans, t-shirt, underwear and shoes. He set these on the chair by the door.

"All night. You had to regrow most of your skin and… a few limbs."

Lucas shuddered at the thought. He raised his head slowly to look

34

down at his body; both arms and legs were there, so his recovery was apparently successful.

"I thought the suit was supposed to protect me," he said.

"It's heat-resistant, but useless against a concussive blast like that," Kowalski replied brusquely. "You destroyed it on your first night out. It's in repair right now."

"Oh, I'm sorry," Lucas said.

"How do you feel?"

"I'm starving," Lucas answered.

"You need to eat," Kowalski nodded. "Healing that much damage takes a lot of energy."

As he spoke, the door opened and two women wearing scrubs entered. They removed the needles from his hand, and the holes closed up immediately. An agent brought a TV table and tray laden with food; the smell made his stomach knot.

"Sit up carefully, honey," the first woman said. She was a middle-aged woman with a round face. She took his hand and gently pulled him upright while the second woman supported his back. Once he was seated, he felt a breeze over his scalp and reached up. His crown was covered in short stubble.

"What happened to my hair?" he asked in surprise.

"What do you think happened?" Kowalski said. "It got burned off. You survived a bomb blowing up in your face and you're worried about your hair?"

Lucas reddened. *The kids at school are going to love this,* he thought with dismay.

"No, you're right," he said, shaking his head.

The women left the room, taking the IV stand with them, and Kowalski set his clothes on the table.

"Can you stand?" he asked.

"Yeah," Lucas answered.

Kowalski turned his back so he could dress. Lucas slid off the table carefully and tested the strength of his legs. They held. He wondered if either of them had been blown off and grown back.

*Like a lizard,* he thought, his stomach turning. It took a few minutes to dress, because he felt so weak. His hands fluttered like dead leaves, and he was quickly out of breath. Kowalski finally turned back around once he was fully dressed, and helped him to the small table so he could eat. On the tray was an omelet and fried potatoes, toast, a sliced orange, a small cup of black coffee and a glass of water.

"I don't drink coffee," Lucas said, grimacing.

"That's for me," Kowalski replied, taking the cup.

Lucas downed the food quickly, and he felt much better. His mind became clearer, and his hands soon stopped quivering. It was a large portion, but within ten minutes it was all gone, except for the orange. He could feel Kowalski looking at him as he sucked on one of the slices. He was pacing the floor and his mouth was tight. Lucas guessed he had something to say.

"Was anyone else hurt last night?" he asked carefully.

"Yes," Kowalski answered. "Two died from infection from the nanomachines. Can you tell me how that happened?"

His tone was cold and measured. Lucas knew immediately that he was in trouble.

"I dropped one of the vials when I shot down that drone - it was a Rising drone, and I felt an infrared beam come out of it. That's what set off the bomb."

Kowalski crossed his arms, leaning back against the wall.

"And what were you supposed to do with the vials?"

"I was supposed to bring them to you," he answered heavily. "But I couldn't do it. They would still be a danger to people, unless I put them where they couldn't hurt anyone else."

"Lucas, I appreciate your heroism, but that wasn't your call to make. And now two people are dead."

"I'm sorry," Lucas answered, and he meant it. "But it would have been more if I hadn't done it! There was no way I could have stopped that bomb from going off, and when it did, all of those vials would have been vaporized and hundreds infected."

"*I know that!*" Kowalski roared, slamming his hand on the table with a loud *bang*, and Lucas jumped out of the chair. "Don't you understand? I know it, and you know it, but the public *doesn't* know it. All they know is what they saw, and can you guess what they're afraid of?"

"Me," Lucas answered, realization dawning on him. Kowalski leaned over him and jabbed a finger at his chest.

"*You.* You're all over the internet now, and they are terrified of you. The President wants you back in hibernation, and my division dissolved."

Lucas swallowed hard. He felt his lip tremble.

"I saved people," he said quietly.

"That doesn't matter. The country is in a panic. Everyone wants to know who you are, and which foreign government is responsible for you."

"Kowalski," Lucas begged. "I can fix it. I can bury this, spam everyone who looks for the story - even make up a few dead ends, you know? Something to make everyone think it's fake."

Kowalski looked away, his hands on his hips. His jaw clenched. Lucas was terrified now. His mind began to race through all the possible ways he could fight his way out of the building, and then go… where?

"I know you can fix it, and you're going to," Kowalski said finally with a level, steady tone. "Bureaucracy being what it is, it'll be days before the higher-ups make any official decision about your fate. During that time, you are going to make yourself as useful and *indispensable* as possible. Bury this story, and stay out of trouble. Go about your day as normally and quietly as you possibly can. One wrong move and you're back in a pod, and I won't be able to protect you. You got that?"

Lucas nodded fiercely, wiping away a stray tear. Thankfully, Kowalski wasn't looking at him; he was checking his phone.

"Now go," he said. "School starts in two hours."

"School?"

"Yes - what did I just say?" Kowalski said impatiently. "Normal, quiet, business as usual. I'll call you if I need you."

Lucas hung his head. Then he felt Kowalski's hand on his shoulder. His eyes were softer now.

"Look," he said quietly. "I know you think you did the right thing, and as your friend, I would agree with you. But as your handler, I am obligated to tell you to keep your head down. This is a matter of life and death - *your* life. Understood?"

"Yes, sir," Lucas answered.

Kowalski swept out of the room, and Lucas was left alone. He sat for several long seconds before the door opened again and he was escorted by men in suits down a long, wood-paneled hallway to an elevator. They took the elevator thirty floors down to a lobby with waxed floors, a fountain, and metal detectors.

"Can you manage your way home from here?" one of the suits asked.

"Yeah, thanks, Jim," Lucas answered.

The men each shook his hand, and he walked through the double doors and out onto the sidewalk. He found himself in the middle of downtown, with glittering skyscrapers towering above him and pedestrians filling the sidewalk. He backed up to be out of the way of the foot traffic as he got his bearings. The bus stop was a block away, and it was ten minutes until the next bus arrived that would take him to the northwest side of town, to his house. In another twenty minutes, another bus would arrive to take him south to school. He decided to wait for the latter. Though he had time, he did not feel like going home. He knew his mother would be freaking out, but he did not have the energy or patience to deal with her. Pulling up the memory file that he had designated as an inbox, he found three unread messages from her demanding to know if he was okay. He sighed, then guiltily typed out a text to reply.

*Hi. I'm fine. Heading to school.*

A new message arrived almost immediately.

*OMG I have been worried sick!!! I was up all night!*

Lucas groaned and rubbed his eyes. *You know I can't die,* he wanted to say, but instead he wrote, *Sorry to worry you. I'll be more careful next time.*

He sat on the bench at the public bus stop, his elbows on his knees and his head in his hands; Kowalski's words weighed heavily on his mind. It wasn't the first time the United States government had threatened to end his life, although he had proven time and again that he was nearly impossible to kill. In the past year, he had been shot (twice), electrocuted, and blown up (now twice). Even at the moment he gained his powers, he had been nearly crushed to death. The nanomachines in his body healed all of it. It wasn't dying that worried him, it was all the creative ways that the government might attempt, and probably fail, to make it finally happen.

*So don't let them,* Lucas told himself. *Prove to them that they need you.*

He looked up as the bus arrived. The brakes hissed as the bus came to a stop, and doors opened. He climbed aboard, then found a seat toward the back. As his brain connected to the onboard wifi, he searched the internet for any video of the bombing last night. He found a few dozen, mostly from high-quality cameras that had filmed the event from afar, or stolen video footage from police body cams. Lucas was amazed as he watched himself catching the bomb's blast in his force field; it felt like an out of body experience. All the feed showed at first was a dark figure, and it was impossible to guess any specific features; he mentally thanked R&D a hundred times over for that mask. He replayed over and over again the moment of the bomb's explosion, when the figure was silhouetted against a brilliantly glowing, white-hot orb, and felt a sense of pride swell inside his chest. Then, as the explosion was finally released and the dark figure went flying out of the shot, he winced.

Lucas had to skim through thousands of individual social media profiles before he found the original owners of the videos, then removed the posts. Then there were the official news stories, which were another matter altogether. He was surprised that any legitimate news stations were talking about him at all; surely they were more likely to assume it was faked. He decided to play that up, swamping each news outlet's websites with angry, anonymous tips that the video was fabricated.

All that done, he sat back, feeling a sense of accomplishment. Then his stomach growled. He was still hungry, even after that large meal back at the field office. He decided to get off early to find something to eat, then walk the rest of the way. When the bus hissed to a stop a few blocks from the school, he stepped off and made straight for a nearby Einstein's Bagels and went inside.

As he stood in line, he noticed five students from his school seated at one of the tables in the corner. He recognized Lily Hofstetter's strawberry blonde hair, and reddened when he realized she was sneaking glances at him over her shoulder. His palms began to sweat as butterflies fluttered in his stomach. Then he realized they were all looking at him. He kept his face forward, pretending to be oblivious, but it was clear that all five were staring. It baffled him. He had gotten used to being ignored all semester, so why the sudden interest?

He placed his order for two bagel sandwiches and chocolate milk, then sat on a bench and waited. In his periphery, he saw Lily and the other students whispering to each other. They couldn't possibly know what happened last night, so what were they talking about? Between his anxiety and hunger, he became increasingly impatient. When his order was finally ready, he snatched it off the counter and hurried out of the restaurant.

As he left, he sensed a text sent from Lily's phone to all of her many friends. Unable to help himself, he intercepted it as it raced through the flowing current of electromagnetic signals. He stopped in his tracks when a picture of himself opened up.

It was taken less than a minute ago, while he was picking up his food at the counter. He saw his shaved head and dark, haunted-looking eyes. The caption on the photo read,

*OMG what's wrong with Lucas Tavera?*

Lucas was perplexed. What was that supposed to mean?

One of Lily's friends replied quickly.

*Stay away if you're smart! He's bad news!*

Lucas couldn't believe it. Why? What had he done wrong? He had done his absolute best to remain invisible, and now... this.

Cheeks burning, he set his jaw and hurried the rest of the way to school. It was still early; the first bell would not ring for another thirty minutes. He finished the bagel sandwiches to stop the gnawing in his stomach, then tossed the paper bag in a nearby trashcan and surveyed the yard. Some kids milled about in the yard, chatting and texting on their phones. Lucas didn't know what to do. He couldn't confront anyone about the texts, because he would have to reveal how he knew about them. Lily had a *lot* of friends; it wouldn't be long before the entire school was talking about him.

"Lucas!"

Lucas spun around. A blond, lanky boy with a pointed face was running up to him with a book under his arm. Lucas immediately tensed.

"Nate?"

"Hey, man," he said breathlessly, stopping right in front of Lucas. "Oh my god, are you okay?"

"What are you talking about?" Lucas replied, startled.

"Wasn't that you, in that video? You - " he looked around, then lowered his voice to a whisper. "You stopped that bomb, right?"

"Yeah, but... how did you know?"

Nate lit up, grinning broadly.

"You're the only guy I know with superpowers, so it wasn't exactly a long shot," he said. "I knew right away when I saw it. Jesus, that was amazing. Were you hurt when it went off?"

"Uh, yeah. It wasn't too bad. I spent the night healing. Lost a few limbs, apparently."

"Dude," Nate cringed. "Which ones?"

"I don't know, I passed out."

"And your hair?"

"Lost that, too. I can regrow skin, but not hair."

"Holy shit," Nate said.

"Yeah."

"I'm sorry, Lucas."

Lucas blinked, surprised.

"For what?"

Nate pressed his lips together and looked away. He didn't seem to know what to do with the hand that wasn't holding the book, and finally put it in his pocket.

"I was pretty scared of you for awhile," he said quietly. "After all that stuff happened, and seeing you almost die again back at your old apartment. It kind of messed me up, you know?"

Lucas hung his head, a hard knot forming in his throat. He knew better than anyone.

"Yeah, me too."

"And I forgot that," Nate nodded. "I couldn't imagine what it's like for you now, until I saw that video last night. It was amazing what you did, and I thought, 'I want that guy to be my friend again.' Not because of your cool powers or 'cause you're a hero, but because you probably need a friend."

Lucas looked up at that and nodded, then smiled.

"You're right. I do."

"Will you be my friend again?" Nate asked.

"Of course," he said.

They shook hands, and Lucas caught another kid staring from a few yards away. He dropped Nate's hand.

"What's wrong with everyone?" he asked Nate. "Why do they keep staring at me?"

"They're just curious," Nate answered.

"About what?"

"Where you've been for the past year. You disappeared, and now you're back and you're different. There are a few rumors floating around as to where you went."

"What do they say?"

"My favorite is that you went to Mexico and joined a gang, but most popular is you went to juvie for fighting."

"That's ridiculous," Lucas scoffed.

"Not as ridiculous as the real story," Nate remarked.

"You've got a point there," he sighed.

"So how did you do it?" Nate asked.

"Do what?"

"The bomb," Nate said, whispering excitedly. "How did you stop that bomb from going off? I know you can talk to computers and make lightning, but I don't know the other stuff you can do."

Lucas glanced around the yard, then beckoned for Nate to follow him. They walked quickly but casually around the back of the school to the teacher's entrance, which required a badge. With a mental command from Lucas, the scanner winked green, and he opened the door. He led the way to the boy's bathroom around the corner. There was one camera in the upper corner of the hall, but he caused it to fritz just long enough for them to get inside unseen.

"Oh man, that was awesome!" Nate exclaimed, once they were in. He dropped his backpack on the floor.

Lucas shushed him, but he was grinning, too.

"Okay, so I used a force field to trap the bomb from going off," he said. "It's the same thing that stopped that bus in July, just a little smaller."

"Can I see?" Nate asked excitedly.

"Yeah, that's why I brought you here," Lucas answered. "Ready?"

Nate nodded, and Lucas held out his hands. Heat began to gather in his chest, then spread across his skin down to his hands. Energy crackled, then sparked, then tiny filaments of light leapt and danced across his fingers.

"Whoa," Nate gaped, staring.

Lucas focused, and the tendrils met between his hands. They began to gather into a sphere about the size of a golf ball, hovering in the air. It was transparent, like glass, but sparked as it were alive with energy. He fed it until it was the size of a softball, and Nate raised a finger to touch it, his eyes wide with wonder.

"Go ahead," Lucas said. "It might shock you, though."

Nate extended a shaky finger toward the sphere and tapped its surface. There was no sound, but ripples of light were sent dancing across the exterior of the field.

"It's so... pretty," Nate commented.

"It can stop bullets, too," Lucas said proudly.

That piercing pain began in his skull, so he dropped his hands and the sphere vanished. Sweat beaded on his temples, and his heart beat quickly.

"That was awesome, man," Nate said with a smile. "So cool."

He looked down and saw the burns coating the backs and palms of Lucas' hands, then frowned. Lucas saw him staring and hid them behind his back, cheeks reddening.

"That's nothing," Lucas said. "They'll heal in a few seconds."

"Does that always happen?" Nate asked.

"Yeah, every time," Lucas replied quietly.

He didn't wait for Nate to say anything else, though he could tell he wanted to. The bell rang, and students began to drift inside. Lucas went to the door and cracked it open, watching. He waited until traffic had gotten thick, then slipped out into the hall. Their first period classes were in the same hallway, so Nate stayed close. Kids pressed in on all sides, and traffic slowed to a crawl. One of the assistant principals yelled over the tops of the students' heads for everyone to quit dawdling. Lucas and Nate finally split as Lucas entered his English class and found his seat, while Nate went to Math. He sat down and rubbed a hand self-consciously over his bald head.

The bell rang, and the teacher turned out the lights and immediately launched into his lecture on *Romeo and Juliet*. Lucas realized that he didn't have anything to write with; his notebook was at his house. No matter; he simply awakened the supercomputer part of his mind and committed everything he heard and saw to his memory files, and resigned to copy it all down later. He listened with his hands folded on his desk, and watched as the teacher clicked through Powerpoint slides, taking mental snapshots of each one.

Forty minutes later, the lights came back on.

"Alright, ladies and gentlemen," the teacher said. "Open your books and complete a summary of Act 4. Whatever you don't finish will be homework."

The students opened the class copies of the textbooks on their desks and set to work, but Lucas still had no pencil or paper. As the teacher passed back graded assignments, he glanced surreptitiously around the classroom, looking for someone to ask. Most of the students had their heads down as they worked, but a few were sneaking hurried peeks at him. One boy looked at him over his shoulder with narrowed eyes, then leaned over to whisper to his neighbor.

"Quiet," the teacher barked.

Lucas waited until the teacher's back was turned, then reached over and tapped the shoulder of the boy in the desk in front of him. The boy turned.

"Hey, can I borrow a pencil?" Lucas whispered.

The boy glared at him, then turned back around.

*Thanks a lot,* Lucas thought, rolling his eyes.

A paper ball landed on Lucas' desk. He looked around in surprise, wondering where it had come from. The teacher was meandering slowly up the row of desks. Lucas picked up the ball and carefully, quietly, began to unroll the paper. On it was a cartoon drawing of himself, with a bald head; his eyes were drawn unnaturally large and orb-like, and he had long vampire fangs.

He stared at it, unsure of whether to laugh or cry. The longer he looked at it, nausea turned his stomach. He hurriedly balled up the paper again as his face and hands grew hot, and he struggled to take another deep, steadying breath.

The teacher passed by him and glanced down his nose at Lucas' empty desk. Lucas expected him to chide him and ask why he hadn't started his assignment, but instead he rolled his eyes and sighed, then walked away. With a frustrated groan, Lucas laid his head down on the desk.

When the bell rang, he was the first one out the door. He hurried down the hall to History. As he rushed along, he felt a tingle up the back of his spine. Over the other students' heads he saw Val Espinoza, Howard Mays, and Darren Jones. They walked three across up the middle of the hallway, and shoved aside students that didn't move out of their way. One of those was Nate, who tried to duck to the side but collided with another kid, then Val shouldered him into a locker.

"Hey!" Lucas said, outraged.

Val gave a short, backward glance as they continued on. The kid Nate had collided with gathered up his dropped books then rushed away without looking up. Lucas hurried up to Nate.

"Are you alright?" he asked.

"Yeah," he said, wincing as he peeled himself off the locker. "Those jerks just can't stay away, can they?"

"Seems not," Lucas replied, glaring at their backs until they disappeared. "Hey, can I borrow a pencil?"

"Sure," Nate said, and dug one out of his backpack.

"And paper?"

Nate looked at him. "Where's your stuff?"

"I didn't sleep at home last night," Lucas answered sheepishly. "They brought me new clothes, but not my notebook."

"Do you need to copy my notes for English, then?"

"No, thanks. I remember everything, I just need to write it down."

"What do you mean, you remember everything?"

Lucas shrugged.

"I remember everything," he said again.

"Like, *literally* remember everything?"

"Yeah, it's all recorded and stored in here," he said, tapping his temple.

Nate squinted at him, notebook in hand.

"You record everything you see?" he said incredulously. "Any other powers you want to tell me about?"

"I also have laser-eyes," Lucas replied with a wink. "Yes, I can record everything, then save it in memory files."

"If you can do that, why do you need to write things down?"

"For appearances, and because otherwise I would be cheating."

"You mean you don't, like, Google the answers on a test?"

"No," Lucas said, offended.

"Why not?" Nate said with a grin. "I would."

"I don't because I can," Lucas answered emphatically. "What would it prove? I'm just trying to lay low here, and be as normal as possible."

They both entered the class, but instead of his usual seat, Nate picked one beside Lucas. Both placed their notebooks on their desks. Music played over the intercom, signaling the last minute of passing period.

"Is that why you won't do anything about Val and his lackeys?" Nate asked in a whisper.

Lucas stared at him. Nate's expression was deadly serious. Now he began to understand why Nate had been so angry with him, but before he could answer, Mr. Cole entered the classroom and started class by taking questions about last night's homework. Lucas sat quietly, taking notes, but his mind was a million miles away. Finally, they were told to answer the questions at the end of the chapter and Mr. Cole allowed them to talk quietly. The class immediately erupted in chatter.

"Yes," Lucas whispered, leaning over to Nate.

"What?"

"The answer to your question," Lucas said. "I leave Val and the others alone because I'm supposed to be a normal kid here. I can't just go and pick a fight with them."

"Even though you'd win?"

Lucas gave a half-smile.

"Yeah… even though I'd win. I'm here to go to school, and that's it. Not to be a hero."

"You could be," Nate insisted.

"No, I can't… I'm sorry."

"What about the stuff you do for the CIA?" Nate asked. He wasn't letting it go. "That's not exactly 'normal' stuff."

"Yeah, but that's outside of school, and it's a secret. I even wear a mask. If I do anything here - anything at all that would draw attention, I'm gone. They'll lock me up and I'll never come back."

Nate looked unconvinced, but said nothing more. In fact, he stayed quiet for the rest of the class period. Lucas wondered if he was going to go back to the full silent treatment. They split up again for the next class, which Lucas used to check news for any more stories about the bombing. Each channel ran a conversation about the aftermath and cleanup, but there was no mention of the mysterious figure; Lucas guessed that his spamming campaign must be working.

At lunch, Lucas got in line and filled a tray with two slices of cheese pizza, a cup of fruit, a cookie, and an apple; he paid extra for an additional sandwich and a bag of chips. He was halfway through the meal at his usual table when Nate arrived with a plate of meatloaf and carrots.

"Wow," he said with raised eyebrows. "Did you really get two lunches?"

"Yeah, I'm starving," Lucas replied with his mouth full.

"Slow down before you choke," Nate said, sitting down. "Hey, what about that Romana chick? Where is she now?"

*So much for the silent treatment,* Lucas thought. He had to admit, it did feel good to talk to someone.

"I don't know," he said. "She's out there somewhere, but I can't find her."

"That's a scary thought," Nate muttered.

"She used to just be in my head, kind of on the periphery where I could feel her, but just barely. Then she spoke to me when the bomb went off. I think she was there, watching."

"What are you going to do?"

Lucas shook his head.

"I can't do anything if I can't find her," he answered, irritated. "It's like she's everywhere and nowhere at the same time; I can't pin her down. Whatever she's doing, it's working."

Then Lucas felt a buzz inside his skull that tickled all the way down the back of his neck. He was getting a phone call.

*Kowalski?*

*Hey, kid,* Kowalski's voice said in his head. *The office got a phone call about a suspicious character found out west, near Odessa. He was injured, so some locals took him to a hospital. A DNA test showed he's a nonhuman.*

"Lucas?" Nate said hesitantly. "Are you okay?"

Lucas held up a hand to quiet him; his heart was pounding.

*An android?* he asked. *Another one?*

*I thought so, until we got a video from one of their security cameras. I just sent it to you.*

Lucas found the email forwarded to him and opened it up. The video was taken from a hallway security camera, and provided a partial view of the room. A person with long, dark hair lay in a hospital bed and appeared to be wrestling with some of the staff. Then, to Lucas' amazement, he tossed one of them across the room, one-handed.

"Nate, check this out," he whispered. He channeled the video into Nate's phone and opened it up.

He played it back, and Nate gasped. Lucas watched, baffled, as a pair of snow-white, angel-like wings sprang from the person's back. They spanned the width of the room and knocked two of the staff out. He leapt off the bed, but seemed too weak to stand. After a few unsuccessful attempts, his wings vanished, and the hospital staff tackled him to the ground. The video ended there.

"What the hell was that?" Nate asked, wide-eyed. "Was that real?"

"I think it was," Lucas replied. "Kowalski sent it to me. Hold on, I'm on the phone with him right now."

*Kowalski, I don't know what I'm looking at here; mythological creatures are outside my area of expertise.*

*Mine too, but unfortunately, this falls to my division. We have to go investigate it, and the higher-ups want the whole operation kept under wraps. As soon as the paperwork comes through, you and I are going to Kermit.*

*Wait, why do I have to go?* Lucas asked.

*Because an indestructible, super-powered android is useful to have on hand, especially if turns out this is another android after all.*

With that, he hung up. Lucas couldn't deny that he was immensely curious about this creature, whatever it was. *But this is way beyond me,* he thought.

"Well?" Nate said. He waved his hand in front of Lucas' face. "Hello?"

"He said we have to go check it out," Lucas said, swatting Nate's hand away. "Investigating weird things are part of the job, apparently."

"That didn't look like an android. Winged people - those are angels, aren't they?"

"I don't believe in angels," Lucas said. "But we don't have any leads on Romana or the Rising, or what they're doing next. I just want to make sure this isn't connected to them."

"Artificial people are real," Nate remarked. "Why can't angels be real?"

"Because they just aren't," Lucas replied. "Everything has an explanation. Supernatural things like angels and demons were made up by people who just didn't understand what was going on."

"A hundred years ago, what do you think people would have called you?"

"I wouldn't have existed, because the science to make me wasn't invented yet," Lucas retorted.

"Whatever," Nate said, throwing up his hands. "You're hopeless."

"I'm just a believer in science," Lucas said with a gloating smile.

The bell rang, and the room was then filled with the noise of chairs scraping as students began to make their way back to class. Lucas got up to throw away his trash. As he pushed his chair back, someone's elbow hit him hard in the back of the head. That was followed by a swinging backpack, apparently full of heavy books.

"Out of my way, freak!" a boy snapped.

"Hey, what's wrong with you!?" Nate shouted, outraged.

Lucas was seeing stars. He leaned forward, rubbing the back of his head while Nate jumped to his feet and made his way around the table. The boy saw him coming and straightened up, squaring his shoulders.

"What, you want to stick up for the freak?" he challenged.

"Nate, stop," Lucas warned.

Nate glared at the smirking boy as he disappeared into the crowd of kids, then hurried to Lucas' side. Lucas had his hand clamped over the back of his head.

"Are you okay?" Nate asked.

"I think so," Lucas answered hesitantly. "Am I bleeding?"

He cautiously peeled back his hand as Nate looked.

"No, just a bruise... well, now it's gone."

Lucas grimaced, standing up. The cafeteria was emptying, and soon they would be the only students left. Two janitors, three tables over, cleared away trash that was left behind. Nate picked up his backpack, his face red.

"Why do you put up with that?" he asked angrily. "You don't have to keep taking that shit; you could just teach them a lesson."

"No, I told you, I can't," Lucas said in a hushed voice. "You don't get it - they don't matter, alright? I've got bigger things to worry about."

Nate gave no reply, but his face grew redder. They walked back to class in silence, but Lucas paused at the door.

"I don't want to end up back in a cell," he said. "If I can't cut it here, that's where they'll send me. Maybe not right away, but eventually. And then, after a few days or weeks, they'll talk about putting me back to sleep. So, as bad as this is, I have to stick it out. There's no other option. I'm sorry, okay?"

He turned away from Nate's grim expression and walked to his desk. As he sat down, a buzz went off inside his skull.

*Lucas,* Kowalski's voice said. *We leave for Kermit at six tonight. I'll bring your new suit.*

# CHAPTER 4

———◆———

*J*ess awoke in the middle of the night to the sound of pounding on the front door. She sat up, listening intently. Arden's footsteps creaked over the floorboards downstairs, then the door opened.

"Hello, we're from the CIA," a man's gruff voice said. "We'd like to ask you a few questions."

"Please, come in," Arden said calmly.

Jess sprang from her bed in a panic. The CIA was here, and they had come to take Martin. She threw on a shirt and jeans, then crept to the top of the stairs.

"What's your name, sir?" the man said.

"Arden Sheffield."

"Are you the only one in the house?"

"No. My daughter, Jess, is upstairs sleeping."

Jess descended the first few steps, straining to see into the living room. She saw a tall, blond man in a suit and tie standing with her father. He looked to be in his thirties, maybe early forties, and was tanned and muscular.

"I'm Agent Seth Kowalski," he said. "I'm with a special task force of the CIA. This is my colleague, Firebolt. He's a specialist we bring on for these unusual cases. Will you take a seat?"

"Of course," Arden said.

The two men passed in front of the stairs, and Jess shrank back. They sat across from each other at the kitchen table. Jess couldn't see the one that Agent Kowalski had called his 'colleague.'

"What about your friend?" Arden asked.

"Pay him no mind - he's just doing his job," Agent Kowalski said dismissively. "You found a boy on the road two days ago, and brought him to the hospital. Is that correct?"

"Yes, he was hurt pretty bad. We got him help."

"Mr. Sheffield, it's very important that you give us your utmost cooperation here."

"I don't understand."

"This situation is very sensitive," Agent Kowalski said seriously. "We need assurance that you will not share with anyone else what you have seen or heard regarding this boy."

"Why?"

"This is not just any ordinary boy; I think you may have guessed that. We don't yet know where he came from or what he is capable of. It is important that we exercise every caution and take no unnecessary risks. Do you have a smartphone?"

"No, sir."

"A laptop?"

"In my office."

"We'll have to confiscate it," Agent Kowalski told him. "It'll be returned after it's been searched."

"Searched for what?" Arden said, confused.

"Does your daughter have a smartphone?" Agent Kowalski asked, ignoring his question.

"Yes, but -"

"Where?"

"I assume it's upstairs, with her. But look, you can't just come in here and take our things without a warrant -"

Agent Kowalski appeared to be ignoring him. He looked back into the living room at something Jess couldn't see, then nodded and turned back to Arden.

"Wake her and bring her down here," he said.

"This is unacceptable," Arden protested.

"Excuse me, sir, you and your daughter have been in contact with an unidentified life form. It is my job to keep you both safe, and I need you to cooperate with me to do this. We can go up there and bring her down forcefully, or you can do it now… the easy way."

Arden pushed back his chair and stood slowly, regarding Agent

Kowalski with silent fury. He stepped toward the stairs, but Jess was already descending, her phone in hand.

"Here," she said indignantly, holding it out.

Agent Kowalski took it without a word, then walked into the living room. There stood a figure that Jess didn't see at first because it blended in with the nighttime shadows. He was slim, shorter than she was, and dressed head to toe in black. He wore a bulletproof vest over a bodysuit, and even had a mask covering his entire head, with a pair of goggles over the eyes. A white lightning bolt symbol stood out brightly on his left shoulder. Jess gasped, realizing that she had seen this figure before. She watched as he accepted the phone from the agent, then laid it across his gloved palm. Nothing happened for several seconds; the figure just stood there, still as a statue, while the phone's screen remained black.

"Her internet searches are problematic," the figure said finally. There was something strange about the voice, like it was distorted, but it sounded male.

"I've seen you before," she blurted. "In a video. You were in Austin."

"Jess, don't talk to them," Arden chided, glaring at the agent.

"Case in point," the figure said, nodding at her.

"You were supposed to take care of that," Agent Kowalski told the figure sharply.

"I did," the figure replied, sounding miffed. "She was pretty determined."

"Can you clear her history?"

"I can do better than that."

Another few seconds went by while the figure remained motionless. Jess was bursting with questions. Here the figure was, the one from the video - right in front of her. Was he an alien, too? And what was he doing with her phone?

"Was that real?" Jess asked. "What happened in the video?"

"Jess, quiet," Arden said sharply.

"Are you an alien?"

"*Jess!*"

The figure raised his head. Jess couldn't see through the lenses of the goggles, but she felt like he was looking at her. She tried to imagine the expression he might have.

"No," he answered flatly. Then he held out her phone. "There. It's just like new."

Jess approached slowly, and accepted her phone back. It had been restored to factory settings.

"Alright," Agent Kowalski said. "I think we have what we need here. Let's get going."

His phone rang in his pocket, and drew it out. "Yes?" he said, placing the phone to his ear.

The figure's posture suddenly changed. He stiffened, then cocked his head. Agent Kowalski looked at him as he hung up the phone.

"What's going on?" Jess asked.

"Looks like we're all going on a field trip," he said.

"What are you talking about?" Arden asked, putting his hands protectively on Jess' shoulders.

"They're having issues getting the ULF to cooperate. We're going to rendezvous with our men at the hospital. You'll ride with us, and once we've picked up the ULF we're all going to Austin."

Jess looked nervously at her dad, but he was glaring at Agent Kowalski.

"You can't just take us from our home," he said angrily. "I want a lawyer."

The agent looked relaxed.

"This is all for your own safety; now, I'm not going to ask again."

Arden looked angry and afraid. Jess worried about what the government would do with Martin, but she was also overwhelmingly curious about the figure in black. He went outside first, disappearing into the darkness, while two other agents in suits and ties entered the house. One of them was a black man with broad shoulders, the other a redhead with tattoos peeking out from beneath his jacket sleeves. Jess wondered if they had been waiting out on the porch. They stood with hands folded while Jess and Arden put on their boots, and Jess put on a jacket.

"Follow me, please," Agent Kowalski said.

Arden and Jess walked behind him with the two agents at their heels. Parked outside in the yard was a large, black van. The back doors were open, and Agent Kowalski stopped there and beckoned for them to get inside. Jess climbed in first, and found the figure in black in the first seat. She slid into the row behind him. Arden sat beside her, and Agent Kowalski took the passenger's seat.

"Go," he told the driver.

The van pulled out of the yard and onto the highway. Outside, the full moon shone on the bare ground, bathing it in a silvery glow. The mesquite trees cast gnarled, twisted shadows, while millions of stars glittered overhead. Jess looked around the silent van, and noticed that the figure in black was staring out the window, too. He didn't move for several long minutes; the sight was almost melancholy. Jess couldn't help herself. She leaned forward.

"Where are you from?" she whispered.

He turned his head, but only slightly.

"Austin," he replied.

"Really?"

"Yes."

"How old are you?"

Jess wasn't sure why she asked that, only that even with his voice distorted, he sounded young. He said nothing, and Jess wondered if she'd offended him. But then, he raised his hand and pointed downward, over his shoulder. She looked, and the screen of the phone she held in her hands illuminated. On it were two text messages from an unknown number:

*13.*

*How old are you?*

Jess stared at the messages, then up at the black figure. His head was turned, but it appeared he was only looking out the window. Did he do that? And if he did, how? Her second thought was that he was indeed very young - younger than she was. How could a kid work with the CIA? While her mind was spinning with these questions, and before she was really sure of what she was doing, her fingers moved, typing quickly.

*15. I'm Jess. What's your name?*

The reply came right away.

*Firebolt.*

Jess was amazed. How was this possible? He was communicating telepathically, through her phone. He *had* to be an alien, or else there was some other explanation for his apparent powers that she couldn't guess. She typed out a response.

*That's not your real name.*

*No. Codename.*

*It means lightning, right?*

*Yes.*

She remembered the video, in which he was struck by lightning. She sat back, baffled, and watched the moon as the van raced down the highway. How did she end up here? Only days ago she would have thought that such things as aliens, or angels, or people who could communicate psychically through a phone were impossible.

Pressing her lips together, she began to type another question, but all the previous messages suddenly disappeared, and the screen went black. The conversation was over.

Lucas was thinking about Jess, and he was conflicted. He was happy that she wanted to talk to him, and didn't seem scared. He was also worried about being too friendly, or sharing more than he should. She would certainly be afraid, if she knew what he really was. It was better not to get involved. He watched the moon through the van window; the landscape outside was so open… and so empty.

He saw the flashing red and blue lights long before they pulled into the hospital parking lot, and he tensed. The town's sheriff and a dozen deputies stood on the front walk with rifles in hand, next to three agents: Figgs, Brown, and Gutierrez. A doctor was also waiting there, wringing his hands. He was a mousy-looking man with glasses that reflected the emergency lights.

Kowalski opened the door and stepped out, then walked up to the agents. He stood with his hands on his hips, and Lucas couldn't hear what he said. Every one of the men standing out there looked hollow-eyed and shaken, especially the doctor. The sinking feeling in Lucas' stomach grew deeper. Something must have happened. His mind opened up, searching through the hospital. He found the security cameras that looked over the ULF's room. Inside, he saw two dead agents and three dead orderlies. Blood splattered the floor, and the door was open.

"Kowalski!" he shouted, and he sprang from the van. He ran straight past them all and up to the front door of the hospital. Through the cameras, he could see something, huge and monstrous, racing through the hallways. Lucas stopped a few feet in front of the doors and extended his arms. A force field materialized at the same time the double doors of the hospital shook. There was a thunderous boom, like a battering ram, and the doors rattled. They opened, just barely, but his force field blocked them.

The agents and cops mobilized to action, aiming their guns at the doors. He spotted Tim and Kenny flanking him, their sidearms drawn. Kowalski got on his phone, and his voice echoed in Lucas' head.

*What the hell is going on?* He shouted.

*Something's trying to get out!* Lucas answered, straining with effort. He was sweating, and it was hard to breathe through his mask. *The agents are dead, and the ULF is gone.*

The light bent and refracted in the air around the doors. The ULF was missing, but what was on the other side of the doors, trying to escape? Was there another creature that the sheriff hadn't told them about? There were two small windows in each door, and he could see something very large on the other side, and the glass was scratched with claw marks. Heart pounding, Lucas searched through the stored memory of the security system. *What happened here?* He only had to go back twenty minutes to find out.

The ULF was still in the bed; it was that long-haired boy with bizarre, bright red eyes. He fast-forwarded a few minutes to the moment the agents entered the room, and the boy began to freak out as they tried to move him to a wheeled gurney. The boy struggled, then suddenly froze. His limbs began to tremble as it appeared he fell into a seizure, but then he began to change. His body began to morph and grow, and the restraints on his arms and legs burst. The bed collapsed beneath him as his back expanded, his arms and legs lengthened, and horns sprouted out of his head. Fur covered his body, and a long tail formed. Then the monster turned on the agents.

"Dear god," Lucas gasped.

The beast hammered the doors again and again, and Lucas held his position until he began to falter. The force field was draining his power.

*It's him! The monster is the ULF!* he shouted over the phone.

Then the pounding stopped. For several long seconds, nothing happened. Lucas released the field, dropping to his knees with dizziness and exhaustion, but Kowalski, the sheriff and his deputies, and all the agents kept their weapons aimed at the doors. Then a window broke, and out tumbled the biggest tiger Lucas had ever seen. It was the size of a horse, and its fur was striped aquamarine and white. A long tail swished angrily, and two giant rams' horns curved out of the top of his head. It snarled, baring long, white teeth at the terrified crowd of officers, and round, yellow eyes flashed.

"Oh, my god!" Kowalski exclaimed, backing away.

Lucas gaped, unable to comprehend what he was seeing. The tiger let out a roar that seemed to shake the earth itself. Lucas had watched the ULF transform, but he still couldn't believe the monster in front of him. *This isn't real… it can't be real…*

"Open fire!" Kowalski barked.

While the cops scrambled to organize themselves, Lucas forced his feet forward. He ran headlong at the tiger and, with a throwing motion, a lightning bolt blasted through the air from his outstretched hand. Thunder pounded and the tiger shrieked as it was tossed off its feet and into the side of one of the police cars, only a few yards from the CIA van. Glass shattered and the metal screeched under the beast's immense weight. After a few, tense seconds, the tiger got back up, its side smoking and its fur singed. As Lucas watched, stunned, the cooked flesh began to repair itself.

*Oh, great,* he thought with dread. *It can heal.*

The tiger shook itself, like it was biting at a fly on its shoulder, then swiped with its paw at the cops that fled for cover. It crouched low and pounced, but a blast of lightning from Lucas stopped it mid-air. He put all of his strength into it, and the resounding thunderclap shattered the windows of the hospital and the surrounding cars. The ground shook as the tiger dropped and squirmed in pain; its greenish fur was scorched and burned away in some places, leaving ugly, blistered patches. A few of the cops nearby readied their guns and one fired in panic, but the bullet ricocheted off the force field that Lucas hastily trapped the tiger with. He created a shimmering dome about six feet tall.

"Bullets aren't going to stop this guy!" Lucas yelled. "Kowalski, tell them to clear out! Evacuate the area!"

While the cops either fled or cleared civilians from the area, Lucas held the force field in place. He knew that he couldn't keep up the battle much longer. He was quickly getting tired, but the tiger didn't seem to be stoppable. He found small relief in the fact that the suit seemed to be doing its job well, protecting him from his own lightning.

The tiger rose awkwardly to its feet, favoring its injured side that was already healing again. It snarled at Lucas, then swiped with its claws at the force field wall. When that didn't work, it lowered its head and rammed the side with its curled horns. It charged again, colliding with the field. Lucas could feel each impact reverberating through his psyche as a stabbing pain in his skull, and his legs were on the verge of giving out.

"I can't hold it forever!" he groaned.

"Alright, on my count, release it, and we'll open a rain of fire," Kowalski barked.

"That won't work!" Lucas called in reply. "It can heal!"

"We have to try!" Kowalski answered. "Goddamned lightning won't kill it, but we have to slow it down somehow. On my count!"

Tim, Kenny, Figgs and Gutierrez gathered on either side of Kowalski with rifles from the truck. Kowalski raised a hand, signalling them to get ready. Lucas slowly inched backwards, putting distance between himself and the tiger while maintaining the force field. It took every ounce of his concentration. Then the tiger stopped charging at the wall. It crouched low to the ground, its face hidden in its paws. Everyone froze, watching and waiting. Lucas strained through the blinding pain to see what was happening. *Maybe it's done fighting,* he hoped, and pleaded mentally for it to stop. *You have to stop, or they'll kill you! Or I will... and then die of exhaustion myself.*

The tiger's back arched suddenly, and then he began to change again. Its fur disappeared, revealing gray, scaly skin. Its forelegs lengthened into muscular arms with four-fingered hands. A second pair of arms burst from its sides, just below the first, and clawed at the dirt. Its ribs swelled and spine lengthened, and its snout became long like an alligator's, with long rows of teeth. A dark mane, like a horse's, grew down its back.

The enormous, reptilian creature was much bigger than the tiger was; it hunched over inside the force field. All four of its clawed hands reached up and pressed against the dome, and Lucas couldn't hold it anymore. Like a balloon bursting, the force field broke, and Lucas collapsed into the dirt. Through blurred vision, he saw the creature rise up to its full, towering height. It had to be nine feet tall, at the very least. Orb-like, yellow eyes fixed on him, and then gunfire erupted.

The creature hissed in rage as bullets punctured its muscled chest.

Kowalski was standing only a few feet away from Lucas with his pistol raised, his face like stone. The monster stumbled a step or two, then dropped down and charged, using all six of its limbs to run. Lucas heard a click: Kowalski had emptied his gun.

"No!" Lucas cried. He hurled a force field, tossing Kowalski out of the way just as the beast opened its jaws.

"Get out of here!" Lucas yelled as Kowalski rolled to his feet, a look of surprise on his face.

The monster was right on top of him; Lucas hastily wrapped a second field around himself just in time. The creature bit down on the force field; two rows of glistening white teeth froze inches above Lucas' face. Enraged, the monster reared back; Lucas could see down its throat as its jaws closed around him again and again with terrifying speed and ferocity. Its claws and teeth slipped, unable to find purchase on the frictionless surface of the field, but the weight of the beast pushed him down, shoving him deeper into a rut it was carving into the earth. He was safely enclosed in his force-field cocoon, but for how long? His mind fogged, and his concentration was beginning to fracture. Three-inch long claws tore at the dirt and clamped around the force field as the frenzied creature hungrily tried to find a way in, and Lucas knew it soon would.

"Stop!" a voice cried, but Lucas barely registered it.

The monster paused.

Spots floated in front of Lucas' eyes; he was beginning to black out now. Saliva dripped onto his mask from the monster's open mouth before he realized the force field was gone. He was stifled by its hot breath, and then a heavy, clawed foot stepped on his lower leg. The bone snapped, and his teeth ground together as tears of pain sprang into his eyes.

"Stop!" the voice cried again. "Martin, stop *now*!"

The girl.

It was the girl, Jess, standing about twenty feet away. The creature was looking at her now, and let out a low growl that raised goosebumps across Lucas' skin, followed by hot breath puffing over his face.

Jess was trembling, but she stood with her head high and arms locked stiffly at her sides.

"Martin," she said clearly. "It's okay. No one is going to hurt you. Now, come here."

The monster hissed in response, but to Lucas' amazement, it stepped toward her. It crept, dragging its four clawed hands, until it was standing directly in front of her. It lowered its head, and she lifted her trembling fingers up to touch the end of its snout.

Jess was staring directly into its face when she saw a change. Those giant, yellow eyes now seemed to actually see her. It recognized her, she was sure of it. Or maybe she was crazy, and this was what it was like staring into the face of death.

The monster blinked twice, then winced. He turned and snapped at his sides, as if he was being stung by an insect. Then Jess saw that he was shrinking. He backed away from her, still flinching at unseen pain. His bones moved and popped out of place, then snapped back together in a different shape. The second pair of arms retreated into his ribs, and the claws disappeared. Slowly, painfully, he returned to the shape of a man, and the dull, gray scales vanished, revealing Martin's olive skin. When the process was all done, he collapsed in the dirt, naked and shivering despite the lingering heat. Jess stood rigid and shaking with fear, unable to believe what she had just seen.

# CHAPTER 5

*M*artin lay still for several seconds, then tried unsuccessfully to lift his head. When he let out a cry of panic, Jess dropped down to his side.

"Help," he gasped, his ruby eyes wide open.

He was covered in sweat, and blue veins stood out in his neck. He reached for her, but his movements were weak and clumsy.

"Jess… Jess," he sputtered, then fell into a violent fit of coughing.

"I'm here," she found herself saying. "Calm down, and just breathe."

His fingers clung tightly to her arms, and his grip was so strong that it hurt. Then she saw Sheriff Owens and several other officers approaching slowly, with guns raised. Arden stood still as a statue six feet behind her, rifle ready and aimed over her shoulder.

She looked back at Firebolt, lying in the dust ten feet away. Agent Kowalski knelt down and said something to him, then shouted to two of the agents. Then he reached out and helped Firebolt sit up. His lower leg bent at an odd angle.

*Martin did that,* she thought, feeling sick.

"Help me," Martin choked out. "What's happening?"

"Try to stay calm," Jess said, watching the cops approach.

Tears streamed down his face. He was bleeding from a cluster of tiny holes in his chest, like someone had stuck him with thumbtacks, and drying, sticky blood coated his chin and neck.

"Martin, listen to me," Jess said quietly. "Do you know where you are?"

He shook his head vigorously.

"Do you know how you got out here, outside?"

He began to turn his head nervously toward the officers, but Jess touched his face with a trembling hand.

"Don't look at them, look at me," she said. "Answer me: do you know how you got outside?"

"I don't know what I did. It all happened so fast. I had no control over myself… there were lights and pain… oh, what did I do?"

"You hurt some people, Martin," Jess said, her voice catching in her throat. "We have to make sure you don't do that again."

He started crying, but with his eyes open, looking up at her. Tears dripped onto the dust.

"It's going to be okay," Jess told him. "These men are going to make sure you stay safe. Don't fight them."

She wasn't sure he could, even if he wanted to. His breath was quick and shallow, and she felt his pulse racing under her hand. The officers were at her shoulder now.

"Don't go anywhere," Sheriff Owens whispered to her.

All at once, Sheriff Owens and another deputy pried his hands off of her. They rolled him over onto his stomach, and held his arms still at his sides. One of the officers put his knee on Martin's back and held his gun aimed at the back of his head, but Martin didn't struggle. A CIA agent injected something into his neck with a syringe. Then, just as quickly, they flipped him onto a backboard with many nylon straps. A blanket was draped over him, and then they began to roughly fasten his arms and legs down. Jess reached out and touched his forehead. He looked like he was about to fall asleep, but he still flinched.

"Don't be afraid, it's only me," she said.

"I am afraid," he said softly, opening his eyes. His voice was barely audible. "I am afraid of myself. What kind of creature am I?"

His red eyes welled with tears, then closed again as something like a muzzle was fitted over his face. It left only his eyes exposed. Then three officers picked up the backboard with Martin securely strapped down onto it, and carried it to the truck. She felt Arden's strong hand take hers.

"Good job, Jess," he said. "That was very brave."

She looked up at him.

"It really was," he said seriously. "I'm proud of you. Scared out of my mind, but proud."

She nodded. Across the yard, Agent Kowalski knelt beside Firebolt, who was sitting up now. He took hold of Firebolt's broken leg, then, to Jess' shock, straightened it out.

"What the hell?" Arden gasped. He was watching them, too.

Agent Kowalski pulled Firebolt up to standing, and they walked together up to the truck, Firebolt leaning heavily on Agent Kowalski's supportive arm. Without a word, Firebolt climbed into the back of the truck alone. Arden stopped Agent Kowalski with a finger on his chest.

"What kind of operation are you running here?" he demanded. "And what exactly is your 'colleague'? My daughter just risked her life for the two of you, and we deserve to know the truth."

"The sooner you get in the truck, the sooner you'll know it," Agent Kowalski replied coolly. "Now will you take your hand off of me?"

Arden retracted his hand, and the agent looked down at Jess.

"Thank you," he said. "What you did was exceptionally dangerous, but very brave. Please, let me help you."

He offered his hand, and Jess took it. He walked her up to the back of the truck; inside, Firebolt sat at the end of a long bench, closest to the cab. Two of the agents - the black man and the redhead - sat on either side of him. Martin lay on the floor of the truck, strapped down to the backboard. His chest rose and fell slowly as a tube fed sedative into him from an IV bag that hung from a hook in the ceiling. Agent Kowalski helped her step up into the truck, and she slid down the bench until she was across from Firebolt. Arden climbed up beside her, then Agent Kowalski came last. The doors of the truck closed soundly.

Once they were moving, Agent Kowalski dug through a cooler that had been under his seat and found a Powerbar. He tossed it to Firebolt, who caught it deftly. He then pulled off the mirrored goggles and his mask. Jess saw now that he was Hispanic, and indeed very young. He had coffee-brown skin and a long, thin nose. His head was shaved, and his dark eyes glinted like obsidian.

"Hi, my name is Lucas Tavera," he said, peeling off a small coin-like device that adhered to his neck. It must have been what distorted his voice, because his words were clear as a bell now. Jess felt Arden tense.

"Are you sure this is a good idea, Lucas?" the black agent muttered.

"She risked her life and saved all of us. They both did, so I think they've earned a little inside information."

"He's a kid," Arden said with disbelief.

"I'm thirteen," Lucas said, raising an eyebrow.

"Are you kidding me?" Arden exclaimed, looking at Agent Kowalski. "You've got a damn *child* working for you?"

"With all due respect, Mr. Sheffield," Lucas interjected, before Agent Kowalski could give a reply. "You've seen what I can do. I'm quite useful, and very difficult to kill."

He pointed at Agent Kowalski.

"This is my handler, Seth Kowalski, and these are my security, Tim and Kenny."

Arden was still furious.

"This is exploitation," he spat. "This is wrong."

"You don't understand the full picture," Agent Kowalski replied calmly. "There are things going on here that you couldn't begin to fathom, so why don't you just take a few deep breaths, alright?"

This was the second time in as many days that Jess had seen her father so angry, and she didn't know how to respond. She wasn't used to being the calm one... and why exactly was she so calm? She realized she should be freaking out, too, yet for some reason, everything made perfect sense. This boy had just saved her life and the lives of everyone at that hospital. Of all the things she had witnessed today, seeing that he was only a child was the least disturbing.

Unsure of how to act, she put a steadying hand on her father's knee and spoke to Lucas, who passively watched the exchange while eating the Powerbar.

"If you're not an alien, then what are you?" Jess asked.

"I'm an android," he answered. "I have nanomachines inside my body that give me the power to control machines and generate lightning."

"No offense, but, um - I thought androids were like robots," Jess said carefully. "You don't seem like a robot."

"No, I'm not a robot," Lucas replied. "I bleed and get tired and hungry just like you do. It's complicated, but let's just say for now that the only difference between me and you is the nanomachines inside me."

"Where did they come from?"

His dark eyes flicked briefly to Agent Kowalski, then back to her.

"I can't tell you that," he said.

"I think we should all just stop talking and enjoy the silence for a while," Agent Kowalski said firmly. "Lucas, you should get some rest. Mr. Sheffield, when we reach Austin, you and your daughter will be debriefed and given a comfortable place to stay until the situation with the ULF is resolved."

Jess looked down at Martin, whose face was sallow, and his closed eyes had dark circles under them, like bruises. His chest rose and fell steadily as he slept. She worried for him, and felt an instinct to protect him out of sympathy, but it was true this boy was dangerous. He couldn't be left free while he had no means of controlling himself. Maybe, this was for the best. If he were contained, help could be found for him without anyone else getting hurt. At least, she hoped that was *all* that the government planned to do.

Lucas leaned his head back against the wall and closed his eyes, his arms crossed over his chest. Jess was immensely curious about his story and how he came to be what he was. Maybe, once upon a time, he was like Martin - frightened and unable to control his abilities, and maybe the government found help for him and it all worked out. And maybe, one day, Martin could be like Lucas - a fierce, powerful hero using his abilities to save people.

"This is ridiculous," Arden whispered in her ear, and Jess was brought back down to reality.

"What?"

"How long has this kid been used by this agency?" Arden hissed. "He's a child soldier - that's wrong, and illegal. We have to find a way to help him. We'll write our congressman, tell the media… something."

Jess didn't know what to say. Even if they did all of that, who would believe them? She wouldn't believe it herself if she wasn't sitting right now in the back of a truck with an self-proclaimed android and a… a… whatever Martin was. She had read dozens of stories like this in the tabloids during her research, and now wondered how many of those were true.

She didn't know how much time passed before she dozed off, leaning against Arden's shoulder, but she felt like she had only been asleep for a couple of minutes when a sound woke her.

Martin coughed.

She opened her eyes. He was lying motionless on the floor, secured by many thick nylon straps. A blanket covered him to his chin, and the muzzle obscured most of his face. She began to wonder if she'd only imagined it, until he coughed again. He sputtered and gasped through the muzzle.

Jess sat up. The two guards, Tim and Kenny, were also watching him anxiously.

"The doc said the sedative would give us ten hours," Kenny whispered to Tim. Tim nodded slowly.

"Think it's running out?"

"I think you'd better wake Kowalski."

Tim slid down the bench and tapped Agent Kowalski's arm.

"Sir," he said.

Agent Kowalski startled awake and looked around. In fact, Lucas was the only one left still sleeping. The others watched, motionless, as Martin twitched, then opened his eyes.

"What do we do, sir?" Kenny asked.

"Wait," Agent Kowalski whispered.

Martin blinked, then searched the ceiling. His eyes widened and his breath began to quicken in panic. Without another thought, Jess dropped down beside him and put a gentle hand on his chest.

"Martin, it's okay," she said. "I'm here."

His eyes found her. She noticed that the shimmering, iridescent spots within his rose-colored eyes seemed to move independently of each other. Among those, there were three in each eye that were darker than the others, and moved as a group. She wondered if that was how he actually saw, or maybe just focused on what he was looking at. Those six scales rolled her direction, and then stayed there. His dark hair was matted to his forehead and neck with sweat.

"It's okay," she whispered gently. "No one is going to hurt you. You're safe here."

He blinked, breathing hard through the muzzle.

"I think he wants to say something," Jess said.

Martin's head jerked slightly.

Agent Kowalski nodded. "Keep him talking," he mouthed.

There were buckles on each side of the muzzle, and Jess fumbled with them for a second before she managed to lift it off. Martin let out a gasp of relief.

"Better?" Jess asked.

"Jess," he said hoarsely. "Am I still here? Am I still me?"

"Yes, you're still you," she answered.

He nodded, clenching his jaw. Tears leaked from his eyes.

"What's wrong?" Jess asked.

"I'm sorry," he croaked.

"For what?"

"I remember it. I remember…" his voice faded.

"Remember what?"

"I was angry," he said, in almost a whisper. "And afraid. It felt like fire raging inside me. Then… I couldn't stop it… it all hurt so much, but I couldn't stop it."

By now, Lucas had awoken. Jess saw him flexing his fingers as he regarded Martin with a cold expression.

"What else do you remember?" she asked quietly.

He fell silent.

"Do you remember your name?"

"Martin."

"That's the name we gave you," she said. "Do you remember the one you had before?"

"There is no before," he answered weakly. "I feel as though I were born only yesterday, into a world of rage, pain, and hostility."

"Awfully poetic for a guy with amnesia," Kenny muttered.

"He's speaking in Spanish," Lucas whispered, looking at Kenny with confusion. "You don't understand Spanish, so how do you know what he's saying?"

Kenny twisted to look at Lucas and paled.

"Because I hear Gaelic," he replied in a constricted voice. "Like my mother and grandmother used to speak it. I haven't heard it in years."

The entire row turned to Agent Kowalski.

"What's going on here?" Kenny said frantically. "What's happening? How's that creature in our heads?"

Agent Kowalski responded by putting his finger to his lips as Martin craned toward the noise, the veins bulging in his neck.

"Where am I?" he said, his tone rising.

"We are taking you somewhere safe," Jess said, her hand on his cheek. "You've hurt some people, Martin."

"Five," he said. "I killed five. And I can't stop it."

His skin began to discolor, and Jess felt his pulse race beneath her fingers.

"I think the sedative has officially quit working," Tim remarked. "Any ideas, Kowalski?"

"Will those straps hold?" Arden asked.

"Not if he changes into something bigger," Lucas answered. "And he could still snap the backboard."

"We could shoot him in the head," Kenny suggested.

"No!" Jess cried, horrified

"You want to shut up?" Kowalski chided Kenny. "Everyone, use gentle tones - we've got a time bomb here."

"There's no time to argue or use 'gentle tones,'" Kenny hissed. "This creature has killed five people already, and two were our servicemen! We don't know what it is, and now it's getting in our heads. If you want to be humane, fine, I promise that it won't feel a thing."

Martin began breathing quickly.

"Jess," he pleaded. "It's happening. I can't stop it."

"Guys," Lucas said with a warning tone, his eyes on Martin.

Martin's face twisted in anguish and he let out a low groan. Kenny drew his sidearm and cocked it back with a click.

"No! Wait!" Arden exclaimed, throwing out his hands.

Suddenly, there was a loud clap of thunder. Through the window into the cab, Jess saw nothing but darkness; the wind howled as it whipped across the road and buffeted the truck. Then the tires screeched, and the truck jerked to a stop. A cannon boom sounded, shaking the windows.

*Another storm*, Jess thought.

Jess and Arden were thrown against the wall, and the backboard slid. Jess found herself falling on top of Martin, but was stopped by some invisible force. Lucas was bracing himself against the wall, his hand outstretched toward her and a look of consternation on his face. *A force field,* Jess realized. He didn't remove the field over Martin until Jess had a chance to right herself, then climb back into her seat.

"Thank you," she began to say, but was interrupted by a series of thuds on the roof. Everyone looked up.

"There's someone on the roof," Arden said.

With a loud screech of metal, the rear doors of the truck were ripped away, and icy wind rushed in. A tall woman stood there, her long, scarlet hair blowing in the strong wind. She wore a coat of royal blue, its collar and the cuffs of its sleeves glittering with tiny rubies and emeralds. Her face was strikingly beautiful, even under streaks of what looked like tattoos that covered her cheekbones and forehead. Most striking of all, her eyes were brilliant, solid red. She drew two short swords that began to glow with white flames, and her lip curled into a snarl.

"Lucas," Agent Kowalski said in a low voice.

"Yeah, yeah," Lucas sighed, pulling down his mask. "Fighting monsters is my thing now, I guess."

The air rushed in like a vacuum and a shimmering wall blasted the tall woman; she was knocked into the idling van ten yards back. Lucas sprang from the truck onto the asphalt, then raced to meet her. Both Lucas and the woman disappeared into the thick billows of dust that swept across the road as thunder rumbled overhead.

At Jess' feet, Martin let out a groan. His skin was fully discolored now, and his joints swelled.

*Oh, no,* Jess thought with dread when she realized what was coming. The straps over his chest snapped as his ribs expanded.

"Everyone out of the truck!" Agent Kowalski shouted.

Arden hooked Jess around the waist and scooped her up, jumping out onto the ground. Cold wind whipped their clothes and raised goosebumps on Jess' arms and legs. Agents spilled out of the other vehicles and began to form two perimeters: one around the truck where Martin was transforming, another at the edge of the ditch where Lucas fought the strange woman. Jess couldn't really see either of them in the darkness, only their silhouettes as Lucas fired a lightning bolt or the woman slashed with her flaming swords, until someone climbed onto the roof of the truck and shone a spotlight on the both of them.

The woman shielded her eyes from the sudden bright light. Lucas hurled another force field at her, but she recovered quickly and leapt out of the way. Despite her impressive height, she was incredibly fast. Lucas seemed entirely focused on keeping distance between them; each time she advanced, slashing with her flaming swords, he released a wave of lightning or barrage of force fields. That's when Jess noticed the way the light from the vehicles' headlights bent and rippled. He had thrown up force fields just inside the perimeter where the agents were posted, keeping her barricaded. She dodged a lightning bolt, then crashed into the near-invisible wall surrounding the two of them.

*He's not fighting her,* Jess saw. *He's keeping her away from us.*

Meanwhile, something clattered inside the truck. Arden pulled Jess behind the van as Martin tumbled out onto the ground, now free of his straps. He collapsed to the ground as his spine grew far out of proportion with the rest of his body; his elbows and shoulders popped out of place, then snapped back together again as his body expanded. He gave a yell that was quickly cut off as his voice disappeared. Fangs grew from his jaw, and an extra pair of arms burst from their new sockets. He continued to grow until he towered head and shoulders over the men as he stood up with a snake-like tongue flicking in and out of his reptilian mouth.

Jess felt herself go weak at the knees with fear, but she did not run. She remembered that terrified look in Martin's eyes before he changed, and knew that he was suffering. *I have to help him,* she thought. *He has no control over himself, but maybe I can stop this.*

"No, Martin!" Jess cried. "Stop! Remember where you are!"

He snarled and stepped forward, then stumbled. His body swayed as if he was dizzy. Something was different this time; he was clearly weaker. But why?

"Martin, listen to me," she said, her voice gentle though her heart was racing. "You must remember where you are. Remember me. You have to calm down."

The monster hissed, his teeth bared. Then he lifted his head and gave a great roar. Jess thought she might faint as the sound reverberated in her ears, making them whine. Arden pulled her back behind the van.

"It's not working, Jess!" he said, but she shook him off. She continued staring into Martin's yellow eyes defiantly.

"Martin, you must stop this now! You can come back!"

"Get down!" Agent Kowalski barked at her. He positioned himself between the van and Martin, then commanded his men to stay back. Martin swiped at the air and hissed after the running agents.

"Lucas!" Agent Kowalski yelled. "Get them to fight each other! Let them take each other out!"

Lucas didn't seem to hear. Jess could see that his movements were slower now; his force-field barricade had begun to dissipate, drifting away in the form of a glittering, glass-like mist.

"Lucas!" Agent Kowalski yelled again as he slowly backed away from Martin's monster form, raising his gun. His eyes were locked on Martin's.

The tall woman dodged another one of Lucas' flying force fields, then attacked with blinding speed. Her swords flashed as they came down over Lucas' head. Jess screamed as his left arm was separated from his body, cut off above the elbow, and dropped to the ground. Lucas cried out and fell to his knees, clutching the stump. The woman didn't give him a second glance; she turned and sprinted up the slope to the road, straight for Martin.

Agent Kowalski spun and aimed his gun at her. Without slowing, she pointed one fiery sword at him and barked a word in an unknown language, and the agent suddenly dropped his gun. It clattered on the asphalt, glowing red-hot. The woman marched up to Martin, and to Jess' surprise, sheathed her swords. Head held high, she stretched out a hand. Martin immediately swiped at it with his great claws, and she jerked back, but her expression remained calm. The monster dropped down on all six of his legs, his breathing slow and ragged, tongue hanging out. His great sides shuddered like bellows as his yellow eyes glared at her.

The woman stepped closer and stretched out her hand again. Jess heard her talking, her voice low and gentle. Jess couldn't understand the words, but it sounded like a strange mixture of French, Spanish, and something else. There was no other sound; the wind had suddenly ceased and the clouds cleared overhead, revealing tiny pinpricks of stars.

The beast snarled, then dropped his head. His eyes squeezed shut as he recoiled backward, flinching away from something unseen. His claws retracted, and his muscles jerked and twitched.

*She's calming him,* Jess thought, exhilarated. *And it's working.*

Slowly, he began to shrink back down. After a lengthy series of painful snapping and crunching sounds, Martin collapsed onto the hot asphalt in the form of a man. His face was haggard, and he rolled onto his back, his breath rasping. The woman stood over him, her shoulders bowed. Jess saw tears glisten on her cheeks.

"What's happening?" Arden said breathlessly.

The woman took off her coat and draped it over Martin's prone form. Her bare arms were tanned and muscular. She wore a bluish-green tunic and tall riding boots, with leather guards around her wrists. Agent Kowalski held up a silent hand at his men; everyone eyed the woman and Martin warily.

"Hello," Agent Kowalski said in a loud, clear voice. "My name is Seth Kowalski. Who are you?"

He took a single, cautious step toward her, with arms raised. Her head snapped toward him, eyes flashing. "Stay back!" she barked in clear English. "This man is dying; I demand that he be released to me!"

"Whoa, slow down," Agent Kowalski said coolly. "We have done nothing to harm him. He came to us injured, and we did our best to care for him. Why don't you tell us your name and what you want? Perhaps we can help you."

She narrowed her red eyes at him.

"I am Larathel," she said. "I am an officer in the Bederian army, and I have come here to claim this man."

"Does he belong to you?"

"He is my commanding officer," she answered. "His name is Sangor, and he went missing from our world. Please, allow me to save him."

"Of course, anything you need," Agent Kowalski replied. "We all want the same thing here."

He called two agents over and ordered them to do whatever the woman asked. They lifted a now-unconscious Martin - or Sangor, as he was really called - into the back of the truck, and Larathel followed.

At that moment, Tim and Kenny appeared, climbing out of the ditch. Tim carried Lucas in his arms; his mask was gone and he hugged the seared stump of his arm. He was horribly pale, and his face was puffy from crying.

"Oh my god," Arden said.

Jess couldn't breathe; her hands felt cold and clammy, and her throat was tight. Tim carried Lucas to the side of the van and propped him up against the tire. He immediately removed his shirt and wrapped it around the wound. Lucas' face twisted in pain and he bit his lip to keep from crying out. Jess clung to Arden, her hand covering her mouth.

"Should we call for an ambulance?" Arden asked.

"No, no," Lucas said quickly through gritted teeth. "No need. It'll heal. I'll be okay."

Agent Kowalski suddenly shoved his way past Arden and Kenny, and dropped down at Lucas' side.

"Lucas, are you alright?" he asked.

He took Lucas' face in both hands, looking him over with surprising tenderness.

"I'm okay," Lucas answered. "It's not that bad."

Agent Kowalski pulled him into a tight embrace, and Lucas hugged him back with his remaining arm. He hid his face in Agent Kowalski's shoulder.

"I'm so sorry," Agent Kowalski said softly.

"Really, I'm okay," Lucas said, though his expression betrayed him.

"No, it was a near miss. She took your arm; she could have taken your head just as easily."

Lucas nodded, and said nothing. He still looked terribly pale and shivered despite the desert heat. Agent Kowalski turned to Tim and Kenny, his face now the semblance of authority.

"One of you needs to go fetch his arm," he said. "It can't be left out in the open. Draw straws or something, but be quick. The other one will stay here and make sure he doesn't pass out. And he needs to eat, whether he wants to or not."

"And," Agent Kowalski added, lowering his voice. "No one is permitted to approach the aliens without me, and no one goes anywhere unarmed. Keep your eyes up."

The other men nodded, faces stoic. Tim volunteered to stay, and Kenny went off in search of the severed arm.

"Now, you two need to come with me," Agent Kowalski said, turning to Arden and Jess.

"Is he going to be okay?" Arden asked, nodding at Lucas. "He doesn't look so good."

"Oh, definitely," Agent Kowalski replied dismissively. "He's had worse."

Arden stopped.

"How can you be so cavalier about this?" he exclaimed. "He's a child, not a soldier, and he just lost his arm! He needs a doctor!"

Agent Kowalski shrugged.

"For what? He'll be completely recovered by evening. As I told you before, there are things happening here beyond your understanding. We've got bigger problems right now; I suggest you shut up and play along."

Arden's fist went flying, connecting with Agent Kowalski's jaw. The agent stumbled back, then righted himself before he fell. At the same instant, Tim and the surrounding agents drew their firearms, aimed at Arden. Agent Kowalski straightened up, rubbing his jaw.

"Dad!" Jess cried out in shock.

Arden's face was red with fury.

"You're the real monster here!" he roared. "You can't just torture and use children for your own secret enterprises! He is a *person*, and he has rights!"

"You idiot!" Agent Kowalski snapped, losing his calm demeanor at last. "You don't know anything about me, or him, or anything that's happening here! I love that boy like he's my own son, and I have been doing everything possible to keep him safe. You have no idea what he's been through or what I've done to protect him from people so evil you can't fathom it. There are people - no, *animals* out there who would do anything to pick him apart, piece by piece, and I will die before I let that happen. *Everything* that I do is for him. Do you understand?"

Arden's mouth twitched, then he turned and walked off as the agents holstered their guns. Jess was dumbfounded. She watched Arden go around to the front of the van, then keep walking; then she noticed Lucas staring at Kowalski, a stunned expression on his face.

"Now, then," Agent Kowalski said, clearing his throat. He straightened his tie, then looked at Jess. "Will you come with me, and represent your family?"

"Um, yes?" she answered hesitantly.

He beckoned her to follow him to the truck. Sangor lay across the floor of the truck, still covered by the blue coat. Larathel crouched over him, one hand on his forehead, the other hovering over the center of his chest. Jess was startled to see that her fingers glowed with gentle, amber light.

"You are Jess?" Larathel asked. She looked up, but didn't stop whatever she was doing.

"Yes, ma'am," Jess answered.

Agent Kowalski helped her up into the truck, and she took a seat uncomfortably at the end of the bench.

"You found him?"

"My father and I did, about forty miles from here."

Larathel's ruby-red eyes studied Jess impassively.

"Tell me everything," she said. "Leave nothing out."

"Well," Jess said slowly. "We were on the way to town when we saw him on the road. He was bleeding... he had been stabbed through the chest. We took him to a hospital, and he healed there over the course of one day, but he couldn't remember anything - he couldn't tell us his name, or where he came from, or how he got hurt. Then he started transforming. He grew wings, then later turned into a tiger-like thing, then -"

"Thank you, Jess," Larathel interrupted sharply, her expression somber. "You have confirmed my worst suspicions."

"What's wrong with him?" Jess asked. "Is he sick?"

"It's a very long story - too long to tell now - but yes, he is very sick. I must focus my energies on healing the worst of it."

Jess looked at Sangor worriedly. Sweat dripped from his brow, and his eyes and cheeks were sunken. Under his eyelids, his eyes darted back and forth, and his lips moved silently.

"Thank you, Lady Jess," Larathel said. "Your actions bought him time. Now, please go; I need to concentrate."

Larathel closed her eyes. Her forehead wrinkled and her hands glowed a shade brighter. Jess wanted to stay and watch, but Agent Kowalski tapped her arm. He offered his hand, then helped her down from the truck. Her boots crunched on the gravel. The rising sun the sun had warmed the air considerably and insects were starting to buzz, hovering over the asphalt. Kenny returned with a small bundle wrapped in a tarp, which he carried to one of the other vans, and Tim sat in the shade next to an apparently dozing Lucas. Arden paced back and forth some fifty yards away.

"Are you alright?" Agent Kowalski asked, though she could have asked him the same thing. His hair was ruffled and a bruise was forming on his chin. His suit was dusty and badly wrinkled.

"Yeah, I think so," Jess answered. "This is... it's pretty wild."

"Yes it is," Agent Kowalski agreed. "Even for me."

"Have you been doing this long?" Jess asked.

"That's a pretty complicated question. If you mean chasing after weird shit - about fifteen years."

"And how long have you known Lucas?"

"Since he was born," he said somberly. Then he lowered his brows at her. "I meant what I said, if that's what you're really getting at. I care about Lucas more than anything else."

"I believe you,' she replied.

"You're very perceptive."

"Thanks."

"Alright then, let's go keep him company, shall we?"

They walked over to the van. Lucas sat cross-legged against the tire, his wrapped stump braced against his chest. His head was leaned back, and his eyes closed. Tim sat with his elbows resting on his knees, the box of Powerbars open in the dirt beside him.

"Has he eaten anything?" Agent Kowalski asked.

"Not yet," Tim answered.

"Lucas," Agent Kowalski said, nudging his shoulder.

Lucas opened his eyes and looked at him blearily.

"What?"

"I hate to bother you about this, all things considered, but I can't get any service out here to call for help. We need another truck brought out here because Larathel stabbed our radiator."

"I told you not to go with Verizon," Lucas said, rolling his eyes. He closed them, then leaned his head back again.

"Yeah, yeah, I know," Agent Kowalski retorted. "Nobody can get any service, and we need to update the field office on our situation."

"I already called for help," Lucas said sleepily. "I sent out an SOS with our location while I was fighting Xena, warrior princess over there."

"How?"

Lucas lifted a hand, his fingers raised. They waved gently, as if to the rhythm of unheard music.

"There's a relay tower about... ten miles away. It's interfering with your signal, but not mine. I can hijack its transmission temporarily to send a message."

"Tell them to bring emergency medical equipment, and a container. Something big to transport our friend, just in case."

Lucas was silent for a few seconds, then opened his eyes.

"Done. It'll be a few hours more before they can get here."

"Thank you," Agent Kowalski replied. "I'll take a group back into town then for supplies. Now eat, please?"

"The pain makes me want to throw up."

"Just try, alright?" Agent Kowalski said more gently. "You need the energy."

He turned and walked back toward the truck, where a few agents were inspecting under the hood. Jess was left there, standing next to the van and feeling awkward.

"Go ahead and take a seat," Tim told her.

"Is that okay?" Jess asked.

"I don't bite," Lucas said dryly. "Unlike your friend over there."

Jess sat down in the shade to Lucas' right. She tried hard not to stare at the stump. Tim stood up and scooted the box closer to Lucas.

"I'll go check on Kenny," he said.

Lucas didn't respond; his eyes were closed again; Jess wasn't sure if he heard him. She gave Tim a jerking nod and he left. Now she was alone with Lucas.

"Is your dad alright?" he asked without opening his eyes.

"Uh, yeah… I think so," she answered. "I've never seen him get so upset. I think the ordeal at the hospital and your fight with Sangor must have triggered something."

He didn't answer. Jess picked up a pebble and drew in the dust with it.

"Are you really only thirteen?" she asked.

He opened one eye.

"Why?"

She was embarrassed now that she asked.

"You seem older. I mean, you don't *look* older; it's just the way you talk."

He gave a light shrug.

"My head's full of information all the time. I guess it rubs off."

"What do you mean?"

"The internet," he said. "My brain's connected to it. There's words, pictures, and conversations going on constantly - and I see and feel all of it. Except out here; there's nothing for miles. It's so quiet."

"Yeah, it's kind of lame."

"No, it's wonderful," he said with a sigh. His eyes had a distant, dreamy look. "For the first time in so long, I actually feel like I'm by myself in my head."

"I can't imagine what that feels like," Jess replied seriously.

"I wasn't always this way," he said, focusing on her now. His firm gaze was penetrating, as if he knew what she was thinking. Jess looked down to avoid it.

"I came in contact with the nanomachines by accident, a year ago," he continued. "But as it turned out, I'm one of the only people in the world who can be infected without dying, so maybe it was destiny, I don't know. They healed me, and gave me these powers instead."

"How long have you been working with the CIA?"

He fell quiet, and his jaw tightened.

"I don't really work for them so much as I *belong* to them," he said finally. "It's not a choice. I'm government property. I have to do what they say, or they'll put me to sleep... permanently."

Jess was confused, and shocked.

"How can they do that? The government can't *own* people."

"I'm not a person," Lucas replied. He said it casually, but Jess detected a tone of bitterness in his words.

"But you said there was no difference between you and me except the nanomachines," she said.

"That's the short answer."

"I don't get it," she said with exasperation. "Then what are you? Human or machine?"

She pointed at his arm.

"You can feel that, so you're not a machine. That's real flesh and bone, right?"

"Of course it is - I'm not a Terminator under all this," Lucas replied. "The only mechanical part of me is the nanomachines. But I'm not human either, or at least not a natural one."

He stopped and looked at the ground shyly.

"I'm sorry, I don't know why I'm telling you all this," he muttered.

"Well, you can't stop now," Jess said, fascinated.

He traced circles in the dirt with one finger.

"I was made by some bad people," he continued. "They built me, genetically, to do ... something. We don't know what, exactly, but it's not good. So, I'm stuck being the property of the US government. As bad as it is working for them, I don't want to go back to the people that made me. The CIA protects me from them, and Kowalski makes sure I don't get put back in hibernation."

"Wow," Jess said, wide-eyed. "That sounds awful."

Lucas nodded. He gazed out at the horizon, his eyes distant. Without saying anything else, he reached into the box for a protein bar. The wrapper crinkled as he opened it with his teeth. Jess was quiet while he ate one bar, and then another. Agent Kowalski and two other agents got into the second van and drove off in the direction of town. Kenny, Tim, and three more agents were left behind with Arden, Larathel, Sangor, Lucas, and herself.

"Can you really regrow your arm?" she asked.

"Yes," he replied. "It's not the first time I've had to, but I was unconscious for it. This time is considerably more unpleasant."

Jess winced at his obvious discomfort.

"Can I get you anything?"

He shook his head, closing his eyes again as he leaned his head back.

"There's not really anything to do but wait."

# CHAPTER 6

*J*ess decided to stop talking. She pulled at the sparse strands of grass at her feet, twisting them beneath her fingers. It was warm, even in the early morning. The pale light of dawn appeared over the horizon, and then golden sunlight broke across the desert. A few hours later, it became unbearably hot. The wind blew dust that got in her nose and eyes. Heat waves shimmered off the nearby road. Tim returned with bottles of water; he gave one to Jess, and she drank eagerly after first rinsing her mouth. He set the other one on the ground next to Lucas, who appeared to be asleep.

The van returned with Agent Kowalski and the others. They brought cases of water and bags of groceries, then made sandwiches and distributed them amongst the men. Tim woke Lucas and coaxed him to eat. Jess sat next to him, both sweating and taking eager sips of water. Arden joined the group after a while, his face red from walking in the sun. He stopped in front of Agent Kowalski, who wordlessly handed him a cold bottle of water. Arden took it sheepishly.

"I wanted to apologize," he said. "I've had time to think about all this, and... I want to help."

"Finally figured out we're all on the same side?" Agent Kowalski said.

"Yes," he answered somberly. "And that I don't have to understand everything to work with you."

"Glad to hear it," Agent Kowalski said. "Will you stay here and babysit the kids while I go check on our extraterrestrial friends?"

Arden nodded. Kowalski took a couple of sandwiches and a bottle of water and walked over to the back of the truck. Inside, Larathel knelt down beside Sangor. He lay flat on his back, his hands limp at his sides. She held his head in her hands, which were both glowing brightly. Her eyes were closed, and her brow furrowed with concentration. She didn't acknowledge him for several minutes, during which time he watched the gentle amber glow of her hands impassively.

At long last, the glow disappeared and she opened her eyes. She straightened up and stretched her back with a tired sigh, then startled when she noticed him standing there.

"Sorry, I didn't mean to scare you," Kowalski said, raising his hands. "I thought you might be hungry."

"Thank you," she replied.

She stepped out onto the ground and looked around. Kowalski offered her a bottle of water, which she accepted. Once again, Kowalski was impressed by her beauty and her height; she was a full six inches taller than he was. She drained the bottle in two swallows, then narrowed her eyes as she spotted Lucas.

"Who is that?" she asked with her thick accent.

"His name is Firebolt."

"A fierce opponent."

"I'll tell him you said so," Kowalski said, then nodded back inside the truck. "How is he?"

Larathel lowered her eyes sadly. "I have placed him in a healing sleep. A great deal of damage has been done to both his mind and body. The body I can heal, but the mind is beyond my skill. To repair what has been done, I must get him back to Beder, our home world."

"Where is that?" Kowalski asked. "Forgive me, but I've never heard of a place called Beder."

She looked up at the sky, brow furrowed. "This is Earth, yes? It is very, very far from here - a universe away. None from our world have visited Earth in millennia."

Kowalski blinked, taken aback. "Wait, what?" he stammered. "You've been to Earth before?"

"No, I have not."

"But Bederians *have* been here?"

"Yes, but to travel here is expensive so it hasn't been done in a very long time. Sangor came on the very last journey, long before I was born -"

"Okay, hang on," Kowalski interrupted. He pointed at the sleeping man inside the truck. "*He's* been here before? But you said it's been millennia since any of your kind have come here. As in *thousands* of years, right?"

She gave him a perplexed look.

"Yes."

"How is that possible? He looks like a teenager."

She raised an eyebrow quizzically.

"I mean he looks young," Kowalski clarified.

"I know what it means," she said. "He *is* young. He was the youngest officer in recorded history, and then the youngest commander of the garrison."

Kowalski was still baffled. He frowned at her. "How old are you?"

"Much younger," she replied. "One thousand, five hundred and eighty-seven years. How old are you?"

"Uh, that's not important," he retreated, frazzled. "Okay - you speak English, so do they teach it over there, or something?"

"*Some* people hear English," Kenny contradicted, shouting from where he stood by the hood of the truck. "Others hear something else. Can you explain that?"

"It is the gift of tongues," she replied. "All Bederians have it. Our magic allows you to hear your first language spoken."

"That explains a lot," Kenny said dryly. "And, what, you understand all of them?"

"Yes," she said. "Because of the magic."

"Magic?" Kowalski repeated.

"Do you not have magic here?"

"Uh, no," he answered with a nervous chuckle. "Not that I know of, anyway."

"But, Firebolt - that was clearly magic that he used, and with impressive skill!"

"He's the product of science," Kowalski corrected. "He was made by people; everything about him can be understood, measured, and repeated."

"That is magic for me," she said, raising one eyebrow. "There is no difference."

"Can you change shape, too, like Sangor does?"

"All Bederians can alter our appearance to some degree," she replied. "But no, Sangor did that to himself, long ago. He was a magical prodigy and pioneered the technique with years and years of practice. He even single-handedly developed the spells to convert excess mass into dimensional energy. He taught his skills to a few others, creating an elite team that used shapeshifting for espionage. In times of war, they travelled between galaxies and dimensions, gathering intelligence."

"Is there a war now? Is that why he came here?"

"He was targeted," she said. "And yes, there is a war. A warlock named Morlann staged a coup and murdered half the royal family in an attempt to take the throne. The palace was quickly overrun, and the residents of the city scattered. Sangor and his elites were escorting the surviving queen, Anthea, to refuge when they were attacked. His team was slaughtered, and he was…"

She stopped, her jaw tight with emotion. Kowalski averted his eyes out of respect and saw that Jess and the others were listening, hanging on every word.

"I was there," she continued in a choked voice. "I saw Morlann himself. He stabbed Sangor, then he and his warlocks cast him into a wormhole, banishing him from our world. It took us twenty-three years to find him, then send me back in time to meet him upon his arrival."

She gave a mirthless laugh.

"As you can see, we miscalculated."

"But, I don't understand," Arden said, moving closer to the truck where Kowalski and Larathel stood together. "We've seen Martin - er, Sangor - heal from injuries that would be life-threatening to any of us; he healed from the stab wound that this, uh… this Morlann person gave him in only an hour. Is that normal for you… um, Bederians?"

"Yes, it's one of our gifts."

Arden crossed his arms and smooth his beard. "So, Morlann had to know he would recover," he mused. "The wound wasn't lethal."

"What are you saying, Arden?" Kowalski asked.

"Well, just that if he wanted to kill him, stabbing him wouldn't be the most effective way to do it. If that was *all* he did, Sangor would be fine now, right?"

"Correct," Larathel answered. "The wound was only intended to slow him down. He did something far worse, which I suspected, but could only confirm if I saw Sangor in person. Morlann took his memories."

Arden and Kowalski looked at each other.

"Um... that *is* terrible," Kowalski nodded. "But how exactly is that worse?"

"He is more than four thousand years old," Larathel said clearly. "All his experience, the spells he used to alter himself, his training - all of it is lost. For him, that is a death sentence; he can no longer control his abilities. Morlann cursed him, then cast him out to be torn apart by his own magic. It was the worst thing he could possibly have done."

The others exchanged stricken, horrified looks. Jess was stunned. She had seen the pain and fear in Sangor's eyes; she could not fathom what it would be like to have all her memories stolen, to feel the pain that he felt and not have any idea why it was happening.

"What can be done?" Arden asked, disturbed. "How do we save him?"

"He must not be allowed to transform again," she said firmly. "The strain of it would certainly kill him. The warlocks still on our side in Beder must open another gate and bring us back. They are the only ones who can undo the spell that took his memories."

"Okay, how long will that take? How soon will you leave?"

"Well, it *is* time travel, so it doesn't really matter how long it takes them to perform the spell, only whether or not they can find us. The gate could open at any moment, or hours from now, or days."

Kowalski wasn't sure he understood all of that, but nodded anyway. He looked at Larathel, his expression serious.

"We want to help you," he said. "We've seen how dangerous Sangor can be, and we believe you when you say that he is suffering. We won't impede you. In fact, if you come with us to Austin, our people can protect you both and give you a comfortable stay until they take you home."

"Thank you, sir," she said. "And thank you for the care you provided to my commander during the interim. We are in your debt."

She gave a stiff bow, her face stoic and eyes impenetrable. Kowalski suppressed a smile. *The soldier attitude must be universal,* he thought to himself.

"Actually, there is one thing you could do for me," Kowalski said. "If you're willing."

"Name it," she answered.

He pointed at Lucas, who slept sitting up against the tire of the van.

"Firebolt, the agent of ours you wounded. Is there any way you could use some of your healing magic on him?"

Larathel shook her head sadly. "I'm sorry, but no," she replied. "To manipulate his cells, I would need to understand his structure and composition perfectly. To gain the knowledge needed to heal my own people took decades of study."

"I understand," Kowalski said, disappointed. "Thanks, anyway."

"However," she said, regarding Lucas pensively. "I may be able to do something."

She walked over to the circle where Tim, Kenny, Jess, and Lucas sat in the shade; Arden and Kowalski followed. Lucas' eyes were closed, sweat dripping from his temples. The left sleeve of his suit was rolled up to his shoulder, and Tim's shirt was wrapped around the stump of his arm, secured with a rubber band. Larathel knelt down in front of him, studying him with an intense gaze. Her scarlet hair flowed over her shoulders and halfway down her back. Up close, Jess could see now that her facial tattoos were a series of fractal spirals in various shades of bright blue ink.

"Lucas," Jess whispered, shaking his shoulder.

Lucas stirred awake and found himself face-to-face with the beautiful woman. Her ruby eyes blinked, and she smiled gently.

"Indeed, you are a child," she said in Spanish. "You fight well for one so young."

"You weren't really trying to hurt me," Lucas mumbled. "Until you got desperate."

Her smile changed to a smirk.

"That is correct," she said. "And I apologize. I would like to make up for it."

Lucas furrowed his brow skeptically.

"How?"

"I have some experience with this type of injury," she answered, then nodded at the bandage. "May I take a look?"

Lucas said nothing, but gave a slow nod. His eyes were only half open, and he looked as if he were on the verge of passing out again. Larathel deftly undid the makeshift bandage then unwrapped it, and Lucas flinched; his jaw clenched and he inhaled deeply through his nose.

Jess took hold of his hand and he squeezed it tightly. She was shocked by how cold his skin was; it felt like ice.

Once the t-shirt was removed, the stump of his arm was revealed. It was cut off just above the elbow, and white bone emerged two inches from the red, exposed flesh. The end of it was jagged, like a bundle of toothpicks.

"Oh, goodness," Tim said, covering his mouth.

"That wasn't there before," Jess noted with wide eyes.

"Yes, it is healing quite nicely," Larathel said. "He is under a great deal of stress. I can't speed the process, but I can ease the pain."

"Do it, please," Kowalski urged anxiously.

Larathel whispered some words in her mysterious language. As she did, an amber glow sparked in her open hand. Lucas' eyes opened wide and startled at the sight of it, his fingers locking around Jess' hand like a vice, but Larathel shushed him like a mother quieting a baby. She placed her glowing palm against his forehead and his eyes rolled back. He slumped against the tire, his breathing deep and easy, and his grip around Jess' hand went slack. Larathel secured the bandage around the wound once more, then stood up.

"Thank you," Kowalski said.

"You're welcome," Larathel said, wiping sweat from her brow. "He is strong, and will recover before long."

"Are you hungry?"

"Yes, very."

She followed him to the cooler. Kowalski gave her a sandwich, which she looked at curiously before taking a bite. Her eyebrows rose, and she nodded appreciatively.

"I consider this an honor," Kowalski remarked with a grin. "It's pretty cool to provide a new experience for a fifteen-hundred-year-old, time-travelling extraterrestrial."

"No matter how long you live, there will always be a first time for something," Larathel said with a half-smile.

A low rumble sounded in the distance. Tim and Kenny stood up to look, and Kowalski squinted at the horizon. The radio in the truck squawked, and Kowalski jogged around to the front, then slid inside the cab to answer it.

*Cobalt, come in, over,* the radio said.

"This is Cobalt, go ahead, over," Kowalski answered, depressing the button.

*Your cavalry is approaching. Is your team ready - over?*

"Ready and waiting, over."

*Ten-four. ETA five minutes, over and out.*

Kowalski got out and returned to the back of the truck where Larathel stood with arms crossed, watching a sleeping Sangor with a doleful expression.

"The rescue team is almost here," he told her. "They've brought a containment unit for your commander. Are you sure he won't wake up?"

"Upon my word," Larathel answered seriously. "The healing sleep is unbreakable."

"That's a relief," Kowalski replied. "I'll tell the others to get ready."

# CHAPTER 7

Jess watched the agents spring into action. They unloaded boxes and large black bags from the vans, and reapplied any gear that had been shed due to the heat. The wind picked up, announcing the arrival of three black helicopters. Two of them landed on the road, and several agents got out to help the others load in. Tim helped Jess to her feet; it was difficult to stand upright while being buffeted by the powerful gales generated by the copter blades. He ran with her to the first chopper, with Kenny and Arden close behind. Kenny carried a still-unconscious Lucas in his arms as they hurried along. Jess was overwhelmed by the roar of the rotors until she was given a radio headset to mute it. Arden strapped in next to her, and Tim and Kenny sat with Lucas between them. Outside and many yards away, Sangor was lifted out of the back of the truck and into some kind of glass pod, with tubes running throughout. Larathel stood nearby, but Jess saw that her appearance had dramatically changed; her hair was a dark, earthy brown, and her facial tattoos had disappeared. Her red eyes, too, now looked ordinary, though from this distance Jess couldn't guess what color they were.

*Wow, she really wasn't joking about this magic stuff,* Jess thought.

The pod was wheeled into a large metal container hanging beneath the third helicopter, which hovered overhead. As the doors closed, Larathel and Kowalski boarded the second chopper, and all three took off. The sun blazed ahead of them as they flew east, the sky like an overturned blue bowl surrounding them from horizon to horizon. Jess watched the brown desert below them give way to green grasses, and farmlands slid past winding roads and intermittent small towns. Arden leaned forward occasionally to look out the window at the land below, his arm securely around Jess' shoulders.

Trees became more frequent, dotting the rocky crags of the hill country. The city of Austin appeared like a silver island amid a rolling green sea. Its towers glinted in the sunlight, and the dark band of a river wrapped around its western side. The helicopters sailed straight over downtown, before slowing and beginning a circular descent. The helicopter that carried Sangor's container paused over a particular building while the other entered a kind of holding pattern. Jess watched as the container was lowered down onto a landing pad, and a group of men ran out to meet it. The doors opened and they wheeled the pod out; the helicopter lifted away, towing the heavy container.

Jess found herself descending toward the skyscraper now. She felt a rushing sensation in her stomach as the roof of the building rose up to meet them. The helicopter touched down, its engine whining and rotors churning the air. An agent leaned over and took Jess' headset from her, then directed her and Arden to the door. As it opened, Arden climbed out and Jess stumbled after him, his hand tight around hers. They ran together, the wind whipping her hair and tugging at her clothes until they reached a door where another agent stood waiting. He beckoned them inside and they found themselves standing before an elevator. A young male agent with curly blond hair smiled and offered his hand.

"Hello, I'm Agent Jones," he said. "Welcome to Austin."

"Arden Sheffield, and this is my daughter, Jess," Arden replied, shaking the agent's hand. "Where are we?"

"CIA field office," he replied. He pushed a button for the 16th floor.

"Are we going to be here long?" Arden asked.

"I don't know, sorry," Agent Jones answered. "I'm just following Agent Kowalski's orders."

"Is there anywhere we can get cleaned up? We've been outside all night."

Agent Jones shook his head.

"I'm only supposed to take you to a room to wait for Agent Kowalski," he said.

"All you guys have the same first names, huh?" Arden quipped.

Agent Jones gave him a blank look as Jess rolled her eyes, mortified.

"Okay, sorry," Arden muttered. "Bad joke."

The elevator chimed, and the doors opened to a quiet hallway lined with blue carpet and dark wood paneling. Agent Jones led them up to a small room with a conference table, a small kitchenette with a coffee maker, and windows that looked out into the hall.

"Have a seat," Agent Jones said. "It shouldn't be long."

He left, closing the door behind him.

Jess picked a chair at the head of the conference table. The surface felt cool under her hands. Tired and dazed, she felt an urge to lay her sun-flushed face on it. Her eyes still hadn't adjusted after the hours of bright sunlight. Arden found a mug and poured himself some coffee, then sniffed the pot and grimaced.

"Better than nothing," he said with a shrug.

He set the mug down on the table and sat, then sighed and rubbed his eyes.

"What time is it?" he asked.

"I don't see a clock anywhere," Jess said, twisting to look. She pulled her phone from her pocket. The screen remained black. "Battery's dead."

"God, I've been awake for what... sixteen, seventeen hours?"

"It's been the longest day of my life," she nodded.

Arden gave an exasperated chuckle.

"What?" Jess asked.

He grinned. "We're in a CIA field office, waiting to be interviewed about a time-travelling, interdimensional wizard."

"A shape-shifting wizard," Jess added. "With amnesia."

"Who's older than Jesus," Arden said with a laugh.

Jess frowned pensively, scratching her chin.

"So... I'm confused," she said. "Are they actually aliens, or not? Where even is that place they said they were from... what was it? Beder?"

Arden sighed. "I don't know," he said, shaking his head. "She said it's a universe away. I thought there was only *one* universe, but I'm starting to question everything I knew. I mean, time travel? Androids? Magic? You could tell me unicorns were real, and I'd probably have to believe you."

Jess nodded, her eyelids heavy. Just then, Agent Kowalski emerged from the elevator followed by Larathel. Jess saw her eyes flash a brilliant sea-green as she glanced into the room, then gave a passing half-smile. Tim and Kenny came next, with Lucas walking between them, still looking very sleepy. Tim had found a new shirt, and Lucas' arm was now in a clean, gauze bandage down to where the wrist would be, and he carried it in a sling. His obsidian eyes met Jess' blue ones as the agents guided him down the hallway and past the door, then the whole entourage disappeared around the corner.

At that moment, a tall man with graying hair and bags under his eyes entered the room. He wore a clean pinstripe suit and carried a silver briefcase. Agent Jones followed him, but stopped just inside the door.

"Hello," the older man said. He gave a smile that looked rehearsed, almost painfully so, and extended a hand to Arden who shook it hesitantly. "I'm CIA director Jensen Dunn, and I'm here to ask you a few questions about the ULF you discovered, and the female that arrived later."

He sat down and opened his briefcase, then removed a small device that looked like a portable CD player with a very old-looking microphone plugged into it. He placed it equidistant between himself and Arden, then folded his hands.

"Jess, you don't need to be here for this," he said, looking at her. "I would appreciate it if you would walk with Agent Jones down the hall. You will be taken with Firebolt ahead to the safe house."

Jess opened her mouth, confused. She wondered briefly how the man knew her name, but that was obvious; Agent Kowalski probably called ahead and told him everything. She looked at her father, who gave her a solemn nod.

"Go ahead," he said. "I'll be right behind you."

Jess stood up and walked around the table to the door. Agent Jones led her down the hall to another elevator. Only Tim and Kenny stood there, apparently waiting.

"She's coming with you," Agent Jones told them.

Jess waved awkwardly. "Uh, hi," she mumbled. "Where's Lucas?"

Tim bobbed his head, nodding in the direction of the hallway.

"Changing out of his suit," he replied.

Agent Jones left, and Jess crossed her arms. Tim and Kenny continued to stand, almost perfectly still. A minute passed, and she wondered if they ever got bored; they watched the wall, their shoulders straight and hands behind their backs. If they didn't blink, Jess would have thought they were statues. She grew tired of standing and leaned against the wall. After another minute, a door opened beside her and she suppressed a sigh of relief. *Finally,* she thought.

Lucas emerged, no longer wearing the black, full bodysuit and kevlar vest. He had on a plain t-shirt, jeans, and sneakers, and looked like he was on the verge of falling asleep on his feet.

"Changing clothes with only one arm... not easy," he muttered as Tim put a supportive hand on his back.

They rode the elevator down to a garage. Two black sedans sat parked in the fire lane; the drivers stood at the front of the cars, wearing black suits with ties and sunglasses, though they were inside a dimly-lit garage. Jess smirked and decided that at least some of the movie stereotypes must be true. She climbed into the back seat with Lucas, while Kenny took the front seat and Tim got into the other car. They left the garage, and Jess craned her neck to take in the full height of the skyscrapers that glittered overhead, and her mouth dropped open.

"First time in Austin?" Kenny chuckled.

"Yes," Jess said. "It's my first time in a city this big."

"What do you think?"

"It's beautiful," Jess answered, taking in the shops, hotels, eclectic restaurants, street art, and the thousands of people that crowded the avenues, either in cars or on the pedestrian walkways. They traveled west and then north, leaving downtown behind, and entered a neighborhood of charming houses with white-painted porches and shutters, flower beds, hedges, and tire swings. Green branches arched gracefully over the street, and kids raced on bicycles down the sidewalks. Golden columns of early afternoon sunlight shone through the changing leaves.

The cars stopped in front of a house with pink siding, a white-columned porch with a swing, and a large magnolia tree. It had small, curtained windows in the front, and a round window peeping from the second story. The magnolia shed its huge leaves, gathered in piles under its wide branches.

"Where are we?" Jess asked.

"My house," Lucas answered, opening the door and stepping out.

Jess blinked, perplexed. The front door opened and an olive-skinned, athletic woman with dark hair dashed out. As Lucas got out of the car, the woman threw her arms around him in a tight embrace, gushing rapid Spanish. Jess didn't understand what was said, but she had never seen such a happy reunion. Kenny came around and opened her door and Jess stepped out onto the sidewalk, embarrassed to interrupt.

"Mom, this is Jess Sheffield," Lucas said, once he'd finally pulled himself away. "Jess, this is my mom, Leah Tavera."

Jess shook her hand shyly. She noticed a small scar near Leah's mouth, and a much larger one on her wrist.

"Nice to meet you," Leah said, somewhat frantically. "Come on, let's go inside and I will get you all something to eat. Lucas, what happened to your arm?"

"It got cut off in a fight," he replied. "Don't worry, it's almost grown back."

Leah's face went white. Tim touched her shoulder gently.

"Oh, *mi Dios*," she gasped. "Good thing it's poker night and your grandma's not home to hear this. You must be starving. Come inside, all of you."

Jess followed Leah and Lucas up the porch steps and through the front door. Jess was impressed by the clean, elegant decor of the house. The living room had dark wood floors, cream-colored rugs, and white furniture. It was simple but chic, and Jess liked Leah's style right away. Lucas flopped onto the couch, his head on a cushion and eyes closed, his bandaged arm across his chest. Tim and Kenny walked with Leah into the kitchen, and Jess heard them conversing as pots and pans clattered. At the dining room table sat a young man in a suit, reading a newspaper.

Jess didn't know what to do with herself. She folded her arms, vaguely admiring the art on the walls.

"You can relax," Lucas said without opening his eyes. "This is a safe place; there's nothing to be afraid of. Just sit down; you're making me nervous."

Jess walked over to the loveseat and sat a few feet away from Lucas. "I'm not afraid," she protested.

"Yes, you are."

Jess sighed, annoyed. "Fine. I'm worried about my dad. He's still at the field office."

"He's fine, don't worry," Lucas said, opening his eyes.

"How do you know?"

"I can see him," he replied. "He's still talking to the director."

Jess furrowed her brow at him.

"No you can't," she said doubtfully.

"Yes, I can. Through the hallway cameras."

Jess stared at him.

"Okay, look," she sighed. "What is this, really? What are you?"

"This is my house," he said. "I told you that already. And I'm an android."

"But you have a mother," she said. "You said that you were made, so how do you have a mother?"

He glared at her.

"It's a long story," he replied. "I don't really want to talk about it."

"Do you have a dad?"

"No."

Jess pressed her lips together and gazed around the room, and observed purple orchids on the coffee table. Another point in Leah's favor. She caught Lucas looking dubiously back at her.

"What?" she said.

"What do you mean, 'what'?" he retorted. "You're the one who's still weirded out. Why? What's your problem?"

"I don't know, it's just - " she stammered.

"You thought I lived in some kind of lab? Or maybe the Fortress of Solitude?"

"A lab, maybe," Jess admitted, her face reddening.

"I'm a normal kid, seriously," he insisted.

"Maybe this is normal for you, but it's freaky from anybody else's perspective."

Lucas narrowed his eyes.

"You know what I was doing when all of this started, when that accident happened?" he said more forcefully. "I was looking for my phone. It was stolen, and I didn't want my mom to get pissed, so I tried to get it back. I got in a fight with the guy who stole it, then ended up in a coma. When I woke up, I was like this. I had to re-learn how to live my life with all of this new stuff in my head, and deal with the fact that I was never human to begin with. And the guy who stole my phone? He was paralyzed, damaged forever, from exposure to the same nanomachines that are in my body right now. He was my only friend while I was locked up... and then my worst enemy killed him."

Lucas clenched his jaw, his eyes full of emotion. Jess had a thousand questions she wanted to ask, but stayed quiet.

"I didn't ask for any of this," he said finally. "But I still have to deal with it."

Neither of them said anything for several seconds. Jess pressed her lips together, waiting until it appeared that Lucas had calmed down.

"My dad and I were just going to dinner when we found a shape-shifter with magical powers," she offered.

"It's a pretty crazy world, isn't it?" Lucas said thickly, rubbing his eyes.

Then he paused. His eyebrows met, and he sat up.

"What's wrong?" Jess asked warily.

"Hand," he muttered.

"What?"

*Now he's going crazy,* she thought, tensing.

He removed the sling, then slowly unwrapped the bandage, starting above the elbow. As it unwound, his brown skin was revealed, whole and without a single scar. The bandage fell away completely, and Lucas flexed the newly-formed wrist and fingers.

"I've got a hand," he said with a tone of awe.

"Wow," Jess gasped.

He rubbed his bare scalp, then sank back into the couch, closing his eyes again.

"Glad that's over," he sighed. "But I'm still so hungry."

"I'll, uh, go check in the kitchen," Jess suggested. She really just wanted some distance. Goosebumps covered her skin, and she tried to push the image of the stump that had once been there from her mind. She got up and walked toward the kitchen. In the dining room, at the round oak pedestal table, the young agent still sat reading a newspaper. He glanced up as she passed, but said nothing. Through the kitchen doorway, she inhaled sweet and spicy smells and heard the sizzle of something cooking. Voices also carried through as Tim and Leah spoke in hushed tones.

"I just don't understand why he didn't check in, that's all," Leah said, sounding miffed.

"There wasn't any service out there," Tim replied. "None of us could call out."

"*Lucas* could," Leah insisted. "He could have told me what was going on. He knows I don't like being kept in the dark… one text would have been fine, just to let me know he was okay."

"Leah, you can't keep coddling him. He can handle himself just fine; you don't need to worry."

A glass shattered and Jess jumped. She shrank against the wall, holding her breath.

"I am his mother, and I will never stop worrying about him!" Leah exclaimed.

Tim shushed her, and Leah lowered her voice, but only by a little.

"*They* are still out there, and that demon could turn up anywhere," she continued hysterically. "Lucas can't beat her - if she comes for him, and he isn't ready -"

"Calm down," Tim reassured her, speaking in quiet, gentle tones. "He will be ready. We both saw him today; he is getting much stronger. If she comes, he'll be much better prepared to handle her. And still, she'd have to get past all of us."

Leah took slow, deep breaths. Jess wondered who "she" was; could Leah mean Larathel? No, that couldn't be it, because Larathel wasn't an enemy. And who was "they"?

Then Leah suddenly emerged from the kitchen. Jess jumped back, her cheeks burning as Leah looked at her, almost accusingly.

"Can I help you?" she said sharply.

"Uh, no - um - Lucas… his arm is all better," Jess stammered. "He wanted to know when dinner was going to be ready."

Leah brushed past her to the living room. Lucas still lay motionless. She bent down and gingerly stroked the back of his hand, and he opened his eyes.

"Come on, honey," Leah said softly. "Let's get you something to eat."

She helped him up, then departed to the kitchen again. Lucas made his way slowly to the dining room on his own.

"That's Agent Kellerman," he said to Jess with a yawn, nodding at the man at the table. "He watches the house."

The young man stood up and offered his hand.

"Jess Sheffield," Agent Kellerman said. "It's a pleasure."

He had an endearing, enthusiastic smile. Jess noticed an earpiece from a radio in his ear. Tim and Kenny came out of the kitchen, carrying dishes full of refried beans, chicken, and Spanish rice. The aromas made Jess' stomach growl. They set these in the middle of the table, then Leah came with a stack of plates.

"Go ahead and help yourselves," she said.

"Ladies first," Kenny said to Jess.

Jess hesitated.

"Lucas should go first," she remarked. "He needs it more."

Lucas gave her an appreciative smile, then picked up a plate. Leah piled it with food and he took a seat. Jess went second, scooping a serving from each of the steaming dishes, then took a chair across from Lucas. Before long, everyone was seated around the table except for Agent Kellerman, who took his plate to a large chair by the window and ate while periodically glancing outside. Dinner had little chatter or excitement; Tim and Kenny talked to each other about sports, but the others ate silently. Lucas quickly finished his first helping and a second, then started a third. Jess watched the whole scene, nonplussed.

The dishes were being cleared from the table when Agent Kowalski and Arden came in the front door.

"Dad!" Jess exclaimed, jumping up.

Arden leaned down to hug her. He carried a shopping bag over his arm.

"I brought you some clean clothes," he told her, showing her the bag. Inside was a new tank top, shorts, and underwear, as well as a shirt and pants for him. He had also brought shampoo and a toothbrush.

"Thank you," she said with relief.

He took his clothes from the bag, then handed it to her. Kowalski disappeared into the kitchen, then came back with a cup of steaming coffee.

"The Sheffields need to stay here," he said, addressing the table. "It may only be for one night, but it could be longer; it's just until we finish the investigation into the ULFs."

"What's left to investigate?" Kenny asked. "The hot alien chick told us everything."

"The administration needs certainty that they're not a threat," Kowalski answered. "That's all I can say. Now, I'm thinking that Arden can sleep in the office and Jess can have Lucas' room, then Lucas can come with me to my place."

"Really?" Lucas asked, sitting up. "I've never seen your apartment."

"Care for a guys' night?" Kowalski grinned.

"Is that okay?" Leah asked. "I mean, will it be safe?"

"Of course, I've got all the best security in place. Though no system comes close to Lucas himself."

He gave Lucas a wink, and Lucas beamed. Then Kowalski turned to Jess.

"Why don't you go ahead and make yourself comfortable?" he said. "I'm sure you'd like to get cleaned up."

"I'll show you upstairs," Leah offered.

She stood, and Jess got up to follow. Between the dining room and the kitchen, a single set of stairs ascended to a dark green curtain. Leah pulled it aside, revealing a spacious loft. At one end was a bed with a greenish-blue bedspread, and at the other stood a blond wooden dresser. The dresser and work desk were piled with what looked like computer parts; there were more than a few exposed circuit boards, hard drives, and an entire laptop in the middle of the desk that had been disassembled, piece by piece.

"This is Lucas' room," Leah said. "You can sleep here. I washed the sheets this morning, so it's clean. Pay no attention to the mess over there. He's always busy with his projects; it's impossible to keep this room neat."

"It's nice," Jess insisted. "Thank you for your hospitality."

"The bathroom is downstairs, just around the corner. You can shower whenever you're ready."

With that, she left, the first step creaking as she descended. Jess dropped the bag onto the bed. Sunlight drifted through the round window, but besides that, the room was dim. She searched along the wall for a lightswitch and found one above the dresser that had been covered with duct tape. Stymied, she hesitated to take it off. She peeled up one corner, then the room suddenly brightened with a faint hum. The naked bulbs along the wall, a desk lamp, and a standing lamp all came on at once. Jess spotted Lucas standing in the doorway and jumped.

"The lamps have switches," he said. "I just don't use them."

"Okay, thanks," she replied, shaken.

Lucas picked up a backpack and began wordlessly stuffing it with clothes from the dresser. Jess gestured at the parts on the desk.

"What is all this?"

"Equipment I found and been trying to rebuild," he answered. "I actually don't know a whole lot about the hardware of computers, so I'm learning."

"Oh, that's cool."

He shrugged.

"It's just a hobby. I have a lot of free time at night, after homework and training."

"Homework? You go to school?"

He gave her a look.

"Okay, sorry," Jess back-pedaled. "I forgot - normal kid. Got it."

"Yes, I go to school," he replied with a huff. "I don't want to do this forever, you know? I figured if I graduate, get a degree, and have qualifications besides just being a living supercomputer, the government will let me go. Like, forever. I could have a normal life on my own, and a regular job."

"I get it," Jess said sympathetically.

"So that's what I'm doing," Lucas continued, fiddling absently with the circuit board. "I've even been taking some online college courses. Eighth grade is pretty easy, since I never forget anything. And I don't sleep, so I've got time."

"Why not?"

"I don't need to, most of the time," he said. "As long as don't need to do some massive healing, I mean."

His expression darkened. He stared at the desk like he was willing it to catch fire.

"It's hard to sleep when you never forget anything," he said slowly. "My brain's always going; it never stops."

Jess couldn't imagine what that was like. Lucas stopped playing with the circuit board and tossed it onto the desk.

"Well, I'd better go," he said with finality. "See you later, maybe."

"Yeah, see you," Jess replied.

He headed toward the stairs, then paused.

"And don't touch my stuff," he told her.

"Of course," she chuckled.

When he was gone, Jess gathered up her new clothes and the shampoo, then descended the stairs to the bathroom. As the hot water ran through her hair and steam filled the bathroom, she realized how completely tired she was. It had been a bizarre day. Kenny had a point; Larathel had been more than willing to cooperate, and she was sure Arden had told the CIA director everything he wanted to know. It shouldn't be long before this adventure was over and they were both going home, back to their normal lives.

# CHAPTER 8

Lucas followed Kowalski outside. He must have showered at the field office, because he smelled fresh, his hair was neatly combed, and he was wearing a clean suit. He tossed Lucas' backpack into the trunk, then they climbed into his black BMW and pulled away from the curb.

"What do you want to do tonight?" Kowalski asked.

"I don't know," Lucas said, surprised by the question. "What do you mean?"

"I mean fun stuff - no working tonight. We can rent a movie, or play some Xbox. I have lots of games - none of them new, however. But if we play Xbox, you have to promise to turn off your brain. No cheating allowed."

Lucas grinned with excitement. "Okay, deal," he said. "Can we order pizza?"

"Didn't you just eat?"

"Yeah, but I'm still hungry."

"Fine, we can order pizza. I don't have any food in the house anyway."

"What's your address? I'll do it now."

Kowalski gave him a sideways smirk.

"1300 East Riverside," he said. "Apartment 13B."

Lucas made the call in his head and began to place the order.

"How do you feel about Canadian bacon?" he asked.

"I'm just a classic pepperoni kind of guy," Kowalski replied.

"Okay done," Lucas grinned. "You still have to pay the guy though."

"I might have you do my taxes for me next," Kowalski chuckled as they drove south.

"Hey, um," Kowalski said after a moment. Lucas looked at him in surprise; Kowalski never stuttered, and he seemed strangely uneasy. "I want to tell you something."

"What's wrong?" Lucas asked.

"I've wanted to talk to you about this for a while, but honestly the thought of that made me nervous," he said, rubbing the back of his neck. "Um, well, you've probably noticed, but your mom and I have been spending a lot of time together."

Lucas froze.

"Yeah?" he said, because he wasn't sure what else he was supposed to say. It wasn't really a question.

"Well, I want to make sure you're okay with it," Kowalski said. "I've known her for a very long time, and I really like her, but I don't want to do anything without your blessing. I really care about you a lot, and... well, my loyalty is to you, first."

Lucas was stunned. He was completely at a loss for words. They pulled into a large garage behind a tall apartment building and parked. Kowalski shut off the engine, then twisted to face Lucas, his hand resting on the back of Lucas' seat. His face was sincere. He looked like a completely different person. His usually sharp eyes were a soft gray.

"I guess what I'm really saying is this," Kowalski said. "Man to man. I want to date your mom, and I'm asking for your blessing."

Lucas took a deep breath.

"She's happier than I've ever seen her, even with all the stuff that's happened," he said slowly. "I think that's because of you. If you make her happy, and you promise to always be there for her, then you have my blessing."

Kowalski lit up and broke into a broad smile.

"Thank you," he said. He extended his hand, and Lucas shook it firmly. "You know what I'll do to you if you hurt her though, right?"

"Nothing, because you still can't kick my ass," Kowalski grinned.

Lucas punched him in the shoulder and they both laughed, then got out of the car. Lucas retrieved his backpack from the trunk and they headed upstairs. The sun had almost completely set, and the city skyline glittered as lights came on.

Kowalski's keys rattled as he opened the door into his apartment. Lucas saw brown leather furniture, a flat screen TV hanging on the wall, and a tall shelf stacked with DVDs. A black coffee table was laden with empty takeout containers. There was no art or photos on the wall, or decorative items of any kind. He walked further inside, and found a kitchen with a layer of dust coating the countertops.

"What do you think?" Kowalski said, tossing his keys into a bowl by the door.

"You need a maid."

Kowalski rolled his eyes.

"You can have the couch," he said. "It's pretty comfortable, not that you'll sleep anyway. I *will* sleep, so I'm going to keep the bed."

Lucas was already perusing the shelf of DVDs.

"Okay," he said. "Where are your games?"

"Let me show you where the shower is first," Kowalski said. "You stink."

The first door on the left led to a tiny bathroom. Lucas took a clean set of clothes from his bag and showered, washing away the sweat and desert dust. He felt refreshed as he dried off and dressed, then finally left the bathroom again. Kowalski stood in the kitchen, popping open a beer. He had removed his jacket and tie, and his gun and badge sat on the end of the counter.

"You want something to drink?" he asked.

"Do you have milk?"

Kowalski opened the fridge and peered in, then shook his head. "Nope. How about juice?"

"You have that?" Lucas asked.

Kowalski unscrewed the cap of an orange juice carton and sniffed it, grimacing. "Does orange juice go bad?"

"Yes," Lucas replied. "And if you have to ask, then I don't think I want any. Could I try some of your beer?"

"Absolutely not," Kowalski said, closing the fridge. "Your mom would murder me. Besides, I don't feel like finding out what alcohol does to androids, particularly a pubescent one."

"Just a sip?"

"No."

"Fine," Lucas said, crossing his arms. "Pizza's here."

The doorbell rang, and Kowalski nudged past him to answer it. He paid the man, then opened the box of pizza on the coffee table and sat on the couch.

"Before you sit down, go pick out a game," he said. "They're in that drawer there."

Lucas opened a drawer beneath the TV and looked over the titles. They were almost all racing games, like *Need for Speed* and the *Forza* series.

"Do you have anything that isn't about cars?" Lucas asked.

"What? I like cars."

Lucas held up a game, eyebrow raised.

"*Sonic All-Stars Racing*? Seriously?" he teased. "No *Call of Duty*? Or *Fallout*?"

Kowalski's smile disappeared. "No. Too many bad memories."

Lucas went cold. He understood completely. He pressed his lips together, then put the disc in the Xbox. As it loaded, he dropped onto the couch next to Kowalski and picked up a controller. Sonic the Hedgehog blazed onto the screen in a cartoonish, electric blue car. Lucas relaxed again as the focus turned to the game. It was harder than he thought keeping the supercomputer part of his brain turned off and playing only with his hands, but he enjoyed the challenge. A year ago, he was instructed by government agents to play a game without his hands, and remembered with amusement how difficult it was. It felt so strange, learning to be ordinary again.

"No offense, but if you had told me a year ago that I would be doing this, with you, I would have thought you were crazy," Lucas remarked, chewing pizza. He had already eaten half the box.

"Same," Kowalski nodded. "But I could get used to this."

Lucas grinned, gentle warmth spreading through him. Kowalski paused the game and set down the controller, then stood up and stretched. "It's late," he said, rubbing his eyes. "I'm going to get some sleep."

"Aw, don't be lame," Lucas teased.

"I gotta quit while I'm ahead," Kowalski replied with a tired smile. "I still can't believe I'm beating you at this game."

"Yeah, well, I've got one metaphorical hand tied behind my back," Lucas retorted.

"Alright, then tomorrow morning, before we head back, we'll play a fair game. You can go all out. Unleash the full might of your power, or whatever."

"You're poking a bear," Lucas smirked. "I don't think you'll be able to take it."

Kowalski responded by humming "Eye of the Tiger" as he carried his empty beer bottle to the kitchen and dropped it into a recycling bin. Lucas started the game again, this time setting it to one player, but was distracted by a thick hum in the back of his mind. He tried shoving it back, but it persisted. Then he spotted something through the corner of his eye that made his heart leap into his mouth.

Standing just behind Kowalski, in the shadows of the hallway, was a girl with long auburn hair and enormous green eyes. She wore a black and gray bodysuit, and her knees bent as if she was ready to pounce.

"Romana," Lucas gasped.

Kowalski reacted in an instant. He sprang for his gun, but Romana was faster; she moved in a blur as she lunged at Kowalski. Lucas generated a force field to throw around him, but stabbing pain filled his mind and it fizzled out of existence. Romana reached Kowalski, who was still reaching for his gun; he looked like he was moving in slow motion. Her pale fingers wrapped around his wrist, and then they both vanished. Lucas was on his knees, panting, in an empty apartment.

The stabbing pain abated, but he still felt a low-frequency hum in the back of his mind, like a swarm of bees.

"No," Lucas mustered, staggering to his feet. "No!"

*He can't be gone,* he thought. *He can't be gone.*

"Where is he!?" he yelled aloud, his body growing hot with rage. He ran through the living room to the hallway, then felt a sickening tug in his gut. The world tipped, and he found himself stumbling into a completely different room. A girl screamed, and Lucas was suddenly lifted off his feet and thrown over the couch. The breath was knocked out of his lungs and his head smacked the floor.

Lucas looked up, bewildered. He was in his own living room, in his own house. But how did he get here? He tasted something metallic in the air, and it felt charged. Then he saw Agent Kellerman and Tim, both with guns raised, then Romana springing over the dining room table, as lithe as a cat. She waved a hand, and Tim was slammed against the wall. Agent

Kellerman fired his gun, but Romana deflected the bullet with a flick of her wrist. Lucas clambered upright and saw that Agent Kellerman had placed himself between Romana on one side, and Arden, Leah, and Jess on the other. Romana glanced at Lucas and startled. She looked surprised to see him there. Lucas didn't understand her reaction, but didn't have time to ponder. Something moved to his right, then a hand shot out of nowhere and clamped over his throat.

Lucas gasped for air as the owner of the hand appeared in view. It was a boy with snow-white hair and pale skin. His eyes were light blue, almost silver, and he wore a black and gray suit just like Romana's, except with what looked like an armored vest. With his hand locked around Lucas' throat, he forced him down onto his back. Lucas began to panic as his mind fogged from lack of oxygen, and he began to feel cold - terribly cold. His heart rate slowed, and it became difficult to lift his limbs. With all his might, he balled his fist and began to slam it down over and over on the boy's forearm to force him to let go. He heard a *crack* as the bones in his hand snapped; it was like he was hitting solid rock. Then he kicked, but his foot went straight through the boy's torso as if it was nothing but air. The boy smiled at the terrified look on Lucas' face and leaned in close, his fingers still clamped over his neck. Cold tendrils touched his mind, shocking his senses.

*You have no idea how long I've been looking forward to this,* a rasping voice echoed in his head.

The boy picked Lucas up with one hand and hurled him across the room toward Romana, who opened her arms and caught him around the waist. Lucas felt that sickening pull in his gut again. The world tipped, and he was dropped onto cool, green grass. Dazed, he struggled to lift his head. It felt like it weighed a ton, and he couldn't get up. He floundered, then finally managed to sit up to see that he was in the backyard with Romana looking down at him. Without a word, she vanished.

His heart raced; he knew he had to get back inside. In his head, he heard Tim shouting for backup into his radio, with no response. Staggering, he forced himself upright and his feet forward. Lightning crackled in his hands as he charged through the backdoor, only to nearly trip over Agent Kellerman. He lay still with eyes open and his face a deathly pallor. Heart in his mouth, Lucas looked around. Tim and Kenny stood in the corner of the living room, Leah and Jess behind them with wide eyes and tear-stained faces. Romana and the white-haired boy were nowhere to be seen.

"Where are they?" Lucas croaked. "Where did they go?"

"Gone," Tim answered, lowering his gun. "And they took Arden."

"They took Kowalski, too," Lucas said through gritted teeth.

Lucas couldn't comprehend it. They took Kowalski, and now Arden. Why? What did they want with them? Rage pumped through his body.

He turned and slammed his now-healed fist into the living room wall. A few bones broke again, but he didn't care. He couldn't think, and he couldn't stop the anger that boiled in his chest. He kicked over a nearby chair. The heat that filled his body culminated in his hands. Tears of rage stung his eyes, and he dropped to his knees. The lights in the house flickered on and off.

"Lucas!" he heard his mother call to him.

"No, don't touch him," Tim warned. "Stay back."

"We should get them outside," Kenny said urgently. "He might lose control."

With a loud popping sound, lightning jumped across Lucas' arms and chest.

*I failed*, he thought miserably. *When it really mattered, I wasn't ready. I failed.*

Kowalski was gone. The Rising took him, and he didn't stop it.

Hunched over on the floor, he took a deep, steadying breath. He swallowed down the heat and the pain, then clenched his fists to steady his hands. Kowalski couldn't be helped if he lost it now. There was work to do.

A few minutes later, there was movement at the door. Someone draped a blanket across his shoulders. Lucas looked up through his tears to see Tim standing over him.

"Come on, Lucas," he said. "It's not over yet. You have to find them."

"I know," Lucas replied hoarsely. "But what can I do? I don't even know where to look."

"They're calling for help at the office," Tim said firmly. "We can start there."

Lucas opened his mouth, but no words came out. He didn't have any left. Tim knelt down and looked Lucas in the eyes. His face was stern, and his dark eyes were bottomless.

"We're going to find Kowalski," Tim told him. "All together. He's important to me, too, so you're not alone here. But you've got strength that none of us have, and we're not going to survive this without you. You've got to be a soldier now and just keep going."

Lucas swallowed hard and nodded. He took Tim's offered hand, and stood up shakily. Leah and Jess stepped cautiously through the front door with a flashlight, gazing around with open mouths at the damage Romana and Lucas had done. Jess was the first to recover.

"Where is my dad?" she asked Tim. Her face was red from crying. "Who were they? Where did they take him!?"

"That was Romana," Kenny answered, entering the house behind them. He carried a large black bag. "She's an android like Lucas. We've never seen the white-haired boy before."

"No, not like me," Lucas objected. "They're better trained. He's one, too; I felt his mind. They both work for the Rising, the organization that made us."

He sighed. "Kowalski was right. They made more than one, so it follows they'd make more than two."

Jess blinked, stunned.

"Okay," she stammered, shaking her head. "But where is my dad? Why did they take him?"

"I don't know," Lucas answered, closing his eyes. "I can't see him. I can't feel Kowalski's phone either, so they must have taken him somewhere far away."

"We got an urgent call for help at the field office," Tim said. "They may have gone there next."

"How? How could they do that?" Leah asked. "How did they just appear in the house and then vanish, just like that?"

"She's a teleporter," Lucas replied. "We were in Kowalski's apartment when she took him. She touched him, and they both disappeared, and then she brought me here, although that may have been an accident. She's teleporting them anywhere she chooses to go."

"Well, that's just great," Kenny remarked dryly. "What about the white-haired boy? What's his deal? He touched Kellerman, but we didn't see him do anything -"

"I don't know, but we can talk about it on the way," Lucas said with renewed fury. "We've got to get going."

"Here's your suit," Kenny said, unzipping the black bag. He tossed Lucas his suit, mask, and goggles.

"Hurry," Tim urged.

Grim-faced, Lucas took his suit and a flashlight upstairs and changed. The left sleeve of the suit ended just above his elbow, but that couldn't be helped. He carried his mask in hand as he emerged.

"Alright, let's go," he said. "Kenny, I need you to stay with my mom. Find my grandma, then come straight back here, lock the doors, and stay ready. I don't know what might happen next."

"Lucas," Kenny said quietly. "There's not much I'm gonna to be able to do if they come back -"

"I know that," Lucas nodded, and Kenny put a heavy hand on his shoulder.

"I'll do what I can," he said.

"No, I'm coming with you," Leah protested angrily. "I'm not letting you out of my sight again."

"No, Mom, I need you to go with Kenny. It's not safe."

She gave him a pleading, helpless look.

"They took Seth," she said in Spanish, her voice breaking.

"*Yo se*," Lucas answered. "And I'll get him back. I know you want to help, and you can. I need you to get Grandma and keep her safe. I can't lose either one of you."

Leah bit her lip, and Lucas squeezed her hand.

"This is what you've been training for," he told her softly.

She nodded, then bent down to kiss his cheek as Kenny shook Tim's hand firmly. Leah looked back once more as she followed Kenny to her small Honda Civic, then got in the passenger's side. As they pulled away, Jess turned to Lucas.

"What about me?" she asked.

"You're coming, because we're going to see the ULFs," Lucas replied.

"How is that going to help us find my dad?" she demanded.

"Whoa, hold on," Tim objected. "We are not putting this girl in danger. She's staying."

"If the office has been attacked, the ULFs will be looking for a fight,"

Lucas said. "They didn't seem like the types to sit out on the action. Especially Sangor. Now, for whatever reason, they like Jess. She's got a connection with them. We need her to come."

Tim puffed out his cheeks and sighed, turning away. That was enough for Lucas.

"Romana and the white-haired boy went there next, so that's where our next clues are going to be," he told Jess. "Let's get going."

# CHAPTER 9

——————◆——————

$T$he three of them hurried to the black sedan parked at the corner. Lucas knew there should have been agents here keeping watch over the house, but the car was empty. Where could they have gone, and why would they abandon their post?

"Where did Jones and Donovan go?" Lucas asked Tim.

"They were already gone when we got out here," Tim answered. "I was wondering the same thing. I can't reach them on the radio."

Lucas tasted that same metallic aura in the air. He opened the door and felt the electrical charge filling the inside of the car.

"Romana's been here," he said. "She took them and teleported them away."

"Okay, that's terrifying," Tim said, eyes widening. "So, they're kidnapping agents now?"

"It seems that way," Lucas replied. "Better stay close."

Tim drove while Jess climbed in the passenger's side and Lucas took the back. He placed the voice scrambling device against his throat, then slipped on his mask and goggles. As they raced up the street, his mind opened up and the sea of electromagnetic signals flooded in. His supercomputer mind quickly sorted through them until he found the feed from the security cameras in the CIA field office. He didn't know what he expected to find, but he was surprised to see empty rooms and hallways. He continued to search until he spotted some bullet holes in the walls and a few bodies sprawled in an office and upper-floor hallway.

"This isn't looking good, Tim," Lucas said.

"What do you see?"

"Almost everyone is gone. There are some dead, but looks like a lot of the agents are missing."

"What about the aliens?"

"I'm still looking for them," Lucas said, closing his eyes.

They would have been held in a secure room, which would not be easy to locate. He only hoped that Romana and the white-haired boy would also have trouble finding them. And if they did, would the Rising take the ULFs or kill them?

*What are you up to?* he thought with frustration. All he felt was chaotic noise.

Then a loud *boom* snapped him out of it as the car rocked. Lucas braced his hands against the seat in front of him.

"Look!" Jess cried.

Lucas looked to his right and saw a fireball bursting from the ground floor of a bank. Another one exploded across the street, out of the top floor of a high-rise; glass and debris showered down from above. People screamed and ran everywhere as cars swerved to avoid them. Thunder echoed throughout the city as plumes of fire rose up from the skyline.

"What the hell?" Tim exclaimed.

"What's happening?" Jess cried.

"It has to be the Rising," Lucas said. "Stop the car!"

Tim pulled over and Lucas sprang out onto the sidewalk. He searched with his mind for any sign of the Rising, but he couldn't find anything. Once upon a time, the Rising used to post a warning twenty-four hours before they set off a bomb, but now there was nothing. No warning.

Another *boom*, from several blocks away. And then another. They sounded like a the beats of a giant drum. The tops of the towers were hidden in smoke and people cried out in panic as they fled in every direction. Lucas' mind was quickly filled with thousands of frightened phone calls to 911 and attempts to locate missing loved ones. The city was in chaos. *What is happening?* he thought, his senses overwhelmed.

An explosion rocked the building right next to the field office, and Lucas was thrown off his feet. He hit the cement, his ears ringing. Screams sounded nearby, prompting him to stagger to his feet. Glass and rubble rained down from above, striking several people running by. Lucas unfurled a giant force field like an awning; the massive pieces of debris and broken glass rolled down it while completely missing the fleeing pedestrians as they crossed the street.

Then one collided with him, knocking him to the ground. The person kept running. He rolled out of the way of the trampling feet, then hands took hold of his arm. Jess was there, pulling him up.

"Are you okay?" she asked.

"Yeah," he said, dazed. "Thanks."

"Lucas, seriously, why am I here? We should be looking for my dad, and if you're not going to do it, then I'm just gonna go on my own -"

"We will find him," Lucas insisted. "But I can't do it by myself. I have an idea that might help us."

"What is it?"

"Larathel kicked my ass when I fought her," he explained. "I didn't stand a chance, and I've got superpowers. She's strong and experienced in battle, and if we could get her to help us fight Romana and the white-haired boy, we'd have a huge advantage. We would finally have someone on our side strong enough to help me fight them. And if Sangor's craziness has calmed down enough that she could get him on board, even better. You're here because you're special, too: they like you, and haven't tried to kill you yet. And, unfortunately, that's all we got going for us right now."

Jess pressed her lips together, giving him a skeptical look. She was becoming increasingly worried. Sirens sounded in the distance, and cars crashed into each other as their drivers strained to look at the pandemonium. The streets were soon impassable by car as traffic came to a stand-still. Tim strode up, his weapon drawn and ready, and gave Lucas a nod. The three of them set off at a run.

Lucas led the way, his mind searching the cameras ahead of them for any sign of danger, and for the room where the ULFs were kept. The elevators still worked, but they took the stairs anyway. With his spectrum goggles, he could see what had left that metallic taste in the air wherever Romana had teleported; there was a residue of energy left behind, hanging like a fog. He found this residue drifting every few dozen yards, usually beside a dead body. Each time they came to a body, Tim checked for a pulse and any injuries. What chilled Lucas was that there weren't any. There were no wounds on any of the bodies, and no blood anywhere.

They were all cold, lifeless, and apparently unharmed - except that they were dead.

"This is how Kellerman was," Tim said. "He just… died. It was the white-haired boy."

"What did he do?" Lucas asked.

"He just touched him," Jess answered. "I saw it; he put his hand on Kellerman's chest, and then he dropped dead."

Lucas remembered that when the white-haired had boy put his hand around his neck, he began to feel cold, too. Like all the energy was being drawn out of him.

"So he kills people by touching them," Lucas said, sickened.

"They took half the agents, and then killed the rest," Tim noted. "But why? What are they going to do with the ones they took?"

"I don't know," Lucas answered. "But we're almost there. I can feel it now."

He saw a room in his mind with reinforced walls and a keypad on the door. The door was still locked, and two dead agents lay outside in the hall. Inside the room was a cot and a sink; Larathel lay on her side on the floor, her two short swords beside her, while Sangor stood with his back to the camera.

"We've got to hurry," Lucas said, filling with dread. "Sangor's awake."

They were in the hall now. Lucas ran ahead, past the dead agents. He invaded the locking mechanism with his mind and forced it open, then burst through the door. Sangor spun to face him. He was shirtless, wearing only black pants and boots. One of Larathel's swords rocketed off the ground and into his hand, and white flames erupted along the blade as he pointed it directly at Lucas. His red eyes reflected their dancing light.

Lucas paused, his hands raised. He looked down at Larathel, lying motionless, and his heart sank.

"What happened?" he asked, looking back up at Sangor.

"Surrender to me now, demon," Sangor hissed in reply. "And I may show you mercy, though you deserve none."

"What?" Lucas said, taken aback.

Tim and Jess arrived behind him, panting. Jess saw Larathel dead on the floor and gasped.

"Oh, my god," Tim exclaimed.

"Sangor," Jess said. "What happened? The white-haired boy - was he here?"

"They were definitely here," Lucas said, waving his hand through the air. "I can feel the residual energy Romana left behind when she teleported."

Sangor continued to point the sword at Lucas, but his head turned slightly toward Jess.

"Surrender this demon to me," he growled. "I demand that justice be done."

"Hey, I didn't kill her," Lucas objected. "But I can help you. I want to stop them from hurting anybody else, but we've got to find them first."

Sangor seemed to falter. His expression looked strained, and the sword began to dip. Everyone immediately tensed.

"Careful guys," Tim whispered. "He could still Hulk out, and it's just us now. We won't be able to stop him."

Sangor lowered the sword completely, and the flames went out.

"You… you're Firebolt," he said.

"Yes, that's right," Lucas nodded with relief. He pulled off his mask and removed the disk on his throat, and Sangor stared at him blankly.

"I cut off your arm," he said.

"No, Larathel did that, but it's okay; it's all better now. What happened to her? How did she die?"

Sangor squeezed his eyes shut like he was in pain. He pressed the heel of his hand to his forehead.

"They came out of nowhere," he answered. "They entered the room, but they didn't come through the door. Larathel… she drew her swords and tried to fight them, but the boy touched her, and it was over. Then they both vanished."

Lucas looked down at her, his heart heavy. Her eyes were still open, back to their natural red color, and so was her hair. It fanned around her head in vermilion rays. Jess bent down and gently closed her eyes, tears glistening on her cheeks.

"What do we do now, Lucas?" Tim asked quietly, leaning close. His hand tightened around his weapon. "This guy's a time bomb that could go off at any second, and his more amicable friend is dead."

"Wait," Lucas said suspiciously. He narrowed his eyes at Sangor and pointed at Larathel's body. "Do you know her? Do you remember who she is?"

"Do you remember who *you* are?" Jess added.

Sangor shook his head, looking confused. He was quickly becoming more agitated.

"There's something wrong," he said. He dropped the sword, then grabbed his head with both hands. "These are not my memories."

"What's he talking about?" Lucas asked Jess, who shook her head, at a loss.

*Something's happened,* he thought. He closed his eyes as his mind entered the cameras, then traveled backward in time until he saw Larathel and Sangor alone in the room. Sangor lay on the cot, seemingly asleep, while Larathel paced, her blue coat glittering as she walked. Romana and the white-haired boy appeared suddenly in the room as if they had stepped straight out of thin air; Larathel immediately drew her two short swords and rushed at them both, but Romana vanished again. The white-haired boy stood his ground, and blocked a slash from Larathel's swords with his bare hands. Lucas saw sparks light off his skin, like it was made of steel. Larathel drew back, ready to attack again, and the boy advanced. One hand clamped over her throat, while the other was placed over her chest. Within seconds, Larathel went limp and sagged in his arms. She tried to pull away from his hands, but seemed to grow weaker by the second.

Lucas felt sick, watching her die. His fists clenched in anger. Then she raised a hand, pointing at Sangor. A golden light flashed, and something like a shooting star flew from her to Sangor's prone form. Then her arm dropped, and the white-haired boy released her. Her body fell to the ground, and he walked back to the door. Romana appeared again, carrying something like a black suitcase. She offered her hand to the white-haired boy, and they both teleported away.

"Lucas?" Tim inquired. "Do you see something?"

"I was reviewing the feed from the cameras," he answered. "Larathel did something to Sangor before they killed her. I saw the golden light."

"Magic," Jess said. "She must have done some kind of magic."

"Like what?" Tim asked, wide-eyed. "What did she do?"

Sangor turned away, pacing furiously.

"Twenty-three years," he said. "That's how long she searched for me. Beder burned... all of it, gone. Morlann... the war..."

"You remember it?" Jess asked him with excitement. "Do you have your memories back?"

"No, he doesn't," Lucas interrupted as it suddenly dawned on him. "He couldn't possibly know how long she looked for him, just like he wouldn't know that Larathel cut off my arm, because he wasn't there. This is going to sound crazy, but... I think he's got *her* memories."

"*What?*" Tim exclaimed.

"She gave him her memories, that's the only thing that makes sense," Lucas explained. "That's what that golden light was. It had to be."

"He's right," Jess nodded slowly, looking down at Larathel's body. "She said that he would die if he didn't get control over his magic, and he couldn't do that without his memory. She knew she was going to die, so she did the only thing she could. She died saving him."

"Jesus, this is crazy," Tim breathed.

"That has to be it," Lucas said. "It's the only reason he's even standing now."

"Would it have cured him?" Jess asked. "Can he transform?"

Lucas shrugged. "I have no idea."

"Well, what now?" Tim asked.

"Maybe he can still help us," Lucas said. "Jess?"

Jess stepped closer to Sangor, who rested his shoulder against the wall. He was tall - at least six feet, even leaning - though noticeably shorter than Larathel was.

"Are you alright?" she asked softly.

He turned his head toward her and blinked his ruby eyes.

"I was a hero, once," he said. "That's why she saved me. When you live as long as we do, your memories become the most priceless thing you own. She gave hers to me because she believed in me."

"She admired you," Jess agreed. "You were important to her."

"But I don't remember anything that I did to deserve that," he said bitterly. "Only the stories she heard. I am empty. Four thousand years of life, reduced to the memory of a child."

"Sangor, your life isn't over," Jess protested. "You can still be a hero! Don't let her sacrifice be in vain."

"I don't intend to," he said, setting his jaw.

He straightened up and strode over to Larathel's body.

"What are you going to do?" Jess asked, surprised.

Instead of answering, he knelt down and removed the sheaths of her swords from her belt and tied them onto his own, then slid both the short swords into them. He went to the cot next; his scarlet coat lay folded at the foot of it. He picked it up and put it on with one sweeping motion.

"Sangor?" Jess asked. "What are you going to do?"

"I have to go home," he replied. "There's still a war to fight, and I have been absent far too long. My people need me."

"What?" Jess said with incredulity.

He brushed past her and stopped at a narrow door that Jess hadn't noticed before, with no knob or handle, only a keypad in the wall beside it. Without hesitating, he jammed his fingers through the cracks around the door, then wrenched it open as an alarm blared loudly, which didn't seem to faze him. It must have been a storage closet of some kind, because it was shallow; he reached inside and pulled his longsword free, then slung it across his back, then strode for the door.

"Sangor, wait!" Jess cried.

But he didn't stop; he walked briskly down the long hallway without looking back.

"What are we going to do?" Tim asked, looking at Lucas.

Jess raced past them both out the door, running after Sangor.

"Follow him, I guess," Lucas answered.

They ran after Jess, who chased Sangor down the stairwell. He wasn't running, but he still moved incredibly fast as he descended the stairs, his strides carrying him impossible distances and his red coat whipping behind him as he rounded each corner. The three of them finally caught up to him in the lobby as he paused, surveying the chaos outside. Jess grabbed hold of his sleeve, breathing hard.

"Where are you going?" she said.

"I told you, I'm going home," he said brusquely. "I'm going to find somewhere to wait for my people to bring me back home, and then I will track Morlann down, kill him, and end this war."

"There's a war going on right here!" she exclaimed, pointing at the windows. "Don't you see that out there? We need you to help us stop this! Our people are in danger, too!"

"This is nothing," he said, with a laugh. "You couldn't possibly fathom the scale of the war I'm talking about. It spans universes. Your planet is so insignificant on the grand scale of things. It's not even strategically important. Let it go; I've got bigger problems to deal with."

Jess stared at him, open-mouthed. Lucas thought she might slap him, but instead she released his sleeve, and he straightened his coat.

"Wait," she said, her voice catching. He stopped at the door and looked back. "Just... just be careful out there."

He smirked.

"The last time I was on this planet, it was Rome that burned," he replied. "I see not much has changed."

As they gaped, his eyes suddenly switched from bright red to icy blue, with an iris and pupil. He stepped outside onto the sidewalk, and the sound of gunshots, car fires, and sirens escaped inside. Lucas watched Sangor cross the street. A few feet away, some men were attempting to move a parked car out of the middle of the road; it jerked forward, then careened straight for Sangor. He hooked a hand under its front bumper and lifted it over his head, then tossed the car aside. Then he walked on, disappearing into the crowd.

"Damn," Tim said. "That guy sure could've been helpful on our side."

"No," Lucas said, looking at Jess. "He was an asshole."

Jess stood with her arms stiff at her sides. Lucas went over to her. He reached up to touch her arm, but changed his mind.

"Are you okay?" he asked.

"Yeah," she said with a sniff. "He's a jerk. What are we going to do now?"

"We're going to find your dad, and Kowalski, and everybody else they kidnapped," he replied. "But it looks like we're on our own."

# CHAPTER 10

K owalski awoke on a concrete floor. He groaned, rolling over onto his back. His head spun, and a wave of nausea washed over him. He hadn't felt like this since his college years, but he really didn't have *that* much to drink. So what happened?

He opened his eyes. The room was dim, and he was looking up at shadowy rafters and old insulation. Nearer than that, there was a set of steel bars. He startled, and quickly rolled over to look around, despite the protest in his stomach. More bars, and a padlock. He was in a cage, maybe eight feet by ten, with a drain in the middle of it. A few feet away, a large man with a salt-and-pepper beard lay on his side, breathing deeply. *Arden.* Their cages were joined, and Kowalski could reach him through the bars. Kowalski crawled over, snaked his arm through and shook him by the shoulder.

"Hey," he whispered. "Hey, Arden. Wake up."

Arden mumbled something, but didn't move. At least he was alive. Kowalski quickly surveyed their surroundings. The room was very large, perhaps the inside of a warehouse of some sort. At least twenty cages lined the wall, forming a narrow corridor; all of them were occupied. He recognized a few of his own agents, men and women, all lying unconscious on the floors of their cages. There were also some men that he didn't know, dressed in military fades. In the cage directly across from him was an old man hunched in one corner. He looked like a prisoner from another era; Kowalski could see a gray beard, rags, and bony bare feet.

*What is going on here?*

His cage appeared to be the first in the row, and to his left stood a silver operating table with heart monitoring equipment and rows of tables

120

bearing other machines he didn't recognize. There was also a strong smell of bleach. Kowalski's heart sank.

Whatever was happening here, it couldn't be good.

Arden groaned, then shifted. He pushed himself up, and Kowalski saw his head bobbing as he took in the cage and the bars overhead. He took a deep breath, but before he could yell, Kowalski clamped a hand over his mouth.

"Shhh," he hissed. "It's me, Seth Kowalski. You've got to stay calm."

Arden wriggled free, but didn't cry out again. He gazed around with wide, panicked eyes.

"Where's Jess?" he blurted. "Is she alright?"

Kowalski bit the inside of his cheek. "I don't know," he admitted.

"What's going on?" Arden gasped. "Where are we?"

"I don't know."

"Do you know anything?" Arden accused.

"I know we're alive," Kowalski replied sharply. "And that's probably not for a good reason."

Arden's eyes widened. "Why not?"

"It means they want us for something."

Arden began to hyperventilate again. "Where'd those kids go? Who were they?"

"The girl's name is Romana," he answered. "She's an android, like Lucas, but she belongs to the Rising. I've never seen the boy before, but I'm going to take a wild guess that he's one, too."

"What's the Rising?" Arden asked, confused.

"Remember when I told you that there were evil people out there that wanted Lucas?"

Arden nodded.

"This is them," Kowalski said. "They made Lucas, but we got a hold of him and now they want him back. I've been tracking these guys for years, trying to take them down. They seem to have stepped up their game."

"They're using *kids*?" Arden exclaimed, disgusted.

"They're not kids - not really," Kowalski corrected. "They were *made*; they're completely artificial. Lucas just seems more human than the others because he was raised like one, but don't be fooled. They are more powerful than you would believe. Romana almost killed Lucas just a few months ago."

"The white-haired boy," Arden said breathlessly. "He killed one of your agents, back at the house... I saw it. All he did was touch him."

"Yeah, that sounds about right," Kowalski muttered. *A killing touch? What'll they think of next?*

"What are they going to do with us?" Arden asked.

"I don't know, but who knows how much time we have to figure it out before the *Children of the Corn* come back? We've gotta get out of here."

At that moment, a door opened in the far corner of the room. Two men in white coats entered and walked toward one of the tables of equipment. One of the men studied a monitor, while another seemed to just stand there, waiting.

Then Romana appeared, apparently out of nowhere. She held a black suitcase in one hand and the white-haired boy's hand in the other. The white-haired boy turned toward the rows of cages and approached slowly, wearing an amused expression. He looked like he was visiting the zoo, studying animals instead of people. Kowalski met his cold, pale eyes and felt chills crawl down his spine. He also noticed that, unlike Romana, he seemed to be wearing some kind of armored vest over his suit.

"Liam," one of the men in white coats called.

The boy's head snapped their direction.

"Go eat and rest," the man said. "Petra will send you his next orders."

Liam narrowed his eyes, but obeyed and followed Romana out. Kowalski strained to get a look at the black suitcase that they had taken from Romana. The men moved it to one of the the tables, then one of them opened it carefully. He snapped on a pair of gloves, then reached inside and removed a long, thin object, wrapped in yellow plastic. He passed it to the second man, who began unceremoniously removing the plastic, revealing a small severed arm. Kowalski gasped.

"Shit," he breathed.

"Is that...?" Arden stammered.

"Yeah, that's Lucas' arm," Kowalski whispered. "They took it from the field office."

Arden croaked like he was about to vomit. "What are they going to do with that?" he choked out.

"Nothing good, we can guess that much," Kowalski snapped. He pounded his fist with frustration on the concrete floor. "Shit!"

The old man across the corridor stirred. He crawled awkwardly to the edge of the cage and peered out through the bars. Kowalski thought he looked especially dirty, like he'd been in that cage for a long time. His beard was stained, and his hair stuck up in wild wisps, but something about him seemed familiar.

"Hello?" the old man said in a shaky, creaky voice. "Is someone else there?"

"Oh my god," Kowalski gasped.

"What?" Arden said, moving closer. "Do you know him?"

"That's Dr. Ari Lytton… Lucas' creator."

# CHAPTER 11

———————◆———————

*J*ess walked between Lucas and Tim through the panicked streets of Austin. People ran in every direction, clutching their belongings and abandoning their cars. The police seemed to be everywhere and nowhere. They yelled at people to get back to their homes and take shelter, while looters ransacked grocery stores and shops in broad daylight. Emergency personnel attempted to put out the fires, and administered aid to the injured right there on the street. A man sat on the sidewalk in the midst of some rubble. Blood poured from a wound in his head, while an EMT tore open some gauze bandages. The man dropped his hand and Jess saw a flap of skin peel back, revealing white bone, and she shuddered.

She jogged to stay as close as possible to Lucas. He had donned his mask again, earning a few weird looks from passers-by.

"This is happening everywhere," he said, his voice distorted again. "Atlanta, New York, Chicago, Denver, Los Angeles… there are reports of bombs set off all over the country."

"Any with nanomachines?" Tim asked.

"I can't tell yet," Lucas replied. "The hospitals are receiving only the usual stuff, burns and broken bones and the like."

They arrived at the car, only to find smoldering flames rising from under its hood; another car had smashed into it, its driver nowhere to be seen.

"Well, that's just great," Tim said, tossing his hands into the air.

"What do we do now?" Jess asked.

"We walk," Lucas replied. "It's not far, only about two miles."

*Through the city, now, in the dark?* Jess thought worriedly.

They set off. It was late, and getting colder. Jess shivered, until Tim took off his jacket and offered it to her. She accepted it awkwardly. Lucas kept a fast pace, almost jogging, and she was soon out of breath. She had never been very athletic, and avoided sports in school. Lucas, however, trotted on with his head high, his form perfect.

*It must be easier for him because he's like a robot,* Jess thought. *He gets tired, sure, but probably not like the rest of us.*

A stitch stung her side, and she wondered if she should ask for break, but was embarrassed to do so. Running between an inhuman android and a government spy, she felt very, very out of place.

Gunshots suddenly rang out, and Lucas dropped to his stomach on the ground. Jess followed suit, with Tim crouching protectively over her.

"What's going on?" she asked.

"Looters," Lucas answered. "Straight ahead. Tim, stay with her. I got this."

He crawled forward slowly. Up ahead, light shone from a corner store's windows, and Jess heard angry shouts and a scuffle. Lucas crept forward at the same moment that two people in ski masks burst through the door, bearing bags of chips and cases of beer in their arms. The one in front also had a pistol in hand. A man wearing a blue smock chased after them, brandishing a shotgun. He raised the gun and fired, and Lucas threw a force field around the robbers. The blast ricocheted off the field, and then, quick as lightning, Lucas swiped the gun out of the man's arms.

"Hey, what's your deal!?" the man exclaimed.

"What did they take, besides food?" Lucas asked him.

"Who do you think you are?" the man demanded. "You're letting them get away!"

"Believe me, if I wanted them, they couldn't escape from me. But if you shoot them, there's no coming back from that. Now what else did they take? Money?"

"No," the man mumbled. "Just the snacks and beer."

"So, nothing worth killing them over?" Lucas asked sharply.

"No…"

"Then forget about it; it easily could have gone a lot worse. If they come back, I'll know, and I'll deal with them then."

Lucas handed the gun back to him, but not before dumping the shells out onto the ground.

"Who are you?" the man said, looking shaken.

"Nobody," Lucas replied.

He turned and walked back to where Jess and Tim waited, then beckoned for them to follow. He led them the long way around the store, through a series of alleyways.

"Lucas?" Jess asked as they walked.

"What?"

"Larathel said that it would be dangerous for Sangor to transform without his memories to control it. I mean, he's got her memories now, but he could still get hurt, so shouldn't we -"

"Let it go, Jess," Lucas interrupted. "He doesn't want our help, and he doesn't want to help us. I'll figure this out and find your dad; we don't need him."

Jess said nothing else. Then they began running again, and Lucas didn't slow until they had entered a neighborhood west of downtown. Sirens still sounded in the distance, and the skyline glowed orange through the haze of burning fires. When they reached the house, Jess' sides hurt and her face poured with sweat from the run. Leah's Honda was parked by the curb, and Kenny stood on the porch. Lucas walked past him and opened the front door. He took off his mask as he stepped inside.

"*Mijo!*" an old woman cried. She was short in stature, with a long braid that was streaked with silver and wrinkles that bunched around her eyes. She embraced Lucas tightly, kissing his forehead and rattling on in Spanish.

Tim entered the house behind Jess, and offered to take the jacket. Jess removed it gladly.

"That's Maria, Lucas' grandmother," Tim told her quietly, nodding at the old woman.

"Oh," she said.

*He's an android, but he's got a grandmother,* she thought. She wondered when he'd explain that.

Spicy aromas filled the house and dishes of food sat on the table, but nobody moved to eat. Leah hugged Tim, and Kenny shook his hand, then all three moved to the kitchen and spoke in hushed tones. Maria followed, and Lucas disappeared into one of the back rooms. Jess was left by herself in the living room.

She sighed, rubbing her eyes, then went into the bathroom under the stairs and washed her face. Her hair was wild and damp with sweat, and dirt stuck to her neck. But she didn't care. Not really. Her father was missing, and she was stuck here in a house full of strangers; two of those people were government agents, and another was a super-powered android. More than anything, she felt like crying. Tears stung her eyes and her throat felt tight, but she swallowed it back. Instead, she did her best to wash the dirt and sweat away with a damp cloth, then smoothed her hair. When she opened the door, she jumped. Maria stood there with a stack of clothes.

"Hello," Maria said. "You must be Jess."

"Uh, yeah," Jess stammered. "Hi."

Maria held out the clothes.

"These are Leah's," she said through a thick accent. "You're about her size. We thought you might want something clean to change into."

"Thanks," Jess said, reddening.

"You should eat something, too," Maria said. "Go ahead and freshen up, then come to dinner."

"Thanks, but I'm not really hungry."

Maria gave her a gentle smile.

"I know, *mijita*. I wouldn't be either, after what you've gone through. But no one is helped by a hungry belly. Now, go on."

Jess nodded, then closed the bathroom door again. She showered, washing her hair, then dressed in the clothes Maria had given her. There was a pair of jeans and a simple, purple blouse. Both fit quite well. She combed out her hair with her fingers, then stepped out. Everyone except Lucas was seated at the table, looking solemn and picking at their food. It seemed she wasn't the only one that Maria had dragged to the table.

"Where's Lucas?" Jess asked as she pulled up a chair.

Tim nodded at the back hallway.

"Working," he said.

"Doesn't he eat?"

"He should, but there's no reasoning with him now. He'll come out eventually."

Jess looked around the table. Tim looked tired, and rested his chin in his hand. Kenny ate slowly, his red hair slick with sweat. Leah and Maria exchanged looks from across the table. Leah's face was strained with worry, deep creases showing in her forehead. Jess noticed some gray showing in her dark hair.

"What's Lucas doing in there?" Jess asked Tim quietly. "How is he going to find my dad - and Agent Kowalski?"

She added the last part after catching a glance from Leah.

"That's a complicated question," he replied. "I'm not one hundred percent certain how he does it 'cause I'm just his security, but I know he can see news reports and look through city cameras - like traffic cameras on the highway and street corners - and from that he basically gets a picture of the whole city. He can see everything that's going on. Now, that's cool by itself, but he can do the same thing in every city in America."

"No way," Jess said skeptically.

"I've seen him do it," Tim insisted. "He found a bomb in LA, about the same time the agents on the ground did - and that was his first time trying. My point is, when he says he's looking for your dad, he's literally looking all over the United States. If he can't find him, I don't think anyone could."

Jess looked down at the table. The real question, the one that she didn't want to voice, was whether or not he could see farther than Romana could teleport. If she could teleport somewhere outside the United States, somewhere beyond his limit, what good would he be?

One look at Leah told her that she was thinking the same thing. Their eyes met, and Jess saw the fear they held.

"Alright, I think it's time we all got some rest," Leah said, looking away. "Jess, you can still have Lucas' room upstairs."

"Thank you."

Everyone got up, and Maria began to wordlessly clear the table. Jess brushed her teeth, then climbed the stairs to the loft. She undressed and climbed into the bed. Downstairs, the clink of dishes eventually stopped, but there was still plenty of movement as the agents made themselves comfortable. She could see lights under the curtain, but those went out eventually, too. Then the only sound was her own breathing.

She didn't know how much time passed before she was jolted awake by a crash. It wasn't loud, but she definitely heard it. She sat up, holding her breath as she waited, but no other sound came. Finally, she crept from the bed and moved to the stairs, and the top step creaked under her foot.

"Jess," Tim's voice whispered from the bottom of the stairs. "Everything is fine, it was only Lucas."

"What happened?" she asked, trying not to let her voice squeak.

"It's nothing," he said calmly. "Just go back to bed."

There was a thump, like an object slamming the wall just inside the office. Where Lucas was.

Jess remembered the way he'd acted when Romana and the white-haired boy attacked, and then she understood. Lucas was angry, and throwing things in frustration.

She quietly crept back up the stairs and slipped back under the covers. Sleep stayed away for a long time as she lay listening in the darkness. Over the next few hours, there were several more muted crashes and, occasionally, the lights in the room glowed briefly with life, then flickered back out.

The next morning, she sleepily descended the stairs just in time to see Lucas leaving, slamming the front door behind him.

# CHAPTER 12

*L*ucas had received a text from Nate during the early hours of the morning.

*Hey, what is going on out there??? Meet me ASAP!*

He was both amazed and relieved that the power grid and phone services were still working. He changed out of his suit, put on jeans and a sweater he got from the laundry room, then headed outside. He followed the signal from Nate's phone to a corner three blocks from his house, where Nate stood with his hands in his pockets and his shoulders hunched against the morning chill. He squinted his eyes when he saw Lucas.

"Dude, you look like hell," he remarked.

"Nice to see you, too," Lucas replied dryly.

"When's the last time you slept?"

"Yesterday afternoon. Didn't really have a choice."

"Do you know what's happening in the city?" Nate asked worriedly. "My dad's been stockpiling food and getting all his guns out of the safe because he thinks North Korea's attacking."

"I wish that was it," Lucas answered. "It's the Rising. They've been setting off bombs and abducting people. Romana and another android took Kowalski. I've been looking for them all night."

"Shit, dude," Nate said, wide-eyed. "Now there's three of you? Can you find them?"

"I've been trying. I still haven't figured out how she manages to keep showing up wherever I am but keep herself hidden. She can see me, but I can't see her. It's like she keeps her brain cloaked. Oh, and she can teleport."

"So, that's it, like - the world's ending now? I mean, what can we do?"

Lucas sighed heavily, leaning against a tree.

"I don't know," he said. "I'm trying to find them, but I don't even know what's going to happen when I do. They're way stronger, and I can't beat them. There's this girl at my house right now who's counting on me to find her dad, and I just don't -"

"Whoa, there's a girl at your house?" Nate interrupted.

"Yeah, she's staying with us. Romana took her dad."

*"There's a girl staying in your house?"* Nate exclaimed. "What grade is she in?"

Lucas narrowed his eyes.

"Um, I don't know, like high school?"

Nate's mouth dropped open. "Dude! What the hell are we doing out here!? Let's go - can I meet her?"

"No! Can we focus, please? Remember the end of the world?"

"Right, right, okay... so we need to stop these other two androids that have kicked your ass twice now. Kowalski's gone, who else you got? Hey - what about that angel you went to investigate?"

"He's not an angel - he's a dick. And he came from another world."

Nate frowned.

"Another world or another planet?" he asked. "Cause there's a difference."

"I don't know," Lucas said impatiently.

"It matters!" Nate insisted. "Is he an alien or something supernatural? He had wings, so I'm banking on supernatural."

"He's *not* an angel," Lucas said flatly. "If you want to call him something, call him a ULF. According to official government records, he's an 'unidentified life form.'"

"Alien, then," Nate grinned.

"Whatever. There were two of them, actually, but Romana and the other android killed the girl one. And that's exactly what I'm talking about - this lady was super-strong and actually knew how to fight, and she had these flaming swords, but they still beat her! I don't stand a chance."

Nate rubbed his chin. "Well, what about the other one?"

"He ran off. He won't help us, I already asked."

"Do you know where he is?"

Lucas dragged a hand over his stubbled scalp with a heavy sigh. "Yes," he admitted. "I might have been following him on the traffic cameras in town."

Nate shrugged. "So, just ask him again."

"Why?" Lucas said incredulously. "What good is it going to do? You didn't meet him, he doesn't want any part of this. Besides, he's completely crazy... like, you have no idea."

"It sounds to me like crazy is exactly what you need right now," Nate replied. "You can't beat Romana by yourself, let alone two other androids who are obviously way better at this than you. You've got no other choice. This is the fate of the world we're talking about, right?"

Lucas groaned, pinching the bridge of his nose. "I'm telling you, this is a waste of time," he said.

Nate looked positively giddy.

"I get to meet an alien from outer space!" he grinned. "And no, it isn't. You need help."

Lucas set off walking and Nate followed, practically skipping. They headed southeast, toward the lake.

"I'm not even sure he really is from outer space," Lucas remarked. "From the way they talked about it, I think it's more like another dimension. Time travel is involved, and they don't use ships."

"This is so cool," Nate said excitedly. "What can he do, besides grow wings?"

"He's strong."

"How strong?"

"Enough to lift a car."

"That's awesome!" he paused, glancing at Lucas sheepishly. "I mean, helpful. Okay, what else?"

"He's a shapeshifter, and supposedly he knows some magic."

"Magic?" Nate said. "Are you *serious?*"

"Yeah, the girl ULF used her magic to heal, but I don't know what he can do."

"Does he have a name?"

"Sangor - whoa, hold up."

Lucas paused. Across the street stood three boys that Lucas recognized instantly: Val - a Hispanic boy with a mohawk - and Howard, and Darren, two former football players with enormous build. Val leaned against a large Dumpster with his arms crossed, while Darren and Howard pushed around a smaller boy who fought to escape.

"Lucas," Nate warned. "It's okay, we can keep walking."

Without realizing it, Lucas had clenched both his fists, his heart pounding. Then he stepped off the curb. Nate caught him by the sleeve.

Howard and Darren picked up the smaller boy and lifted him into the air, then began lowering him head-first into the open Dumpster despite the boy's whimpered protests.

"Hey!" Lucas exclaimed, wrenching away from Nate and crossing the street.

"Lick it," Howard told the boy. "Lick it."

The boy struggled; his frightened squeals echoed inside the metal container. Val noticed Lucas first. He straightened up and glared at Lucas. Darren saw him move and looked over his shoulder, then nearly dropped the boy in surprise. Lucas was less than twenty feet away now. Howard and Darren pulled the squirming boy from the Dumpster and released him onto the ground. His clothes reeked, and for some reason he was dripping wet. He peered through dirty Coke-bottle glasses.

"Holy shit, it's Lucas Tavera," he squeaked.

"Get out of here," Lucas told him.

The boy practically melted with relief. The gravel crunched under his shoes as he fled at a sprint. Lucas glared at Val, Howard and Darren. They stood side by side, regarding him warily. Val spoke first, sticking out his chin.

"What do you want?" he asked in Spanish.

"I don't want anything from you," Lucas answered.

"We heard what they been sayin' about you."

"Yeah? *Que has escuchado?*"

"That you went to juvie for fighting. Maybe you've gotten tougher since that day we pounded you in that warehouse."

As Val spoke, the two other boys were moving, circling around him. Darren positioned himself on Lucas' left, while Howard covered his right. They were attempting to corner him. Nate had crossed the street and appeared right behind him. Lucas held up a hand, then motioned for him to get back.

"Yeah, I got tougher," Lucas growled. "But the truth is so much better."

"Well, you know what? I don't believe any of the things they say. I think you're still that same little wussy kid we used to beat the shit out of… and you're way past due for another beating."

"You don't want to do that," Lucas said. "I'm giving you all one last chance to walk away."

Val smirked, but he had a nervous look in his eye.

"Come on," Nate said, stepping forward. He put a hand on Lucas' elbow, but addressed Val. "Hey, we got no beef with you, man. We'll go, and you can promise to leave us alone. Deal?"

Val ignored him. He stepped closer, looking down his nose.

"You really don't want to do this," Nate blurted. "I would seriously consider just walking away."

"Shut up," Val spat in English. He narrowed his eyes at Lucas. "You talk big."

"And you picked the wrong day to piss me off," Lucas said as he glowered.

Val gave a subtle nod to Howard and Darren, who began to close in. Lucas shouldered Nate aside as they each grabbed one of Lucas' arms. Val pulled back his arm, fist aimed at Lucas' face. At that instant, Lucas released a force field that rippled out of his body and sent all four of the other boys flying. There was a rapid popping sound as electric current raced across his skin. His eyes flashed as heat overwhelmed his body. He marched straight for Val, who looked up at him from the ground with amazement and fear.

"Lucas!" Nate cried.

Lucas raised a hand, then fired a lightning bolt straight at the Dumpster. Val squealed in fear, thunder clapped, and the metal container jumped backward several feet. A wisp of smoke rose from a blackened spot on its front.

Then Lucas pointed one red, blistered finger at Val's face.

"*Eres un demonio*," Val whispered, eyes wide.

"Why does everyone keep calling me that?" Lucas remarked, then spoke in low, even tones. "Unless you want to know what it feels like to be barbecue, you'd better stop harassing other kids. I will know if you don't, and I will come find you."

Val nodded vigorously, his jaw clenched tight. He got to his feet, then hurried away. Darren and Howard both followed, giving Lucas a wide berth. They glared at Nate, then fled up the street.

Nate clapped Lucas on the shoulder, receiving a static shock.

"Ow!" he yelped.

"Sorry," Lucas said.

"No, no, don't apologize - that was amazing!" Nate gasped. "And totally, completely terrifying. How's your hand?"

"Healed," Lucas replied, flexing his fingers.

A slow clap sounded. Lucas startled, and looked up to see a gray-haired man in a green canvas jacket watching them from under a tree.

"Impressive," he laughed. "That was very entertaining."

Lucas stared in shock as the old man stepped closer; his gray hair stuck up in every direction and he carried a large backpack. His jeans were worn and dirty, with large scuffed-up boots, and he smelled strongly of alcohol. Then Lucas saw the ruby pommel of a sword peeking out from beneath the backpack.

"Sangor?" Lucas said, eyes wide in disbelief.

"Indeed," he replied with a sly smile.

"*That's* the alien?" Nate whispered, leaning close. "That doesn't look like the guy from the video."

"He's a shapeshifter," Lucas explained. "He can look like anyone."

"Then why would he want to look like Nick Nolte?"

Lucas rolled his eyes, then turned back to Sangor.

"What are you doing here?"

"I was in the area. Would you like to see my humble abode? I'll take you."

Without waiting for an answer, he staggered away. Lucas had a sinking feeling in his stomach. He beckoned for Nate to come along, then followed after Sangor, who led them a few blocks closer to the river. The water reflected the gray clouds, and a cool breeze blew. They passed a few burnt-out cars and emergency crews still trying to put out the smoldering fires and sweep up glass in the streets. Nate stayed close, eyeing the destruction with his mouth hanging open. Lucas kept his jaw tight and his mind open to the nearby street cameras. The last thing he wanted to do at that moment was run into more looters.

Sangor stopped at a two-story house with boarded-up windows, surrounded by a tangle of overgrown trees. The mailbox was missing, and beer bottles littered the crooked porch. He went around the back, then slipped in through the broken screen door. Lucas and Nate followed, and were greeted by the horrible smell of urine and trash. Sangor took off his backpack and dropped it off the floor, then spread his arms like a showman. Graffiti coated the walls, and broken glass scattered over the dusty floorboards. There was a stained mattress on the floor and a mess of blankets; several nests like these sat in other corners of the room, and Lucas was fairly certain that one of them was occupied.

"Sangor," he said hesitantly. "Ummm... why are you staying here?"

Sangor shrugged, then lifted a bottle of amber liquid.

"They had alcohol," he replied, taking a drink.

"How do you even know what that is?" Lucas said with disbelief. "Jesus, it's been one night - *one night* on your own and you end up here!? What's wrong with you?"

Sangor gave him a dangerous glare.

"Did you forget that four thousand years of my life was stolen from me?" he said, his tone rising. "I was a hero of war. I fought armies, saved the galaxy numerous times, had the recognition of royalty... and now I can't remember any of it, except bits of stories told to someone else. It's like it never happened. Morlann knew what he was doing, sending me to this meaningless corner of the universe. He didn't want to kill me - he wanted to torture me."

He took another long drink, then dropped into a nearby chair.

"What kind of accent is that?" Nate asked quietly.

"Bederian," Sangor grunted. Then he squinted at Nate. "Who is that?"

"My friend, Nate," Lucas answered. "He's cool."

Sangor raised his eyebrows.

"Well, then I can relax."

He sighed deeply, and his eyes became solid red once more. The bones in his face ground together as it restructured itself, becoming decades younger, with a straight nose and sharp jawline. Long, dark hair flowed over his shoulders.

"Oh, shit," Nate said, going pale.

"Sangor, listen," Lucas interjected. "You could still save people. Jess was right, you can still be a hero. You could help us save our world, and then maybe we could work together to get you back to yours."

"I don't need your help," he replied, waving a hand dismissively. "My people will find me and bring me home. It's better that I stay in one place; if I travel too much, it will make it more difficult for them to locate me."

"What about *my* world?" Lucas pleaded. "People are dying out there, and you could do something about it!"

"As I told your friend, I don't care about your world. Generations of you have lived and died during my lifetime, what's a few more? Why should I risk my life for mayflies?"

Lucas seethed. Heat filled his hands.

"Because it would be the right thing to do!" he shouted.

Sangor was suddenly on his feet, and perfectly steady.

"You had best watch your tone, child," he said in a low voice. "You forget yourself, and to whom you speak. I am the commander of the garrison, the hero of the Battle of Corvakt, and you will address me with respect."

Lucas couldn't take it anymore. He took a deep breath to suppress the lightning surging through his veins, then leveled at Sangor.

"You keep calling yourself a hero, but you don't have a right to that word anymore," he said. "You don't remember your life or any of the stuff you did to earn that title, only the way that Larathel remembered you. She looked up to you, and you know what? I think she was mistaken."

He gestured at the surrounding filth.

"*This* is you, the real you, without all the banners, flags and showmanship. You're not a great hero, you're a coward. I thought I needed you because I'm not a soldier, and I never wanted to lead anyone. But I can see now that I'd be a hell of a lot better at it than you."

Sangor narrowed his eyes, a vein bulging in his neck. Lucas wondered if he might have gone too far, and waited for Sangor to suddenly shift into some monster again. Instead, he hurled the bottle over Lucas' head. It shattered on the wall.

"Get out!" he roared.

"Way ahead of you," Lucas replied, glaring at him. "C'mon, Nate."

He turned to the door, and Nate followed eagerly. Then Lucas paused, looking back over his shoulder at Sangor, anger still boiling in his chest.

"Larathel died saving you," he said. "This sure is some thanks for the sacrifice she made."

Before Lucas could blink, Sangor had whirled around, his hand outstretched. Lucas felt himself lifted off his feet and flying up toward the ceiling. Reacting instantly, he hurled a force field at Sangor like a baseball pitch. It slammed into him, knocking him backward into the drywall. Lucas landed on his feet as Sangor dropped to the ground with a heavy thud. The wall crumbled behind him, and Sangor's head sagged against his chest.

Lucas looked down at him, feeling nothing but disgust.

"Maybe one day you'll deserve her respect again," he said.

Then he and Nate walked out.

# CHAPTER 13

——————◆——————

*K*owalski gaped at the old man in the cage, his weepy eyes peering between the bars from beneath a mess of gray hair.

"What do you mean, that's Lucas' creator?" Arden whispered hoarsely. "Like, he literally built Lucas?"

"He made the nanomachines that give Lucas his powers," Kowalski explained. "We think the Rising actually did the building part, like putting him together, though we're not sure. Maybe now we can finally find out…"

Arden shook his head. "When did my life turn into a science fiction movie?" he sighed.

"I've been living a science fiction movie for the past thirteen years," Kowalski said. He turned back to the old man. "Dr. Lytton? Is that you?"

"Yes, who are you?" the man said in a creaky voice.

"My name is Seth Kowalski and I lead a special task force with the CIA. We've been searching for you since you disappeared."

Dr. Lytton gripped the bars of his cage. "You're too late," he said shakily. "You've got to get out of here and warn everyone."

"Warn them about what?" Kowalski asked.

"They're planning something terrible… no one is safe. What they've created here using my work… Petra is insane. It's complete madness."

"Sir, what have they done with your work?" Kowalski asked carefully. "Is there a way to stop it?"

"This isn't what I intended," the old man croaked. Tears glistened on his cheeks. "I wanted to help people. I never wanted any of this."

"Doctor, listen to me," Kowalski said, losing patience. "Try to focus. The androids - is there a way to stop them? Can they be killed?"

"It doesn't matter. More would come."

That sent chills crawling down Kowalski's spine.

"How many are there?" he asked, his throat tightening.

"Thousands… maybe more," the old man answered.

"Shit," Kowalski said, jumping up. He turned to Arden, his face pale. "We've got to get out of here."

"How?" Arden said, standing.

Kowalski felt his way around the perimeter of the cage. The bars were thick, and the door pressurized, secured with an electronic locking system.

"There's gotta be something," he said under his breath. "Some weak spots, maybe."

"Here," Arden called.

He was kneeling down in a back corner of his cage. He dug into his pocket and retrieved a quarter, which he fitted into one of the bolts.

"That's going to take forever," Kowalski chided.

"Just keep a lookout, alright?"

Kowalski watched the doors, but he was antsy. After a minute, he glanced back at Arden, who was still trying to work the bolt loose, then sighed, resting his forehead against the bars.

"Kowalski, sir? Is that you?" said a voice from a few cages down.

"Donovan?" Kowalski inquired. "If you're here, then I'm guessing the safe house was hit."

"Yes, sir," the agent answered heavily. "She jumped us. I'm sorry."

"There's nothing you could've done. Romana took us all by surprise; I didn't fare much better against her."

"Do we have a plan, sir?"

"Not a good one," Kowalski muttered.

Then he heard the clink of metal on the concrete floor as Arden freed the first bolt.

"I stand corrected," Kowalski noted, impressed. "Wow, you've got some strong hands."

"I used to do grunt work on the oil fields, until recently," he replied, then grinned. "And maybe a little boxing back in my twenties."

The other agents who'd woken up craned to look, perking up at each clatter of a bolt hitting the floor. Kowalski, too, began to grow more excited. Finally, half an hour later, Arden stood up.

"Here we go," he said in a low voice.

He gripped the bars and widened his feet. With a grunt, he pushed the side of the cage open. Kowalski winced at the loud screech and everyone in the room froze, waiting for a response, but none came.

"Okay, great," Kowalski whispered. "Get me out next, and we'll both try to find a way to call for help."

It took another thirty minutes, but Arden managed to get the bolts removed from one side of Kowalski's cage. Together, they pushed the metal apart and Kowalski slipped out.

"Alright!" Donovan exulted in a hushed voice.

"Well done," Kowalski said quietly. "Let's go."

He put a hand on Arden's back and together they crouched low, hurrying toward the operating table. Kowalski motioned at Arden to stop, then they both began searching through the equipment.

"What are we looking for?" Arden asked.

"Anything we can use to call for help, or that might give us a clue as to what these guys are up to… or both."

The tables were piled with a lot of electronic monitoring equipment, along with a bunch of hoses and vials. The rest looked like items from any ordinary doctor's office - stethoscopes, cotton balls, and rubber gloves. Kowalski found a scalpel and gripped it in his fist.

"Alright," he said, glancing at Arden. "Let's keep going."

They tiptoed to the wide double doors and Kowalski paused, listening. He heard voices on the other side, so he directed Arden to follow him to the back of the room. There, a smaller door opened into an enormous hallway with empty carts parked every few feet and a series of closed doors on either side. Kowalski jogged ahead, glancing over his shoulder for cameras. He saw none, but that didn't mean there weren't any. They had to move quickly. He cautiously peeked through the window in the first door and saw only shelves of cardboard boxes. At the next door, he froze.

"Oh my god," he breathed.

"What is it?" Arden said, standing on his tiptoes to see.

Inside, a woman lay strapped to a table, an IV needle in her arm. Under the breathing mask over her mouth and nose, she looked young, possibly a teenager. She wore a short hospital gown; tiny electrodes appeared to be stuck all over her forehead, and dozens of tubes fed into each of her outstretched arms. Machines surrounded the table she lay on, along with glass containers of multi-colored liquid.

"Dear god, what are they doing to her?" Arden gasped.

"My guess, the same thing they did to Lucas' mother," Kowalski said through gritted teeth. "We didn't shut them down after all, they just moved their operation."

His jaw clenched, he moved down to the next door and saw the same setup: a young woman strapped to a table and surrounded by machinery. The only difference was that this girl had pink highlights in her hair, and cuts and bruises covering her arms and legs. Kowalski's stomach turned as they passed five doors in total. Five women. All strapped down and asleep.

"They could be using them to test the nanomachines, but I didn't see any in there," Kowalski said in a tight voice, dragging a hand through his hair. "When we raided their operation in California, the women they'd taken all died of infection from the nanomachines, except for Lucas' mom. We got her out and nine months later, Lucas was born. But he doesn't share her DNA. Maybe they needed something else."

Arden looked sick. "Could *that* be what they're doing with them?" he asked. "Using them like… like a… mill?"

"Maybe," Kowalski nodded, equally horrified. "Let's keep heading this way, there might be a way out further on."

"What? No!" Arden objected. "We have to save them!"

"We will, when we come back with Special Ops," Kowalski said. "We can't do anything for them right now, and we've wasted enough time here as it is."

"We can't leave them here!"

"There are two of us, and five unconscious girls. How do you propose we carry them out? We can't go back and bring the rest of my agents over - that would take too much time and half of them are still unconscious. Our best option is to get out of here as quickly as possible and bring back help. Do you still trust me, or not?"

Arden looked conflicted, but said nothing. Kowalski nodded once, then turned and jogged the rest of the way up the corridor. They passed through the set of double doors at the end and were met by two men in white suits. Kowalski sprang into action, slamming his fist into the first man's mask and the scalpel into his ribs, then bringing his heel down onto his knee. He gave the man another hard punch to make sure he stayed down. Arden took his man down with a haymaker, then a kick to the chest. The man dropped, and did not get up.

"Good job," Kowalski said, panting.

"I think I pulled something," Arden grunted, rubbing his shoulder.

They ran on, then skidded to a stop at a set of sliding glass doors that led into a room lit with soft blue light. The ceiling was more than twenty feet high, and suspended from it were dozens upon dozens of bags made of clear plastic. The bags were filled with gallons of clouded fluid, and each one contained a baby floating freely, connected to several thick cables in its stomach and spine. A blinking green and yellow light hung above each bag, and an ECG machine beeped. Some of the infants twitched their fingers, grasping with their tiny hands. One opened its mouth in a yawn.

Arden and Kowalski stepped close to the glass, gaping.

"What the hell?" Arden gasped.

"This is really, really bad," Kowalski said seriously. "This is beyond bad."

"Are those… androids?" Arden gasped.

Kowalski nodded slowly.

"I think so," he said, eyes wide. "This isn't terrorism… this is a takeover. They've got enough here for a full-scale invasion. The world wouldn't stand a chance: online networks, communication, infrastructure - they could destroy all of it, bring every country to its knees. They could take over everything."

"What should we do?" Arden asked, panicked.

"I… I don't know," Kowalski replied.

Arden spun around, searching the walls, floor, ceiling… then he grabbed Kowalski's shoulder.

"Well, come on, let's go get help," he said shakily. "We've got to go warn somebody, right?"

Kowalski wasn't listening. He looked at the keypad on the wall by the door, then raised his foot and kicked it. Sparks flew, and an alarm blared.

"What are you doing!?" Arden cried.

"I have to stop this," Kowalski growled, prying the door open.

He walked inside and located a wide control panel. He strode over to it and Arden raced after him, then caught him in a bear hug.

"No, stop! I can't let you do this!" he cried.

Kowalski squirmed, but Arden was strong. They both crashed into the wall, and only then did Arden let go.

"What's wrong with you?" Kowalski exclaimed, staggering back. "I have to destroy these things! The world depends on it!"

"I can't let you kill them," Arden said, gasping for air. "It would be wrong. There's got to be another way."

Kowalski couldn't believe what he was hearing. He pointed up to the nearest android, which floated in its bag ten feet above his head. Its fingers twitched near its mouth.

"*That* is not a child!" Kowalski yelled at Arden. "It's not human! Two of those things kidnapped you, did you forget that? They are dangerous, and have to be stopped before people die. Did you hear me? *People!* Human beings will die if I don't do this!"

Arden met his glare defiantly. "They're innocent," he said quietly.

"That doesn't matter," Kowalski replied. "They are weapons. And they will be used like weapons."

"What about Lucas?" Arden challenged. "You said you loved him like a son. Why is he different? Because you know him?"

Kowalski didn't know what to say. He dragged a hand through his hair, then kicked a cart in frustration.

"Yeah," he muttered. "He's different. I'm sorry, but I have to do this."

He turned back to the control panel, and Arden didn't move to stop him. Instead, he covered his face with both hands. Kowalski took a few seconds to study the buttons and dials, his hands shaking.

"You're out of time," a soft, reedy voice said. It sounded like sandpaper.

The men whirled around to see the white-haired boy, Liam, stepping into the room. Kowalski's eyes widened as he realized that half the boy was missing - it was hidden in the wall. The android was in the process of emerging into the room from the corridor *through the wall*. He brought his other foot out, then squared up at the men, a smile playing on his thin lips. Kowalski lunged and Arden ran, but the android was too fast. He tapped Kowalski on the forehead with a hand that felt like it was made of rock, and the agent was out cold.

Machines beeped. Blood rushed in his ears, like waves crashing on a beach. He woke up feeling like he was trapped on a merry-go-round, and his stomach lurched. Acid rose in his throat, and he leaned over in the chair he was sitting in and vomited onto the concrete floor. He wanted to wipe his mouth, but his hands were tied to the arms of the chair.

Gasping for breath, he looked around. His vision was blurred, but he made out men in white coats and an operating table with a figure lying down on it. He recognized the barreled chest and graying beard.

"Arden," Kowalski groaned.

Arden muttered something. In fact, he was talking a lot. More of Kowalski's surroundings began to take shape. Arden was strapped to the table, and the men in white coats were hooking electrodes up to him. Information was displayed on each of the half-dozen monitors in scrolling green letters. Arden kept talking in a low, hushed voice, then Kowalski realized he was praying. According to the monitors, his heart was racing, and Kowalski saw sweat drip from his forehead onto the metal table.

"Hey," Kowalski said, clearing his throat. His vocal chords felt like they were filled with sand. "Hey, what's going on here?"

A tall man with dark skin and neatly-combed hair appeared, stepping up from behind Kowalski. He was accompanied by Liam, who walked a few steps behind him.

"Seth Kowalski," the man said with a smile. He spoke with an elegant French accent and wore a white shirt and trousers, and silver-embroidered vest. "You have been a thorn in my side for quite some time now."

"The pleasure's all mine. Who are you?"

"Gabriel Petra. The rightful owner of the boy you call Lucas."

"Ah, yes, you've met," Kowalski said with a short nod. "Where are you from, if you don't mind me asking?"

"Morocco," Petra replied flatly.

"Sweet, I loved *Casablanca*," Kowalski grinned. "And sorry to burst your bubble, but you don't actually own him anymore, the United States government does."

The man's smile widened as he interlaced his fingers.

"As a matter of fact, he *is* my property, and nothing you do or say will change that. Nothing Lucas can do or say will change it. I designed him, engineered him, and gifted him with his abilities. What does that make you? A thief. And thieves get punished."

"What about Lucas?" Kowalski said, suppressing the fear that rose in his chest. "If memory serves, he made it very clear that he has no intention of joining you."

"Alas, he is still only a child," Petra replied softly. "He doesn't know what he wants. He'll have to be taught a lesson, and that's why you're here."

Kowalski's stomach turned somersaults. "What are you going to do?" he asked.

"That depends on your friend here," Petra answered, glancing sideways at Arden.

One of the white-suited people approached the table, wearing a mask and carrying a metal tray of at least a dozen cylinders that glowed a bright, electric blue. *Nanomachines.* Kowalski immediately tensed, fighting his bonds.

"You asshole!" Kowalski shouted at Petra. "Don't do this!"

Petra gave no response. His eyes were fixed on the white-suited person, who picked up one of the glowing cylinders and fitted it into a syringe, then slid the needle into the inside of Arden's elbow. Arden went from weeping to screaming at the top of his lungs and thrashed so hard his wrists were quickly rubbed raw. The ECG machine that monitored his heart let out an alarming screech.

"No!" Kowalski yelled, rocking his chair.

Petra gave the attendants a nod, and another one approached the table. He adjusted the setting on one of the IV bags, and, after a minute, Arden's thrashing slowed. Another minute passed, and he lay still, the ECG machine beeping steadily. Petra walked over to the table, looking the unconscious Arden up and down, then checked the monitors. Kowalski watched all of his, his heart pounding and his body wracked with chills of terror.

"Well done, everyone," Petra smiled. "Liam, you can come over now."

Liam emerged from wherever he had been hiding in the shadows, looking a little green. He moved closer and then stopped, cocking his head to the side. For an entire minute, nobody moved, then a wicked smile spread across his face.

"Excellent," Petra said, then addressed one of the attendants. "Take them both to the next room. Keep me updated on any changes."

Kowalski watched breathlessly as Arden was wheeled out with Liam walking close behind.

"Now, who's next?" Petra said, spreading his hands. His dark eyes fixed on Kowalski. "How about you?"

Two men in dark suits began to undo the bonds on Kowalski's wrists and ankles. The second his hands were free, he hurled a punch, connecting with one man's jaw. Petra laughed as the men struggled, exchanging punches until Kowalski found himself overpowered. They backed him into the table, then forced him down onto it. Panic began to blind him.

*What's wrong with me?* he thought. *I should be better than this!*

But he had to admit that he was afraid. Far too afraid to think clearly.

He was strapped onto the table, his whole body shaking. The white-suited people began to attach leads and electrodes onto his forehead and arms. The machines beeped, betraying his racing heart. Then came the attendant with the syringe of glowing blue nanomachines.

*Dear god,* Kowalski thought, his heart in his mouth.

The needle was inserted into his arm, and the plunger pushed thousands upon thousands of microscopic machines into his bloodstream. His veins glowed blue for a brief second, and then that faded. He felt something cold travel up his arm and into his chest, and then a feeling like ice attacked his skull. The sensation spread, and he couldn't hold back the scream of pain; darkness began to fold across his mind.

*I'm sorry, Leah.*

# CHAPTER 14

---◆---

*J*ess wandered downstairs, wearing the clothes that Maria had given her. She rubbed her eyes and yawned; three hours of sleep was not nearly enough to counteract the exhaustion of worry, not to mention running all over the city. Wandering into the living room, she found Leah, Kenny, and Tim, looking just as sleep-deprived as she felt.

"He's not picking up," Tim said.

"Oh, god, do you think that Romana may have taken him?" Leah said, covering her mouth.

"Are you guys talking about Lucas?" Jess asked.

"Do you know where he is?" Tim replied.

"He left this morning," she answered. "I saw him walk out the door."

"Did he say where he was going?"

"No."

Leah crossed her arms, her hands trembling. Tim put a gentle hand on her shoulder.

"I'm sure he's fine," he said.

Leah didn't look convinced. "I'm going to go train," she said, pulling away.

She walked through the kitchen to the garage. Tim looked at Kenny, who shook his head. Both were wearing civilian clothes now and Kenny's tattoos showed on his arms, covering them all the way down to his wrists in Celtic knots and other weird patterns. He sat down in one of the easy chairs with a cup of coffee as Tim turned to Jess.

"Well, you'd better get some breakfast," he said. "Maria made some fantastic *migas*."

"What, that's it?" Jess exclaimed. "We're going back out, right? My dad is still out there, and we have to look for him!"

"There's not much we can do until Lucas gets back. When he does, we'll reconvene and come up with a plan."

"So that's all? We're just going to sit around?"

"And rest," Kenny added, sipping his coffee.

Tim looked apologetic.

"It's a good idea to use the time right now to eat and rest up, so we're ready to go as soon as we hear from Lucas," he said. "I'll keep calling him, and let you know as soon as I reach him, okay?"

Jess crossed her arms. She wasn't hungry, but walked to the kitchen anyway. It smelled like coffee and fried eggs. Maria was kneading a large lump of dough with her bare hands, her sleeves rolled up to the elbow. She wore an apron, and her graying hair was pulled back in a long braid that hung to her waist. She looked up and smiled as Jess entered.

"*Buenos dias, mijita*," she said. "How did you sleep?"

"Not well," Jess admitted.

"Me neither," Maria replied with a slow nod. "I worry for my grandson, and all that he has to worry about. You worry, too?"

"Yeah, for my dad. He's still out there, and… I know that Lucas is looking, but… I just feel like it's not enough. I want to help, but I don't know how."

"When you feel like things are out of your control, it's good to do something productive. I'm old, and there are many things I can't do anymore. So, I do what I can; I make bread."

"Where did you learn to do this?" Jess asked, watching with interest as Maria flipped the lump of dough, then sank her fingers deep into it.

"YouTube," she replied.

"Oh."

"You should eat," Maria said, nodding at a cast iron pan on the stove. It contained a mixture of scrambled eggs, tomatoes, and tortilla strips - and smelled wonderful.

"Well, okay," Jess said with a shrug. She helped herself, then poured a cup of coffee. She normally didn't drink coffee, but Arden did, and it comforted her to see the steaming mug sitting there. She tasted the *migas* and her stomach responded by growling ferociously, so she finished the whole plate.

"Good?" Maria asked with a smile.

"Good," Jess nodded shyly.

"What does your father do for a living?" Maria asked.

"He used to work for an oil company," Jess answered. "He worked out on the rigs til my mom died. Then he quit and decided to become a writer."

"Why that?"

Jess shrugged.

"I don't know," she said, leaning against the counter with her arms crossed. "My mom always hated that he was gone so often. She talked about him doing something safer and closer to home. She wanted a farm and a vegetable garden. And I guess since he never did it while she was alive, he felt obligated to do it after she died."

Maria looked at Jess with soft, gentle eyes. Jess felt like they were looking straight through her.

"How did she die?" Maria asked.

"Cancer," Jess replied. "Two years ago."

*And I can't lose my dad, too. I just can't.*

"I'm sorry for your loss."

"Thanks," Jess said, twirling the end of her hair. Her eyes stung, so she turned away to hide them. "And thank you for breakfast."

"Oh, *de nada*," Maria said. Even her voice smiled, and it made Jess want to hug her.

She was distracted by the sound of a phone vibrating. Back in the living room, Tim's phone vibrated. Jess listened as he answered the call, hoping that it was Lucas finally making contact, but the conversation sounded formal. Tim said "yes, sir," and "no, sir" enough times that Jess concluded that it definitely wasn't Lucas on the other end.

"*Mijita*, honey, can you reach that bowl for me?" Maria said, pointing to a light blue ceramic bowl high on a shelf.

"Oh, sure," Jess said.

She stood up on her tiptoes and retrieved the bowl, then set it on the counter. Maria picked up the dough with both hands, then dropped it into the bowl with a satisfying *plop*.

"Can I help with anything else?" Jess asked sheepishly.

"Oh, no, sweetheart," Maria replied as she covered the dough with a damp towel. "I can finish up here. But you could go check on Leah; she's working in the garage and I am sure she could use some help."

She nodded to the door, then gave Jess a wink. Jess furrowed her brow, confused, but went to the door anyway and opened it. She saw Leah in athletic shorts and tank top, her hands and wrists wrapped with tape. She was barefoot and stood in front of a large punching bag that hung from the ceiling. Jess watched, perplexed, as Leah threw a few quick jabs, then swung a kick that hit the bag with a loud thump. The bag swayed, and Leah assumed her stance again. Jess looked back at Maria, who gave her another wink.

*Okay...* she thought. *Leah definitely doesn't look like she needs help.*

She stepped further in, then closed the door. Leah didn't seem to pay attention to her; she kept hurling punches, bouncing on her toes as she moved around the bag. Jess curiously watched everything she did. Leah threw another kick, then paused, giving Jess a hard look.

"What are you doing here?" she asked, panting.

"Uh, well, I heard you in here," Jess lied. "I... um, I thought maybe you could teach me some of that."

Leah stepped away from the bags, rubbing her knuckles. The bag swayed back and forth slowly.

"Well, I don't know much," she said, breathing hard. "Seth taught me a little - Agent Kowalski, I mean. He used to train me and Lucas."

Jess looked at the scar on her chin. She noticed that it made a slight dimple, then looked somewhere else so Leah didn't think she was staring.

"Where did you get your scars?" she asked.

"I made a lot of mistakes when I was younger," Leah answered with a tone of hesitation. "And got involved with the wrong people."

Jess pressed her lips together, wondering if she had been too nosy. Leah took a drink of water from a plastic bottle, then appraised Jess with furrowed brows. Then she sighed.

"I can teach you what little I know, if you want," she said finally. "It might be better than nothing."

She motioned for Jess to get up and follow her to the bag.

"Okay, so you want to stand like this," she said, staggering her feet, and Jess mimicked her. "Then close your fists. Make sure your thumb is on the outside so you don't break it... like this. And when you hit, extend your arm and rotate your hips, like this."

She modeled punching the bag, moving her hips as she did so. Then she stepped back, and Jess tried it. She hit the bag and felt the sting in her knuckles right away.

"That's going to happen," Leah told her after Jess winced. "It will hurt a lot worse if you actually hit somebody. Keep going."

Jess punched the bag again, trying to hit it as hard as she could though the pain surprised her. Leah adjusted her stance, nudging her feet into the right position.

"Put your hips into it," she said. "It'll extend your reach and give you more power. Men have power in their arms; women need to use their entire body. Rotate like that - that's where your strength comes from."

Jess was soon sweating, and her heart pounded with the effort. After a few minutes, Leah showed her how to kick, and that hurt her feet, too. She continued practicing for the next twenty minutes, then Leah called for a break. Jess dropped down and rested her head on her knees, breathing hard.

"No, stand up," Leah told her. "You'll never catch your breath that way. Put your hands on your head."

Jess did, and winced at the stitch that had formed in her side.

"How long have you been doing this?" she asked Leah.

"Not long. I'm still new at it, too."

"Why did you want to learn?"

"Every girl should have the skills to defend herself," she said. She sounded casual, but her tone was dark and her eyes flinty. Then Leah grimaced and put her hand to her stomach.

"Are you okay?" Jess asked.

"Yeah," she answered, rubbing her stomach. Her brow furrowed. "I just had a weird feeling. It's nothing; I probably just need some more water."

Jess watched Leah wince again, then she led the way back into the kitchen. Leah poured two glasses of water and gave one to Jess, which she gratefully accepted.

"What you'll want to do is start running; that will build up your endurance," Leah explained. "Seth told me that your skills won't mean anything if you get tired faster than the person you're fighting."

"Wow," Jess shook her head. "I didn't know there was so much to it. Watching Lucas and Larathel, well, they both just made it look so easy."

"And look how Larathel ended up," Leah remarked grimly. "These people we're up against are no joke. They've killed Larathel and nearly killed Lucas once before. It's going to take everything we have to take them down. It's going to take all of us."

"That's what I'm afraid of," Jess replied, looking away.

A knock pounded on the door, and Jess and Leah both jumped.

"Ladies," Tim called from the living room. "You'd better get over here."

Tim opened the door, and a lanky boy with blond hair and a pointed face hurried in. His face was red, and he was breathless.

"Nate?" Leah said, hurrying over. "What are you doing here?"

"He brought a friend," Kenny said before Nate could answer.

Kenny was gazing intensely through the blinds. Jess peeked through, and was stunned to see a young man with long dark hair standing on the sidewalk, wearing a green canvas jacket, dirty jeans, and heavy boots. He wore a backpack, and the ruby-pommeled hilt of a sword peeked out over his shoulder. Instead of bright red, however, his eyes were icy blue; he looked straight at Jess and gave a half-smile, then raised his hands over his head, palms out.

"Uh, hi, Mrs. Tavera," Nate stammered. He looked like he was about to cry; his chin trembled, and his face was bright red.

"Nate, what's going on?" Leah said warily. "Is that him? The alien?"

"What's he doing here?" Jess asked bitterly, crossing her arms.

"It's about Lucas," Nate blurted, his voice breaking. "He's gone. Romana took him."

"What!?" Leah cried.

Tim grabbed hold of Nate and forcefully whirled him around.

"Explain, *now!*" he said sternly. "What happened?"

Nate's face grew redder, and a few tears leaked out.

"Lucas and I went to see the alien and convince him to help," he stammered. "He said no, and Lucas got mad, and then the alien got mad, so they fought and then we left. We were walking home when Romana appeared out of nowhere and touched Lucas and then they both just disappeared. I freaked out and and started to run here, and then... he just showed up and told me to take him here."

Tim moved toward the door, but Leah caught his arm.

"We shouldn't let him in," she objected. "Not with Lucas gone."

"Believe me, a door wouldn't stop this guy," Tim said dryly. "He's in his right mind now; if he wanted to hurt us, not even Lucas would be able to prevent that."

He opened the door and stepped out. Kenny continued to watch through the window, his hand resting on the gun at his belt and his eyes narrowed. Tim stopped halfway down the front walk and stopped, his hands on his hips.

"What do you want?" he said. He spoke loudly, but his tone was easy.

"I've had a change of heart," Sangor replied. "I want to help you."

"Oh yeah?" Tim scoffed. "What changed your mind?"

Sangor's eyes dropped.

"Lucas visited me, and... well, he had a great deal to say. He convinced me that my time on this world would be best served aiding you in your struggle."

"Those are some flowery words," Tim replied. "Where is Lucas now?"

"That's also what I came to tell you," Sangor said darkly. "He left, and I followed. I tracked his scent to that boy, and found him alone." He nodded toward the house, and Nate seemed to shrink. He inched closer to Jess, who leaned away from him, puzzled.

"And then...?" Tim prompted.

"He told me that the demon girl, Romana, stole Lucas away," Sangor continued. "She is the same one who was there when Larathel was killed. I want to help you find Lucas, and then I will kill both Romana and the white-haired demon."

Tim crossed his arms, then looked back over his shoulder at the window. Leah shook her head, biting her lip, but Kenny shrugged. Tim visibly sighed, then motioned for Sangor to follow him inside. The door opened, and Sangor looked around curiously at the furniture, at Leah, and then at Maria, who had emerged from one of the back rooms holding a rosary. Jess noticed right away Sangor's greasy hair and the strong smell of alcohol.

"Do you have a plan for fetching him back?" Sangor asked, dropping his backpack on the floor. He propped his sword up against the couch, still in its gleaming sheath.

Kenny said something in a bizarre, rolling kind of language that Jess had never heard before, then sighed heavily.

"What was that?" Tim asked, glancing at him in surprise.

Kenny blinked, looking confused, and then his cheeks reddened.

"Sorry, that was Gaelic," he explained. "That's what I heard, so answering in it was like a reflex. God, this is gonna be annoying."

Tim shook his head, then addressed everyone else.

"No, we don't have a plan for getting him back. Or what we're going to do about Romana and the rest now that he's gone. I mean, he *was* the plan."

Leah put her arms around Maria as tears welled in her eyes. Jess felt her anger rise.

"Well, we have to do *something*!" she exclaimed. "We can't just stay holed up in here, hoping he'll come back!"

Sangor gave her a look of amusement, his lip curled in a half-smile.

"You're right," Tim replied. "I got a phone call from the President earlier this morning. He wants to see Lucas and will be demanding answers. If Lucas has been taken, he'll need to know that. We've got to tell him what happened, then come up with some kind of contingency plan."

"President? What is that?" Sangor asked, confused.

"The leader of our country," Jess answered.

"Like a king?"

"No!" Tim and Kenny said in unison.

Sangor raised his eyebrows, and Jess shrugged.

"Sort of," she said dismissively. "That's not important right now."

"If Lucas has been captured, then that could very well be it, for all of us," Tim said. "We need to tell the President, and let the world know what they're up against."

"And then what?" Kenny asked anxiously.

"Evacuate the cities, tell everyone to get somewhere safe," Tim replied. "And pray."

# CHAPTER 15

Lucas and Nate walked together back toward downtown. The day brightened as the sun rose higher, and black smoke stood out starkly against the white sky. In a way, the destruction looked sadder in the daylight. Black, gaping holes yawned from the buildings that had been gutted by the bombs; paper and trash drifted across the pavement, pushed along by the chilly wind, and broken glass glittered on the asphalt.

A few emergency vehicles remained parked in the streets as crews of city personnel dug through the debris for survivors, or evidence as to who the bombers might be. Lucas noted that the Rising was named nowhere in the media. News anchors speculated about the culprits, throwing out possibilities like gang wars, anarchists, or foreign terrorists. Political pundits across the country blamed North Korea, China, Russia, Iran, and Saudi Arabia, all demanding that their leaders own up to the attack. The ones that actually made statements obviously denied any role in it. A few fringe news outlets blamed the United States government itself, calling it a set-up to start World War III. And one website, TheyAreAmongUs.com, actually pinned the destruction on Lucas:

*On the ground sources confirmed that the mysterious "Figure in Black" was present during the explosions in Austin, Texas. Did he have a hand in these explosions? Are there others like him? Witnesses to the abductions across the country report seeing similar figures appear and then vanish. Are these strange beings from another world? What kind of power do they have? Have the Martians finally decided to wage an open attack?*

"This whole country is in a panic," Lucas said. "The abductions happened across the states. The Rising took a lot of people."

"What for?" Nate asked.

"I don't know. And I don't know how to stop it, either."

"Well, on another note, what are you going to do now that Val knows what you can do? Are you worried he might tell somebody?"

"It doesn't really matter now," Lucas replied. "And I don't really care anymore. I mean, look at all this. The world's never going to be the same. I think the public has much bigger things to worry about, and... I don't know, maybe I'm tired of hiding."

"My friend, the superhero!" Nate cried gleefully. "That would be so cool!"

"Whoa, I didn't say anything about that," Lucas said, though he smiled. "Besides, superheroes still wear masks, or at least have a secret identity. I'm talking about just being me... no masks, no secrets, and no one to answer to. I don't know what that looks like yet, but that's the dream."

"Do you have a superhero name?"

"The CIA codenamed me 'Firebolt,'" Lucas answered.

"Awesome," Nate said with wide eyes.

He picked up a stray newspaper as it blew by, then balled it up and threw it at Lucas who caught it with a grin, then chucked it back. They tossed it back and forth as they walked, skirting around alleys and freezing as an emergency vehicle passed with its lights on, but no siren. The sun was getting higher, and Lucas frowned at the sky.

"You'd better get home," he told Nate. "Your parents are looking for you; they're calling around the neighbors."

"Oh, okay," Nate said, crestfallen. "Yeah, guess I'd better go. Well, keep me updated when you find Kowalski, okay?"

Lucas offered a smile, though inside his stomach tightened. *If we survive,* he thought. "Yeah, I'll call you," he said.

Nate turned to go, and Lucas felt a deep hum reverberate through his skull, like a train was passing nearby. He tasted something metallic in the air, then felt a cold hand grip his wrist. His stomach lurched, and the world tipped. Something sharp hooked his insides and seemed to fold him in half. He landed hard on his back, feeling like his skin was on fire. He rolled carefully, struggled to get up onto his hands and knees, then vomited violently. He coughed, unable to hold anything back in his stomach. Finally, he rolled over, gasping for air. His guts felt like they'd been twisted into a pretzel.

"Teleportation is a real bitch," a soft voice said. "But you get used to it."

Lucas looked up and saw a slim girl with auburn hair standing by his shoulder.

"Romana," he choked out, tensing. He couldn't get up.

It occurred to him that was the first time he'd ever heard her speak out loud. Her voice was... different. It had a musical quality to it, but there was no time to contemplate that. Cold wind blew against his face. He was on all fours in short, stubbled grass. Ice glistened on the ground beneath his fingers, and he shivered. Stretching out before him was dark blue water, rippling with white-crested waves beneath a dreary sky.

"Where are we?" he asked.

"St. Paul, Alaska," she replied, not looking at him. "I read about it in an atlas in Petra's office. It's great for birdwatching."

He staggered to his feet, worried he might throw up again. The acid burned his throat and his muscles still twitched, but he remained upright.

"Why did you bring me here?" he asked.

"To talk," she replied, finally fixing those enormous green eyes on him. "Tell me, what do you feel?"

"Like I was put through a blender," he answered, hugging himself. "And I'm f-freezing."

It bothered him that she didn't seem to notice the cold. Maybe that was just the way she was - no emotions, no feelings.

"No, what do you feel inside your head?" she said more sharply. "Reach out."

He lowered his brows at her. There had to be a catch. Why would she want him to do that? What could she gain?

"You're wondering what I could possibly get out of asking you to open up your mind," she said in that musical voice. "But that's just the thing, isn't it? I already have everything you've got to offer. I'm in your head, always, because you've never learned to keep me out. I know where your friends are, including the ones I've taken from you. I know what you're thinking all the time. So, it's a simple request. There's no trap here."

He felt like he could drown in those bottomless green eyes. She was right, of course. He could feel her in there, but when he probed for her thoughts, he only hit a wall. It hummed, like an electrified fence. With a sigh of resignation, he closed his eyes and opened his thoughts outward. Instead of the kaleidoscopic rush of lights and noise surging through his mind, he found only a few tiny stars representing the quaint town on the other side of the island. They were like a couple of boats lost on a sea of darkness. He reached farther and farther, widening his search and found a few dozen more pinpricks of light, drifting in that vast emptiness, but that was all.

"It's so... quiet," he said softly.

"Yes. It's wonderful, isn't it?" she asked.

Lucas ran a hand over his scalp. It really was - the creeping, prickling feeling was completely gone from his skin, and the noise that always raged in the back of his mind was silenced. Then the thing he never expected happened: Romana removed herself from his mind. It was like the Niagara Falls had suddenly been turned off; he hadn't realized how much space her presence had taken up in his head until she pulled back. She really had been everywhere, filling up caverns in his thoughts that he didn't even know he had. She must have seen everything he had ever done, heard everything he heard. He would have been scared, but an overwhelming silence echoed, and he realized that he was truly was... finally... alone in his mind.

He dropped to his knees as a hard knot formed in his throat. All he heard were the birds, singing to each other as they swooped over the hilltops, and all he saw were the slowly drifting clouds and the cresting waves. The icy wind roared against the cliffs and whistled over the craggy outcropping a hundred feet below the spot where he knelt.

"You forgot what this was like," Romana said. Instead of in his head, her voice was several feet behind him and almost carried away by the wind.

Lucas wiped a tear away from his cheek.

"What did you do?" he choked.

"Nothing," she replied. "I only left you alone. This is what you had, once upon a time, back when you were the only one in your head."

He bowed his head, pressing the heels of his hands to his eyes. *Was that only a year ago, when this was all I knew? It feels like an eternity.* He missed it, dearly. He missed true silence, to think only his own thoughts and to feel nothing but the wind, sunlight, and his mother's arms around him. He wondered, if there was a heaven, if this was what it would feel like. Maybe this is what he would feel when he finally died. Just silence.

"Why?" he said, looking back at Romana. "Why did you bring me here? Why haven't you killed me?"

"I told you, I only wanted to talk," she replied.

"I don't want to talk to you," he said bitterly. "Besides, what's there to talk about? You know everything I know. You said yourself there's nothing left for you to get out of me."

"And that's why I know you haven't seen the whole picture," she said in her soft, cool voice. "I don't want to take anything from you, Lucas; I want to offer you something. You can have this, what you're feeling right now, all the time. Forever. I could leave you here; there's a town, not far from here. You could live the rest of your life here in peace. You could finally rest."

"If I do what?" he asked suspiciously.

"If you stop. Just don't come back. Stop what you're doing. Don't fight, and don't come after us."

He couldn't believe what he was hearing. *Stop? Stop what? Stop losing?*

"But I haven't done anything," he objected. "I haven't stopped you at all; I haven't won a single fight against you. There's nothing I can do, no way to -"

Then it dawned on him. He stood up, his eyes widening.

"Unless, there *is* something," Lucas said. "There is a way, isn't there? And you know what it is."

Her passive, emotionless eyes looked away and Lucas saw a change. It was fleeting, but it was there. For a moment, without his powers in the way and her mind imposing itself on his thoughts, she was just an ordinary, thirteen-year-old girl, just as lost as he was.

"You *care*," he said with disbelief. "You're not trying to prevent me from stopping the Rising - you're protecting me!"

Her eyes flashed. "I'm doing my job," she said with venom.

"No, you're not," he insisted. "That's why you brought me all the way out here, so they can't find you. You want me out of the way, not because you're worried about the Rising, but because you're worried about *me*. It's true, isn't it?"

She bit her lip. The wind blew her hair across her face, and she brushed it aside. "I saw you broken," she said quietly.

"When you killed my friend," Lucas growled.

He clenched his fists as lightning crackled across his chest and into his hands. Romana looked unfazed.

"I didn't have a choice," she said.

"Yes, you did. You didn't *have* to commit murder. You could have left, or fought back with me, but instead you killed a helpless -"

"I know!" she shouted.

Her hand shot out, and Lucas saw the air ripple like water. Something hard struck him in the chest, then wrapped around him. It was the strange, invisible force that emanated from her. His arms were locked at his sides as his ribs cracked. He couldn't speak or catch his breath, and Romana's green eyes flashed with fire. But Lucas wasn't afraid, because tears trickled down her cheeks. She wasn't a monster anymore; she was just a girl.

"I know what I did!" she screamed at him. "I saw it all in your head and I felt his life being extinguished. I know what he meant to you. I know! I know!"

Lucas couldn't breathe to make a response. But he was so stunned, he forgot what he would say anyway.

"You don't understand - you just don't get it!" she shrieked. "You don't know who these people are or what they're capable of, but I live with them! They made me what I am - trained me, taught me everything I know! And whatever you think of me, Liam is so much worse. He *likes* it, what they make us do!"

*Liam,* Lucas thought. *That must be his name… the white-haired android.*

"Romana," Lucas gasped. His chest burned.

She released him, and he dropped onto the grass. As soon as his ribs healed, he took a great, gasping breath. Romana covered her face with her hands.

"Tell me," Lucas said, straightening up. "Tell me about the other android."

She shook her head and turned away. Lucas took several deep breaths; his head spun and his thoughts were sluggish, but he had to press on.

"You don't get it, you just don't get it. You still don't see… " Romana stammered.

"Romana, you're scared, I can see that," he said. "And I know that you'll never be free as long as you're with them."

"But at least I'll be alive," she replied. He could see the terror plainly in her eyes and it radiated into him like heat. He wondered if he felt it because of their mental link, but that was turned off. "They'll kill you, Lucas. They know how."

"How?" he asked. "I don't even know how to kill us."

"A shot to the back of the head."

Lucas' hand traveled up to the base of his skull. Of course, it made perfect sense; he knew what it was. That black, perfectly circular space in the back of his brain where the nanomachines nested. How many times had he come so close to destroying it?

"Permanent death," Romana said. "You won't come back."

"I still have to try," he said, trying to sound confident. "There really is a way I can stop them, isn't there? You have to tell me."

She looked down, shaking her head.

"Romana, please," he begged. "Help me."

"It took Liam longer to get control of his powers," she said, almost in a whisper. "He can change the strength of the bonds between his molecules, to make himself stronger or denser, and even to pass through walls. But it's dangerous to become intangible; you might fade away altogether."

"What are you saying?" Lucas asked.

"He can't do it well," she continued, looking steadily at Lucas. "It's hard, and he's nearly disappeared completely numerous times. There's a device implanted in his chest that brings him back together again. If that's destroyed, he'll fade."

"If it's that easy, why haven't you done it?"

"It's *not* easy," she retorted. "He knows what his weakness is and he protects it fiercely. I don't want to die, but if you're willing to take the risk, then I'm telling you what you can do. There is a very strong chance you will die if you try this."

"Like I said, I have to do it," Lucas replied. "I have to protect my family."

Romana shook her head. "I tried to protect you, Lucas," she said.

"You could help," he told her. "We could take him down together."

"How about I just agree not to kill you?" she replied, suddenly a stone wall again.

He gave her a sad look. Her eyes were flat once more as she extended a pale hand.

"Ready to go home?"

"Wait," he said earnestly. "Teach me how to block you out. How do I do that?"

"You're out of favors."

"Come on, I need to know how to do that or there's no way I'll succeed. Liam will see me coming a mile away."

Her eyes locked on his, and he felt her mind flood into his mind like an avalanche of bricks. He tried to resist, throwing up walls or stabbing back just as she had done to him, but his defenses were crushed the moment they were formed. She swept through him and settled at the back of his mind, humming like a purring tiger.

*You already know how to do it,* her voice echoed inside his head. *You could have kept me out, you just didn't want to.*

*Yes I did! I just couldn't! Help me -*

She grabbed his hand, her fingers interlacing with his. The sharp tug hooked his insides and he was flipped onto his back. The world spun, and he landed heavily on a hard floor. He lurched, swallowing back the acid that burned in his throat, and his arms and legs trembled uncontrollably.

"Lucas!" his mother's voice cried.

He lifted his head to see her running to his side. He was back in his house, lying just behind the dining room table.

"Mom," he coughed.

She helped him up. As she hugged him tightly, he spotted Maria, Jess, Tim, and Kenny, and was surprised to see Nate and Sangor.

"What happened?" Tim asked urgently. "Nate said Romana took you!"

"She did," Lucas replied as Leah helped him painfully to the couch. He sat down, hoping the world would stop spinning.

"What did she do to you?" Nate asked, his face stained with tears.

"Did she hurt you?" Leah added.

"No, she just dumped me on this island in the middle of nowhere. She wanted to talk."

"We tried calling you," Kenny said.

"I couldn't feel anything out there," Lucas said apologetically. He chose not to say how nice that was, or how deeply he actually wanted to stay.

"Jesus, so she really had you," Tim commented.

"Yeah, she could have killed me if she wanted, or just left me there to find my own way back, but she didn't. She's trapped, and she wants out."

"What are you talking about?"

"First," Lucas said, leveling his eyes at Sangor, who was seated in one of the chairs, his hands folded calmly. "What's *he* doing here?"

"I came to help," Sangor answered.

"I thought you didn't care about us or our 'insignificant' problems," Lucas replied in Spanish.

"See?" Kenny blurted, pointing at Lucas. "It's a reflex, isn't it?"

Lucas ignored him, and continued glaring at Sangor.

"You were right," Sangor said, lowering his eyes. "You showed me that I had failed; the hero I used to be is gone, most likely forever. I cannot sit by, longing for a past that no longer exists."

He stood up, towering over Lucas. Tim and Kenny tensed, their hands creeping to the guns at their belts. Then everyone gaped in surprise as he knelt down in front of Lucas with his hands open, palms turned upward.

"I will follow your lead," he said. "I serve you now, until I am dead or you release me."

Lucas looked at the others for help. He didn't know what to say. For several long seconds, nobody knew how to respond. He was relieved when Sangor stood up once more.

"Um, thank you," he stammered. "I, uh, I'm honored. You can sit down now."

He did, and Lucas tried to gather his thoughts. The silence was heavy and uncomfortable.

"We still need a plan," he said. "Romana told me that the white-haired android, Liam, doesn't have full control of his powers. He's got a device in his chest that helps him; it's basically keeping him alive. If we can destroy that, he'll be out of the game and we might actually have a chance, especially if Romana keeps her word and doesn't kill me."

"What did she want from you?" Tim asked. "Why is she helping you?"

"She wanted me to stay out of it," Lucas answered. "She asked me to stop fighting, and to leave them alone. I realized it was because she was scared, and wanted to protect me. She is really terrified of Liam, and wants him dead just as badly as we do."

"Can't blame her," Tim remarked.

"Yeah," Kenny said slowly. "Okay, this is all helpful, but we still don't know where they are."

"San Diego," Lucas said suddenly. He saw it in his head, almost like a memory.

"How do you know?"

"I just do," Lucas answered, and the humming sensation in the back of his mind strengthened.

*Was that you, Romana?*

Kenny crossed his arms, giving him a skeptical look.

"I have my doubts about this Romana girl," he said. "She killed Brick, kidnapped Kowalski, Arden Sheffield *and* you, and now all of a sudden she wants to help?"

"I know how it sounds, and I had my doubts, too, but you didn't see her. She's just as scared as we are."

Kenny and Tim looked at each other. Leah covered Lucas' hand with hers, and Maria squeezed his shoulder. Jess sat on the loveseat, while Nate leaned on the back. All looked tired and strained.

"Lucas, I have the utmost respect for you," Kenny said slowly. "I really do; you've saved my life more than once and you know that I trust you, but I don't trust Romana. How do we know she's not lying?"

"Because... I just know," he said. *Because she's in my head and we've been connected for months,* he thought. "Please, you just have to trust me."

"Okay," Tim said with a shrug. "So we've finally got something to give the President."

"Wait, what?" Lucas said in surprise.

"President Rourke called. He wants to meet you, personally. He wants answers, and now we've got some. I'll call him back, and we'll arrange the meeting."

"The President wants to meet *me*?"

"Wow, that's so awesome!" Nate exclaimed.

"Yes, so you'd better eat and rest up," Tim told him.

"Come on," Leah said, pulling him to his feet. "Let's eat, and then you need to sleep."

She walked him to the kitchen, and although he was sure that he was far too tired to eat, he gratefully devoured the homemade bread and cold chicken that Maria prepared for him. Then he went upstairs and dropped onto the bed. He was asleep within seconds.

# CHAPTER 16

*J*ess watched Lucas head up the stairs. She couldn't believe that this Romana person genuinely wanted to help... after all, she had kidnapped Arden! She was definitely complicit in all this. It had to be a trap. And even if it wasn't, they should be trying to find a way to get to San Diego as fast as possible.

"What now?" Jess asked Tim, though it was really more of a demand. "Are we going to San Diego?"

"Hang on," Tim said.

He removed his phone from his pocket and dialed, then strode into the next room while Kenny followed. Sangor sank back into the chair, examining his nails, while Nate dropped onto the loveseat beside Jess.

"Hi," he said with a grin. "I'm Nate Wissen, Lucas' best friend."

"Jess Sheffield," she said, raising one eyebrow.

"Lucas said the Rising took your dad."

"Yeah," she replied darkly.

"I'm sorry," Nate said, scooting closer. "They almost killed me three months ago. One of their big goons even punched me in the face. I was scared for my life."

"That's awful."

Jess wasn't looking at Nate; she was watching Sangor, who hid a smirk.

"How did you get mixed up in all this in the first place?" Nate asked.

"Jess," Sangor said, standing up. "Would you be so kind as to show me where I could clean up?"

"It'd be my pleasure," she replied sardonically.

She led him to the bathroom under the stairs, opened the door, and flicked the light on.

"You probably don't know how to work the shower," she said. "The left knob is for hot water; the right is for cold."

She turned to leave. Sangor stood in the way.

"Jess," he said.

His tone was serious. She looked up at him; his eyes were still icy blue, but bore a hint of sadness.

"I wanted to apologize," he said quietly.

Jess crossed her arms.

"Unless you can turn into a giant dragon or something and fly me to San Diego, we don't have anything to talk about," she said acidly.

"No, I can't do that," he replied, crestfallen. He looked embarrassed. "I still can't use my magic, and… I'm afraid to try, after all that happened."

"Look, I don't really care," she told him. "You can say what you want to Lucas, but I don't buy it."

She tried to edge around him, but he put his arm out, blocking her way.

"I haven't forgotten what you said," he said earnestly. "Each time I was lost inside myself, you pulled me back. I remember your kindness and bravery. It saved me, Jess."

"You talk a lot, but when you actually had a chance to show me your gratitude, you threw it all back in my face. I'll believe you've changed when I see it with my own eyes. Now, let me pass or I'll hit you; I don't care how strong you are."

He blinked, taken aback, then dropped his arm. Jess swept past him and stormed back into the living room. Nate's cheeks reddened as he quickly looked away; Jess knew he had heard everything. She didn't care, she dropped back down onto the loveseat with a huff. Nate fidgeted, twiddling his fingers.

"Did you really just tell off a super-strong alien?" he asked.

"Yeah, so what?" Jess said, tucking her hair behind her ear.

"Wow, that's so cool. I mean, Lucas did it, too, but I can understand that because Lucas can, like, zap him and stuff. That's really brave of you."

"Yeah, well, somebody had to do it."

"He still scares the hell out of me," Nate replied.

"Okay," Tim said, returning with phone in hand. "We're going to meet the President at ABIA in three hours."

"The airport?" Jess said, lighting up. "And then we'll go to San Diego, right?"

"Yes, but don't get excited," Tim said. "We're not just going to go charging in there without a plan, or backup. I reached out to some of my old contacts for a plane and anybody willing to go with us. We'll need Lucas to do some reconnaissance and pin down the exact location, then get us a full read of the place."

Kenny was typing on his phone.

"I can get us some equipment," he said. "Cheng said he could help out with that, and a chopper for extraction."

Nate was bouncing up and down in his seat.

"This is so awesome!" he said to Jess. "This is like *Mission: Impossible*, but with real government spies!"

"Don't you have a family?" Jess replied, annoyed.

Tim looked up from his phone. "Yeah, what are you still doing here?" he asked. "Go home, your parents are probably worried about you!"

"Are you kidding?" Nate said. "I can't go home now, things are just about to get real! I can help - I've helped Lucas before!"

"This isn't a game!" Tim snapped. "Go home, now!"

Nate stood up glaring at Tim, then stomped out. Jess looked at the two agents, then decided she'd better make herself scarce before they decided that she was in the way, too. Leah and Maria talked in low, serious voices in the kitchen, so she got up and headed for the stairs. As she climbed, Sangor exited the bathroom below her. His hair was wet and he smelled like shampoo; he wore a different shirt and the black pants that he had arrived in. She continued up the steps, keeping her eyes forward so that if he looked at her, she didn't have to make eye contact. Pulling back the curtain, she saw Lucas lying on his back on the bed. She'd forgotten he was sleeping up here. Kicking herself mentally, she began to back away. Then she saw Lucas blink, then sit up and squint at her.

"Jess?" he asked. "What are you doing up here?"

"I don't know - I'm sorry," she said. "I was just looking for a place to be alone... I forgot you were sleeping."

"Well, I wasn't really anymore," he said with a shrug. "You can stay, if you want to."

He hung his legs off the bed and scooted over to give her room to sit down. Gray morning sunlight drifted through the round window, and the dozen or so bulbs around the room glowed gently to life, brightening up the dim room. She noticed the hard drives stacked against the wall were humming, and the laptop on his desk was repaired and powered on. She sat down on the bed and he ran a hand over his scalp with a tired sigh.

"Are you alright?" she asked.

"Yeah," he said with a shrug. "I just have a lot on my mind."

"That's a bit of an understatement for you."

He chuckled, but it was half-hearted.

"Yeah, I guess it is," he said. "How about you? How are you holding up?"

Jess shook her head.

"Sorry, stupid question," Lucas said sadly.

"I don't know what else to do," she replied. "My mom would say to pray. I'm starting to think that's the only option."

Lucas gave a mirthless laugh.

"You don't pray, either, I'm guessing," Jess said, looking at him.

"No," he replied. "Maybe I would have, a long time ago. But there are too many questions now that I don't really want to ask."

"Like what?"

He looked away, his brows meeting.

"Like, does something like me even have a soul?" he said. "God didn't make me; people did. Evil people. I don't think if I prayed God would even hear it. It probably wouldn't count."

Jess covered his hand with hers, moved with pity. He pulled his hand away and wiped his eyes, even though there weren't any tears.

"Can I tell you a secret?" he said.

"Sure," she answered hesitantly.

"Romana took me to this place, an island in the Bering Sea. It was so remote, with no cities or highways, only a tiny town with less than a thousand people. It was quiet enough that I really felt like I was alone in my head. I've felt that way before, when I'd first been locked up by the CIA and they put me in this cell, underground. I was scared for my life then, but this time I wasn't. I should have been, because I was alone with Romana and she could have killed me easily, but instead I was just thinking how tired I was."

He looked down at the ground as he fidgeted with a piece of lint from the bedspread. To Jess, he looked so young and small.

"I'm sorry," he said softly. "I knew I had to come back, because Kowalski and your dad are still missing and I have to find them, but I have to be honest, I guess… I still kind of wish I'd stayed."

Jess wasn't sure what she should say, once she realized he was making a confession. She wasn't angry at all, but beginning to remember that he was still only thirteen.

"Thanks for telling me," she said finally. "But I'm not mad. It's totally reasonable for you to feel that way, after all the stuff you've been through."

He raised one eyebrow. "But you were mad at Sangor for not wanting to help," he said.

"That's different," she objected. "He's a lot older than you, and he wouldn't help for selfish reasons."

Lucas didn't look convinced.

"It's completely normal, Lucas," Jess said emphatically. "It makes complete sense for you to feel the way you do. It's human. And the really cool thing is that you keep helping anyway, and doing the right thing. That's bravery."

"I guess so," he said.

"You said you didn't think you had a soul," she said. "I think you do. You're good, Lucas."

He gave a small smile. "Thank you for saying so," he said.

The laptop made a beeping sound from the desk, and Lucas looked at it. Some of its internal components began to whir, and then the hard drives ran as well, their fans blowing.

"Are you doing something with these?" Jess asked him.

Lucas seemed to think for a minute.

"Yeah," he said hesitantly. "Can I tell you another secret? This one's pretty… well, it's pretty big."

Jess blinked.

"Um, okay," she said.

He sat back, crossing his legs. Then he picked at another piece of lint as he seemed to gather his thoughts. He did not meet her eyes as he took a deep breath before he spoke.

"So, androids can… um, well, we can read each other's minds. It's not like literal mind-reading though; the nanomachines we have inside us, like, talk to each other and it's like we can hear each other's thoughts and even see what the other one is seeing. I've heard what Liam was thinking, and Romana has been in my head for a long time. So, anyway, I have a lot of government information in my head because of the work I do, and it's got me worried about how much Romana or Liam might have seen."

Jess gaped at him.

"They can read your mind?" she asked.

He nodded, still not looking at her.

"Yeah, and I don't know how to keep them out yet," he admitted.

"Can you read their minds?" she asked.

"Only when they let me. They're a lot better trained than I am."

"This is huge, Lucas," Jess said with incredulity.

"I know," he said, crestfallen. "That's why I've been thinking about what would happen to all the stuff in my head if this didn't go well. After what happened to Sangor, you know, losing his memories, I've wondered what would happen if they got in my head and took all of it, you know? So I started downloading my memories to these hard drives, to keep them safe."

Jess looked at the hard drives stacked by the wall. She counted six.

"You're downloading your memories?" she said, pointing a quivering finger at the metal boxes. "They're in there?"

"Everything that I am," he nodded. "Everything I know, it's all there. Just copies though; I still remember it all."

"When did you do this?"

"About five minutes ago."

"Jesus," Jess breathed, rubbing her eyes. "Wait, so what's going to happen if they take you?"

"A couple of things," he answered. "I'm going to wipe my own mind clean, and then you need to shoot me in the back of the head, at the base of my skull. That's the only way to kill me and to make sure I don't come back. I'll die for real."

Goosebumps rose on Jess' arms. She felt a bit sick.

"Wait, why me?" she asked.

"Because I don't trust anyone else," he said. "Tim and Kenny have worked with me and fought beside me, but I don't trust the government

171

with the knowledge of how to kill me. Only a few days ago, they were ready to put me to sleep again forever. You've kept a level head through all this, and that makes me think I can trust you to kill me when the right time comes. Can you shoot?"

"Yes, but, Lucas - " she said, but no other words came. Now he was finally looking her in the eyes. His black eyes pierced into her blue ones.

"This is really important," he said. "I would rather die than be taken by the Rising again, but I don't trust the people that kept me prisoner for nearly a whole year."

"I understand," she said heavily. "I really do, but all the stuff in your head, how do you know they don't have it already?"

"They might," he nodded. "Romana said they already have everything they want from me. But in case that isn't true, everything is on those hard drives where it'll be safe."

"Do Tim and Kenny know she can read your mind?"

"No," he admitted.

"Don't you think they should?" she pressed.

"No, because I would only get locked up again," he said earnestly. "They wouldn't understand. I can handle this, and I'll figure out how to keep the other androids out of my head eventually. I just can't get put into another hibernation pod; I'm the only chance we have of winning."

Jess cleared her throat, then sat up straight.

"Okay," she said firmly. "If you do everything you can to get my dad back, then you can count on me to kill you when the time comes."

"Thank you," he replied. "And don't tell them any of the stuff I just told you. Promise?"

"Don't make me regret this," she replied. "I promise. Now, we need a plan. Tim said we're going to meet President Rourke at the airport, then get some people together to go to San Diego."

"There's no need," Lucas said, his eyes suddenly becoming distant. "Six helicopters took off from a shipping facility just outside San Diego city proper. That has to be them."

"What? How do you know?"

"The military was just alerted about it," he said. "But I can't see them. Romana or Liam must be blocking me; that's the only way."

"Where are they going?" Jess asked.

172

"The report said they were headed east."

"Then we have to get ready," Jess said seriously. "The President is coming here, too."

Lucas nodded. "He's probably the target," he said. "It would make sense."

"He'll be in danger if you guys start fighting."

"Let's go tell the others," Lucas said, jumping up.

They hurried down the stairs. Tim and Kenny were both on their phones, while Sangor sat back in one of the easy chairs. He stood up when Lucas entered and stood rigid.

"There's a squad of helicopters coming this way from San Diego," Lucas announced. "I think it's the Rising."

"Hang on a minute, sir," Tim said into his phone. "I'll call you back."

He hung up, then looked at Lucas.

"How do you know?" he said.

"I can't see them at all," Lucas said. "Not even on satellite. Romana or Liam must be shielding them somehow. It has to be them."

"He's right," Kenny said, hanging up his phone. "The Air Force is on high alert. They shot down a police chopper on their way out, and now they've crossed state lines."

"How many of them are there?" Tim asked.

"Six Blackhawks, all packing some big guns."

"Okay, so the Rising is on the move, and the President's about an hour out," Tim said pensively, rubbing his chin. "He's got to be protected, and he'll want you specifically. Kenny, call all our guys back and tell them to meet us at ABIA. If it's really them, at least we'll be outside the city to limit civilian casualties. And Lucas, you'll have backup if they come to you."

"Backup would be nice," Lucas agreed. "And if Liam is there, I need to try to destroy that device."

"No, you need to stay close to the President," Tim objected. "Your force fields are his best protection."

"Yeah, Lucas," Jess said, giving him a look. "You're the *last* person who should be going straight for Liam."

Lucas opened his mouth with indignation, then closed it again and hung his head. "Yeah, you're right," he said.

"Sangor," Jess said, looking at the alien. He had been sitting with his fingers steepled, listening wordlessly to the conversation.

"Yes, my lady?" he said coyly.

"You should go after Liam. Do you remember what he did to Larathel?"

"Vividly," he replied, eyes flashing. "But I serve Lucas. I take orders from him and no one else."

Everyone looked at Lucas, eyebrows raised, and Jess rolled her eyes.

"Sangor," Lucas said heavily. "This is what I want you to do."

"Then he shall indeed die."

"Liam is your priority," Tim joined in again, looking hard at Sangor. "You have to kill him, but you can't let him touch you. Romana, either."

"Are you going to be good for this fight?" Kenny broke in, looking doubtful. "I mean you're not going to suddenly transform and create more problems for us, right?"

Sangor's face became stony as his cavalier attitude disappeared.

"That won't be a problem," he said.

"Are you sure?" Lucas asked. "I mean, it's actually kind of important that we know if you have that... well, if you have that under control."

Sangor looked down. Jess saw his fists tighten, his knuckles white.

"Truthfully, I don't know," he admitted. "Larathel's memories helped, and gave me access to her magic, but she knew very little about shape-shifting on the scale that I did. That area of my mind is still very... tumultuous. I don't know that I will ever be able to do it on purpose again, but I think I can prevent it from happening by accident."

Tim and Kenny looked at each other, then Tim crossed his arms.

"Well, what do you think?" he asked Lucas. "You're in charge of him now."

Lucas' face was solemn.

"I know what it's like to be broken, and to have stuff in your head that doesn't belong to you," he said. "I think we should give him a chance to prove himself. Besides, we're going to need all hands on deck for this."

Sangor lifted his head, and his face brightened slightly.

"Alright," Tim said. "Everyone suit up, then. We've got to hurry."

# CHAPTER 17

enny carried some large black bags out to the car from the office. Sangor stood up and searched through his backpack for his coat, which he put on. The rubies and emeralds in the collar and cuffs of his sleeves glittered as he took the two short swords and strapped them to his belt, then slung his longsword across his back.

Lucas looked around, confused. "Where's my mom?" he asked.

Tim put a hand as heavy as lead on his shoulder.

"Come with me, I'll help you with your suit," he said.

Lucas followed him upstairs and found his suit and vest. Tim picked up the vest and held it out with both hands. Lucas sensed that he was about to say something, and waited impatiently.

"We sent your mom and grandmother ahead to the next safe house," Lucas said. "We're moving them."

"What do you mean?" Lucas said, his voice rising. His mind opened outward, searching the city for her phone's signal. He couldn't find it anywhere. "Where's her phone?"

"We destroyed it," Tim said. His tone was carefully measured, like Kowalski's used to be when he was telling Lucas something he knew that he didn't want to hear. Lucas braced himself for what would come next.

"You can't know where she is until this is all over," he said.

"Why not?" Lucas asked, his heart pounding.

"You've been compromised, Lucas," Tim replied. "I know that Romana's in your head, and you told me yourself that Liam was, too. They've caught us by surprise every single time, and I figured out that it's because of you. It has to be. You're a mole."

"No I'm not!" Lucas said, indignant. "I would never betray you to the Rising!"

"It's not your fault," Tim said calmly, unflinching. "You can't help it; but they know everything you know, so we have to limit the information you have access to. Your mom's location will be kept secret until you either defeat the Rising, or learn to conceal your thoughts."

Lucas' face felt hot. He clenched his fists, trying to remain calm.

"I don't know how to do it," he said shakily. "Romana is already there; I can't keep her out. I tried, I promise."

Then he saw the way Tim was looking at him. He wore a sympathetic expression, and it was genuine. He wasn't yelling at Lucas or accusing him, just stating facts.

"Wait," Lucas said. "Why haven't you knocked me out already? I know the plan, which means Romana does, too."

"You trust her, don't you?"

Lucas hesitated. He had to admit to himself that he didn't.

"I think she wants to be saved," he answered.

"And I think that you want to save all of us," Tim said. "You want to protect this city and your family, and you've given everything you have to prove that over and over again. Yeah, I could put you to sleep again until we get to the safe house, but we need you for this fight. I trust you to figure this out. You have to."

Lucas met his dark eyes and felt like he'd grown a foot taller. Tim smiled, then held up the kevlar vest. With a strong hand, he ripped the *CIA* patch from the back, then he held it out to Lucas. "You're your own man," he said.

"What if the President feels differently?" Lucas asked.

"I've got your back, whatever happens."

He gave him a stiff nod, then walked back out through the curtain. Lucas swelled with pride, though his hands still shook with anxiety. He quickly dressed in his suit, vest, and gloves, then picked up his mask and goggles. He stared at the mask for several seconds before dropping it back on the bed.

*I'm my own man,* he thought. *That means all of me.*

He started toward the stairs, then stopped and turned around, taking in the room. If he and his family really weren't coming back to this house, then he figured that he should probably pack some clothes. He grabbed a backpack and began to stuff underwear, pants and shirts into it, and then remembered the hard drives. Those would need to come, too.

*But it would be safer if I didn't know where they are*, he thought. *Since we're taking every precaution...*

He took his backpack full of clothes downstairs. Tim stood in the living room, texting on his phone.

"Ready?" he said. "We're running out of time."

"Uh, yeah, almost," Lucas answered hesitantly. "Um, so there are some hard drives up in my room that I downloaded with all my memories, just in case something were to happen to me. I think it would be better that I didn't know where those were hidden, you know?"

Tim's face was stoic.

"Understood," he said. "I'll have someone take care of it. Now, head out to the car; we've got to go."

"I will, but there's one last thing I need to check," Lucas told him.

He hurried to the back of the house, where his mother's and grandmother's bedrooms were located. He stopped at Maria's bedroom first; the drawers were open, and her personal items were missing from the top of her dresser and vanity. Next, he went to his mother's room. The closet door stood open, the hangers empty. He grabbed a few books from the shelf, and found his baby book, her clay bowl and carved turtle still there. He exhaled sharply. She must have been so worried, helping Maria get packed that she left without them. He carefully wrapped the bowl and turtle in a couple of his t-shirts, then tucked them inside the backpack. Then he picked up his baby book, and a folded piece of paper dropped out onto the carpet.

He picked it up, then unfolded it curiously. It contained his mother's handwriting. His heart skipped a beat.

*Lucas,*

*If you're reading this, then your grandmother and I have already been moved to the new safe house. And, as I expected, you checked to make sure that we were both taken care of. Tim explained everything - how you can't know where we are, and I understand. I hope you do, too. I know how you must feel, and my heart aches for you. You already have so much on your shoulders, and have been through more than anyone should. I want you to know that I am so proud of you. But there is something else I have to tell you: I am pregnant. Seth doesn't know yet, but the baby is his. I hope to tell him together, once you've brought him back. You are so strong, and I know that you will make it through this. We will be together again soon. All of us.*

*With love,*
*Mom*

Lucas stared at the note. He read through it again. And again. Anger boiled inside of him. He couldn't believe it. Kowalski had asked for his blessing, but had already been seeing his mother behind his back. That was as good as a lie.

*Kowalski, you asshole!* Lucas thought, blinded by anger. *How could you? How could you be so goddamned selfish!?*

He didn't understand. What was the point of asking? Was it out of guilt? Blood pounded in his ears as rage filled him. It became heat, and the paper note began to smoke, then was licked away by flames. He clenched his fist around the burning paper, which stung, but the burns quickly healed. He pounded his fist against the wall, electricity crackling across his skin. *I should just leave you there for the Rising… that's what you deserve.*

No, he knew he couldn't do that. His mother would never forgive him. Unless she didn't know… he could say that he simply didn't get there in time. Besides, Kowalski could be dead already, for all he knew…

*Stop, stop!* he told himself, shaking his head to clear it. *What's wrong with you? This is Kowalski! Asshole or not, remember what he means to you. God, why is this so hard!?*

He pressed the heels of his hands into his eyes. Then, steeling himself, he stood up. *Time to go.*

# CHAPTER 18

*H*e walked outside, his head high but his face was still warm. A large, unmarked van sat parked by the curb between two black SUVs. Kenny stood at the backdoor of the van and took Lucas' backpack before helping him inside. Jess and Sangor were already seated in the back; Sangor's longsword lay across his knees. Jess' sandy-brown hair was tied up in a ponytail, and she wore jeans, boots, and a kevlar vest over her t-shirt. Lucas' heart fluttered and he quickly looked away.

"No mask?" she said.

"Nope," he replied, taking a seat across from her. "If I live through this, I'm not going to hide what I am anymore. However this goes down, the world's never going to be the same."

"You think they're going to be more accepting of androids, if you save the world?"

"I don't know - maybe," he said. "I'm just going to be me, and hope for the best."

"Well, you're pretty cool," she replied with a smile.

He found himself smiling back, and Sangor sighed audibly.

"You two are adorable," he said dryly, and Lucas' cheeks reddened. Then something occurred to him.

"Hang on, what about you?" he asked.

Sangor shrugged. "What about me? I can blend in anywhere, on any planet."

"You're an interdimensional, shapeshifting wizard," Lucas pointed out. "You're not subtle. Your true form was seen by everyone at that hospital. We can't risk anyone recognizing you."

Tim climbed in the back as Kenny shut the doors.

"Does President Rourke know about Sangor?" Lucas asked.

"Not yet," Tim answered sheepishly. "That bit of information never got to him, before the field office was attacked and the ULF disappeared. He's got enough to worry about, with a terrorist group starting a full-scale war on the homeland."

"Okay, so you've got to disguise yourself then," Lucas told Sangor.

"I'm already wearing one," he protested.

"You need a better one; we can't have you getting shot or put in a lab; we need you. All anyone has to do is hear you talk to know you're something different. You know all languages, right? Can you control what language people hear you speak in?"

"Yes," Sangor replied.

"Then here's what you'll do: make your eyes look like mine, and then you can be my cousin from Mexico. And only talk to me, in Spanish."

"*That's* how you'll keep him beneath suspicion?" Tim asked dubiously.

Lucas shrugged.

"In my experience, people don't pay much attention to you if they can't understand what you're saying," he said. "And they'll already be preoccupied worrying about me, anyway."

"If that's what you want," Sangor said with a sigh. "Hold still."

He leaned forward and stared hard into Lucas' eyes. A second later, his blue eyes turned dark brown, almost black, and adjusted shape. He sat back, and Jess raised her eyebrows.

"Wow," she said. "Yep, I'd buy it. You two definitely could be related."

"*Encantado,* Martin," Lucas said, shaking Sangor's hand with a smile.

With a jolt, the van pulled away from the curb. It took them nearly an hour to reach the airport, and all the while Lucas kept tabs on the group of Rising helicopters. He still couldn't see them, but he could follow the communications concerning them. They were on a direct course for Texas, and now had an escort of military jets.

"They're almost here," Lucas said.

"Why haven't they been shot down?" Kenny asked.

"They claim to have hostages on board," Lucas replied.

"Like my dad?" Jess gasped.

"And Kowalski," he nodded.

"Have they made any demands?" Tim asked.

"We know what they want," Lucas said darkly.

They arrived at the airport and continued driving directly onto the tarmac. When the van came to a stop and the back doors opened, Lucas saw a white Boeing 747 parked a hundred yards away from a wide hangar, and surrounded by a group of black sedans. Men in dark suits and sunglasses stood at the foot of the stairs. Lucas could feel an enormous amount of radio communication filling the air. He also saw military vehicles: Jeeps with guns mounted on top, and soldiers standing by. Even more filled the hangar.

*I sure hope that's our backup,* he thought warily.

"Come on, Lucas," Tim said, climbing down. "Jess, you wait in here with Kenny."

Jess opened her mouth to protest, but Lucas held out a hand.

"Hold on," Lucas said. "You'll need to be able to talk to me. Give me your phone."

"It's dead," she replied.

"I know, and I can take care of that."

She handed it over, and Lucas took off one of his gloves. With a breath, energy flowed into it through his palm. The screen illuminated, and he passed it back.

"There," he said. "My number is programmed in, just select 'Firebolt.'"

"There is no number, just a bunch of boxes," she said, frowning at the screen.

"Trust me, it'll work," he replied.

Then he climbed down, and Sangor followed. Together, they walked with Tim to the stairs that led up to the door of Air Force One.

"We're following your lead, Firebolt," Tim whispered, leaning over. "You're in charge from here on out."

Lucas' heart beat faster. They climbed the stairs, and he found himself inside a very clean, spacious plane. The carpet was white, and everything was trimmed with walnut wood. There were also screens everywhere, all playing live news reports about the incoming choppers. Now that Lucas could actually see them on those screens, his jaw clenched.

A short man with white hair and a round face stood up. His jowls sagged, and his eyes had heavy bags under them. He wore a clean suit and red tie with an American flag pin. He was surrounded by a group of five other men in suits with earpieces, and they all stood up when he did. He walked briskly down the length of the plane and held out a hand to Lucas.

"President Jason Rourke," the man said. "And you must be Lucas Tavera, AKA Firebolt. It's fascinating to finally meet you."

Lucas shook the President's hand firmly, though he felt a bit dazed.

"Uh, it's a pleasure to meet you, too, Mr. President," he said.

"Mr. Carter, thank you for service, and diligence," President Rourke said, shaking Tim's hand. Then he turned to Sangor and blinked his weepy eyes. "And who is this?"

"Martin Sangor," Lucas answered quickly. "He's with me, and he doesn't speak English. Martin, *saluda el presidente como lo hice.*"

"*Es un honor,*" Sangor grunted, offering his hand.

The President shook it, looking flustered. Then he beckoned to the chairs.

"Well, please, sit down all of you," he said. "Director Dunn briefed me on your past encounters with this organization, the Rising, and I am convinced that you are both useful and necessary in dealing with this threat."

"Thank you, sir," Lucas replied. "But there's not much time. They are on their way here now, and you'll soon be in a lot of danger."

"That's why I've asked you here," President Rourke said. "I am aware of your impressive abilities and accomplishments. I want your personal protection, and for you to keep me updated on everything that happens as we engage this terrorist group."

*What Liam and Romana will let me see,* Lucas thought to himself.

"I can protect you, sir," he said heavily. "And I will do my best."

The President smiled excitedly.

"Excellent," he said. "I've read your file, and I know that you can see through cameras, even across the country. You're the very best form of remote surveillance I could possibly have access to."

"Yes," Lucas said. "I'll do my best to keep tabs on the enemy."

"And you're untraceable?"

"Yes."

"You could tell me of any dangers or threats, even on the other side of the country?"

Lucas didn't answer. He didn't like the way the President was looking at him.

"Of course, this will all have to be kept secret; no one could know, especially my rivals. This Rising organization made you, and if the public knew that I had you spying on them for me, well... they wouldn't trust you. It's quite understandable. But I can offer you the very best living conditions for you and your mother, and all expenses paid. I think we'll be very happy working together."

"Hang on, I haven't agreed to anything yet," Lucas objected. "I'll consult privately, but I won't work for the government any longer."

"Well, you don't have much of a choice, do you?" President Rourke said casually, spreading his hands. "If you didn't work for me, what would you do? Child or not, you can't be allowed to roam freely with all the information you've had access to; your time working for the CIA practically guaranteed that you could never have a life of freedom. You're too valuable. No one else can be allowed to get their hands on you."

Lucas glared at the man, laying his hands palm-down on the table.

"I decline," he growled.

"That would be very unwise," President Rourke replied slowly.

"I know what it is you really want, and I won't do it," Lucas said. "I won't spy on innocent people."

The President scoffed, looking offended.

"That's not what I want at all, I only want you to help me root out enemies of the State, like the Rising. They could have been stopped a long time ago, if I had known about you. And we could prevent more like them from coming to power."

"And how do you think that happens?" Lucas snapped. "It will always come down to ultimate surveillance, where no one can be trusted and no one has freedom. That's the way it always ends, and I won't do it."

"Very well," President Rourke said dangerously. His beady eyes slid to Tim. "You know what to do."

Lucas froze. He tensed, preparing to fight, but to his great relief Tim shook his head.

"I'm with the boy," Tim said coolly. "He's right, sir."

"This is ridiculous," President Rourke said, outraged. He jabbed a finger at Lucas. "This creature will never make it off this plane! I want him back in a pod!"

Lucas raised a hand.

"As a matter of fact, I will walk out of here," he said, fighting to keep his voice level. "One thing that wasn't in those files is that I can record everything I hear and see, and I've recorded everything you've said since we came on board. You've got three seconds to let me walk out of here, or I will send it to every news outlet in the country. We'll see what your rivals think about it."

The President's face reddened. Then a tickle climbed up Lucas' skull.

*Incoming.*

"They're here," he gasped.

A sound like thunder grew louder and louder, raising goosebumps on Lucas' arms and the back of his neck. He jumped up and rushed to a window. Sangor was on his feet as well.

"We're not finished here!" President Rourke snapped.

"Yeah, I think we are," Lucas replied. "Sir, do you have a safe room on this plane? Something bulletproof?"

"Yes, in the back," one of the secret service agents replied.

"It's time to take him there, now," Lucas said. "Go!"

Romana's voice hummed inside his skull, making him freeze.

*Too late,* she said.

"They're firing rockets!" Tim exclaimed.

Outside, explosions sounded and the plane was rocked by the force. Lucas saw a ball of fire billow upward, and shrapnel ricocheted off the windows. Wisps of smoke trailed through the air, and he knew more were coming. With a breath, he closed his eyes and raised his arms. He imagined a dome falling around the plane. As he opened his eyes, a force field descended from above. It was more than fifty feet high and two hundred feet across, and the sunlight bent in rainbows through the rippling energy. The secret service agents and the President gaped in awe, craning to look through the windows. Lucas gasped; his skull felt like it was being split in half. He felt the rockets glance off, and heard distant explosions. Then the field vanished.

Lucas wobbled, then sagged against Tim.

"Well done," Tim told him. "Now it's time to go."

He half-carried him to the door, with Sangor on their heels. Outside, the six helicopters were descending, the wind generated by their rotors blowing sparks and heat from the burning Jeeps across the tarmac.

"They're landing," Tim said.

Soldiers surrounded the plane with weapons ready. Lucas spotted Jess and Kenny just inside the hangar, and felt some relief.

"Hold your fire!" an officer shouted. "Remember, they have hostages!"

As the helicopters drew nearer to the ground, men began to drop out. They each carried M4s, and wore military vests over civilian clothes with a black band over their upper arms. They began running as the soldiers unfolded thick metal barricades between them and the plane, then readied to fire; the hostages drew nearer, and Lucas saw the man in the lead. He had broad shoulders and a thick, muscular neck, and blond hair.

*Kowalski.*

He lurched forward, but Tim held him back.

"Stay with the plane, Lucas!" he barked. "Protect the President! We'll take care of this."

He felt ice running through his veins. It was *definitely* Kowalski, though he looked different; his face was twisted in rage. Just behind him came Arden, Jess' dad, with an M4 in hand. But why? Why are the Rising sending out the hostages, and why are they carrying weapons?

"Fire at will!" the officer shouted.

"No!" Lucas cried.

As the gunfire opened up, Lucas hurled a force field that stretched in front of Kowalski and the other hostages, wrapping around them like a fence. A few didn't stop running in time, and barreled straight into it like zombies. The bullets glanced off, ricocheting in every direction. The soldiers ducked and the officer shouted at Lucas in outrage.

"What's wrong with you?" he cried.

"Those are civilians!" Lucas yelled in reply. "They're the hostages!"

"Yes, and they're attacking us!"

Sure enough, Kowalski, Arden, and ten other hostages in front all knelt down with weapons raised; they opened fire, and Tim hurled Lucas to the ground behind the fuselage, then dropped down beside him. Sangor crouched over Lucas, covering his head. The soldiers all fled for cover behind the vehicles and barricades. Lucas couldn't believe what was happening. Why were they attacking?

A buzz went off in his skull. It was Jess.

*Lucas, what is going on? Why is my dad doing this?*

*I don't know,* Lucas admitted, his head spinning. *Kowalski would never do this; he'd never hurt his own people. The Rising must be forcing them to do it, somehow.*

Then he went cold. He remembered Brick, just before he died, when he was controlled by Romana. She spoke through him, making him say what she wanted.

*Mind control,* he realized. *They're being mind-controlled.*

*What?* Jess exclaimed.

He opened his mind outward, searching for the tell-tale electrical signal that would only be there if his worst fears were realized. His consciousness surrounded Kowalski's mind, probing. He found it. A flicker of light, and then the stab of pain as he was forced back out, but not before he heard the echo of a foreign voice. It hissed in a reptilian kind of way.

*I can feel their minds,* Lucas told Jess. *They've put nanomachines in their heads.*

The foreign voice began to form words that snaked their way into Lucas' mind with an ice-cold touch.

*Hello, Lucas,* it rasped. *Welcome to the game.*

Lucas wanted to cry. *Please, no. Not Kowalski.*

"They've all been infected with the nanomachines," he said out loud, though hoarsely. "Liam is controlling them. They're being forced to do this."

"My god," Tim exclaimed. "And they're not dead? How is that possible?"

"I don't know, but we have to stop it, and we can't let these soldiers kill them - they can't help what they're doing!"

"Got it," Tim said, getting up. "Sangor, you're on. You've got to stop Liam before any of these innocent hostages get killed, or kill one of us."

Sangor drew the two short swords, and they glowed with white flames. His eyes switched to solid red. No point in a disguise now.

"Just tell me where he is," he growled.

*The helicopter!* Jess' voice shouted in Lucas' head. *There's one that hasn't landed yet!*

Lucas looked. Indeed, there was one helicopter that still hovered high in the air, making small circles above the hangars. Lucas tried to force his mind inside it, but saw only a white haze. He could see it plain as day with his eyes, but in his mind, it was like the helicopter wasn't there at all.

"Up there," he pointed. "He's gotta be in there."

"I'll bring that bird down," Sangor snarled.

He stood up, then took off at a sprint, his red coat flapping behind him. Gunfire still rained down from the formation of hostages, so Lucas threw out a force field to provide cover. Sangor sprang on top of a Jeep, then launched himself high into the air. He rose fifty, then a hundred feet, sailing over the roof of the hangar toward the helicopter.

Tim whistled in amazement, his eyes wide.

"It's really lucky for us that guy's on our side," he remarked.

Lucas saw the air ripple. It was like a heatwave, moving underneath the helicopter's skids. Then it raced down to meet Sangor. It whipped into him, sending him flying off to the east, to the other side of the barricade where the hostages were. Though he fell more that half a mile, he flipped in the air, then landed on his feet.

*Romana!* Lucas thought in outrage. *I know that was you! Why are you protecting Liam? Let us have him!*

*I have to survive, Lucas,* came the calm reply.

"Romana's on that chopper, too," he said out loud to Tim.

"And Sangor needs help," Tim remarked. "I'm gonna go help him; Lucas, *stay with the plane.* Got it?"

"Got it," Lucas nodded frantically. "Go."

Tim took off running. Across the tarmac, Sangor was in the middle of a crowd of ten hostages who all shot at him at once, though the bullets seemed to bounce off of his coat. He used his flaming swords to slice through their weapons, then tapped them on the head with an open palm. One by one, hostages dropped to the ground, unconscious, though more were still making their way around to the plane. Lucas forced them back with a field as Sangor knocked them out with the hilt of his sword.

"Perfect!" Lucas cried, raising his fist. "Way to go!"

Gunfire rang out from their side of the barricade, and two hostages fell with bullets in their heads. Lucas hurled another shield to protect the rest, then took over the soldiers' radios as more hostages poured from the other four helicopters.

*Don't kill these Rising operatives!* he shouted angrily at the soldiers. *They are the hostages, and they don't know what they're doing!*

He felt another buzz.

*Jess?*

*It's Kenny. We have to get the President out of here.*

*Any ideas?*

*We just have to clear a path for them to move the plane so the pilot can take off, then protect it from getting shot down once it's in the air.*

Lucas surveyed the scene. Besides two cars, the plane was surrounded by five helicopters, plus one in the air. His mind raced. Liam and Romana were still up in the chopper. Why? Both could do a lot of damage down here, if they chose to fight. Lucas guessed that Liam must need a clear view of the scene to control everyone in it, like a chess master with a view of the board. And Romana... she's his protection, in case anyone attacks the chopper. It's smart to keep her beside him. He looked back at the plane; the President and his secret service were still holed up inside. They would not be in any immediate danger as long as Romana stayed up in the sky.

*Alright, I'll work on it,* he told Kenny.

He summoned energy into his hands, then blasted the nearest car with a force field. It skidded back a few feet, its tires screeching, then settled again. Lucas dropped his arms, panting with exhaustion. *I can't do this,* he thought to himself. *It'll take more energy than I have.* He looked back over his shoulder, searching for help. Tim was fighting with Arden, trying to wrestle a rifle out of his hands; just behind him, Kowalski karate-chopped a soldier in the neck.

He spotted Sangor as he knocked out a woman who had been trying to climb over the barricade.

"Sangor! I need help!" Lucas called, waving his hands. Gunshots rang out, and bullets whizzed past his head. He threw up a force field, then gasped to see it was Kowalski who fired on him. *Come on, man,* Lucas thought sadly.

Sangor landed at his side and sheathed his swords. His red eyes flashed and he was breathing hard, but smiling. Lucas noticed more than a few bullet wounds healing in his chest.

"I need you to move these cars," Lucas told him quickly. "We need to give the President room to fly out of here."

"You're helping the man who showed you such disrespect?" Sangor inquired.

"Yeah, well, it's the right thing to do," Lucas said with resignation. "Once these cars are out of here, we'll get rid of the helicopters."

"As you wish," Sangor replied.

He approached the first vehicle, which was riddled with bullet holes. With a groan and creak of metal, he hefted it over his head and hurled it away. The car spun in the air, then crashed to the ground fifty yards away. Lucas focused on the helicopters. With his mind, he found the controls of each aircraft and commanded the computers to overheat and destroy themselves. One by one, the rotors slowed and the choppers settled to the ground. He tried to lock onto the one still hovering above the hangar; maybe he could force it to crash with Liam inside, but had no such luck. He was still blocked out.

*You're wasting time,* Romana said in his head. *You should be getting away from here. I can take you... you don't need to fight.*

*Or you could help me,* Lucas answered with irritation.

*I can only protect you for so long,* she said.

*What does that mean?*

*He's growing annoyed with you.*

The second car was hurled away, and Sangor walked up beside him, dusting off his hands. He looked up at the helicopter and growled.

"Enough playing," he said through gritted teeth. "It's time to end this. Now, it's my turn to fly."

He took his sword from his back and drew it; flames erupted along its length. Then he removed his coat and dropped it on the ground.

"Whoa, whoa, Sangor, wait," Lucas said with surprise. "We still need to move those helicopters over there. What are you doing?"

"Stand back," Sangor said.

He arched his back and gave a pained yell. His bare back seem to bubble, then two great wings erupted from it. Snow-white feathers gleamed in the sun, and they spanned twenty feet across. Sangor crouched as his wings opened, then beat downward. The force generated by his wings caused Lucas to stumble backward, shielding his face. When he looked up, Sangor was already high in the air, soaring toward the helicopter.

"Sangor, wait!" Lucas yelled.

"Lucas!" Tim called frantically. "We need you!"

Three hostages had cleared the barricade, with Kowalski in the lead. He gunned down a soldier, then punched out Tim who attempted to tackle him. Lucas saw with shock that very few soldiers remained alive, while he counted eight hostages not yet unconscious. Kowalski, Arden, and a brown-haired woman that Lucas didn't recognize were marching straight for the plane. Five secret service agents raced down the stairs with guns raised.

"No!" Lucas shouted.

He wrapped a force field around Kowalski, Arden, and the woman, encasing them in a giant, shimmering bubble. His mind in agony, he lifted them up, then carried them backward beyond the barricade while the secret service agents looked on in wonder. The field vanished, dropping them in a pile. After a few seconds, Kowalski got up and continued moving, his face completely expressionless.

*Kowalski stop, please stop,* Lucas begged.

He charged with his mind again, pounding desperately on the barrier surrounding Kowalski's thoughts, but was forced back again by stabbing pain. Liam wasn't going to let him usurp his control.

A loud crash caused him to look up. Sangor swooped under the skids of the helicopter; Lucas could see Romana leaning out the door, her hand outstretched. Sangor's wings locked, then one of them snapped backward at an unnatural angle. He cried out, then began to fall. Twisting in the air, he drew back his hand, then hurled the sword at the underside of the chopper. It pierced through to the cockpit, its flames licking the helicopter's belly, and the aircraft wobbled. For a split second, Lucas could feel its computers in his mind before they completely shorted out. It began to lilt as the rotors slowed, then came crashing down onto the roof of the hangar. Smoke and flames billowed high into the air.

Sangor used his one good wing to glide, then landed at a stumbling run beside Lucas before his wings vanished. He smiled broadly.

"Good job," Lucas said with a grin. "You used your magic and didn't go crazy. How do you feel?"

"I wasn't sure it would work," Sangor replied, breathing deeply. Sweat poured down his face. "But I feel good. I am ready to finish this."

"Then let's go. We still need to move those other choppers."

They took off at a run, but were stopped in their tracks as Liam dropped down onto the tarmac. The concrete cracked beneath his feet as he landed. He straightened up, his pale eyes twinkling as his thin lips curled into a smile. The eight hostages suddenly stopped fighting and looked at Lucas.

"Your time is now at an end," they all said in unison, and chills crawled down Lucas' spine. "The Rising will reign victorious."

"I've dealt with bullies like you before," Lucas replied, glaring at Liam though he shook with fear. "You won't win."

"We already have," said the eight voices. "Because you haven't yet learned how to play the game. But your time is almost up, and I will take the pleasure of killing you myself. You are obsolete, accept it."

Out the corner of his eye, Lucas spied Romana. She appeared beside Kowalski, as if stepping out of thin air. She grabbed his hand, then they both vanished. Sangor drew his two short swords and raised them, roaring loudly. Lucas watched it all as if it happened in slow motion. As Sangor brought down his swords, Romana and Kowalski appeared just behind Liam. Romana reached over and touched Liam's hand, and they both disappeared, leaving only Kowalski standing directly in the path of Sangor's swords. Then Kowalski stepped forward, placed his pistol under Sangor's chin, and fired.

"No!" Lucas cried out in shock.

Sangor's knees sagged, blood leaking out from the open top of his head. He flopped limply onto the ground and Kowalski stepped over him, his face completely expressionless.

"No, no, no no!" Lucas yelled. He ran at Kowalski, throwing up a force field the same instant Kowalski raised his gun again to fire. The bullet bounced off, then Lucas hurled his fist at Kowalski's face. The agent deflected the punch with ease, slamming his own fist into Lucas' side. Ribs cracked, and all the air rushed out of his lungs. Kowalski swept one of his legs and hurled him onto the ground.

"The only way to stop me is to kill me," he said, leaning close with his hand on Lucas' neck.

Lucas glared through his tears.

"That's not you saying that; it's Liam," he choked out. "This isn't you, Seth."

"You have a lesson to learn," Kowalski said in that flat, cold voice. "It's that the old world must pass away for a new one to come. But don't be afraid; Kowalski won't kill you. Remember? I said I want the pleasure of doing that personally."

Kowalski pressed the barrel of the gun to Lucas' forehead.

"I will not lose you," Lucas said through gritted teeth.

He threw his arms out and a force field blasted upward, knocking Kowalski high into the air. He landed hard on his back and let out a groan. Lucas rolled to his feet, his muscles screaming with exhaustion, and waited. Kowalski did not get up. The remaining hostages still advanced on the plane, and the secret service agents scrambled to fight them off. At least they were knocking them out with the butts of their pistols instead of shooting them. Lucas could see a small gap between the helicopters; the plane may be able to fit if he widened it just a little.

He summoned energy into his hands; his reservoir was shrinking. Spots showed in his vision, and his arms felt like lead. He had already conjured more force fields today than he ever had in his life. With a yell, he flung everything he had at the helicopters in a V-shaped field. They crashed apart, then he ran to the stairs and shocked the hostages battling their way up with a few small bolts of electricity. They collapsed, unconscious but still alive. Lucas spotted Arden among them.

"Go, go!" Lucas yelled at the secret service agents. "Get the President out of here!"

"It's too late," one man replied. "He's already gone. We were coming to help you."

"He's gone?" Lucas gasped, his stomach dropping to his feet.

"The girl and that white-haired boy took him," the agent said.

Lucas staggered, catching the rail of the stairs to keep himself steady.

*I failed again,* he thought.

He fell to his knees, tears leaking down his cheeks. He was so tired, and now he was defeated. He had lost.

# CHAPTER 19

———————◆———————

*J*ess stood in the doorway of the hangar, her phone frozen in her hand and static crackling in her ear. She watched Lucas collapse to his knees, his head in his hands and his shoulders bowed. A cool wind whipped across the tarmac, threatening to blow him over, and he didn't fight it. He looked so small and broken.

Less than twenty feet away, Sangor lay on his back on the pavement. His legs were bent at an awkward angle beneath him, and his head was blown open. The blood that pooled around him was dark, almost black, and his red eyes stared up at the sky. Jess couldn't breathe. This couldn't be real… he can't be dead.

Sirens sounded in the distance as the remaining soldiers immediately set about gathering the hostages. The ones that hadn't been knocked out stood around blinking with confusion, like they'd just woken from a dream. The soldiers handcuffed and led them roughly into the hangar, then set them in a group on the floor. Jess spotted Arden being escorted over by two men in dark suits, and her heart leapt. He looked pale, and dark circles showed under his eyes; sweat darkened the front of his shirt, and he had bruises on his cheeks and forehead, but Jess was only thrilled to see him alive. He saw her and began to pull away from the men who held him as his eyes lit up.

"Jess!" he cried. "Jess! You're okay! Oh, thank God!"

"Daddy!" Jess exclaimed, but Kenny clamped a hand around her upper arm.

"Don't, Jess," he said firmly. "You have to stay back."

"What?" she gasped. "Why? He's my dad!"

"He might not be, not anymore," Kenny replied. "You saw what he did. We don't know what they've done to him, or how deep it goes. Trust me, you need to keep your distance."

Jess felt a hard knot form in her throat as the agents led Arden over to the others, his hands cuffed behind his back, and ordered him to sit down on the ground. Huge tears leaked down his ruddy face. Jess looked pleadingly at Kenny.

"He recognizes me," she cried. "It's still him. Please, can't I go?"

Kenny shook his head.

"I will restrain you myself," he said gruffly. "Nobody goes near them until they've been thoroughly checked out."

Then Kowalski appeared, and Jess saw the same pleading, earnest look on Kenny's face as he watched him forced down onto his knees, his hands cuffed. A matted patch of blood was drying on the back of his head. Kowalski sat, his face drawn and his eyes hollow. Kenny clenched his jaw, and Jess touched his arm sympathetically. Whatever was going to happen next, she realized, it was going to be hell for everyone.

All of the hostages gradually became more alert, the sleepy, dream-like look in their eyes replaced by horror and panic. They talked loudly over each other, and some sobbed on the ground.

"I didn't do this!" one cried.

"It wasn't my fault," another wailed. "I didn't want to do any of it, but I had no control!"

"What happened? Please tell me how this happened! I want to go home!"

The room was soon filled with terrified, shouting voices while the soldiers looked at each other helplessly. The only two people who stayed quiet were Kowalski and Arden.

"How will we know when they're safe?" Jess asked quietly. "Who's going to check them out?"

Kenny nodded over his shoulder. "Lucas. He's the only one who can safely go near them. It has to be him."

Tim entered with a frail-looking Lucas beside him. A huge cut bled from the bridge of Tim's nose and he favored one leg, but still he walked with his head high and a steady hand on Lucas' shoulder until they reached the cluster of hostages. Then he backed away, leaving Lucas standing in front of the group, alone. Jess remembered what Lucas had said about how the nanomachines could talk to each other, which meant he could read the minds of other androids that had them in their heads, and she had a bizarre thought: If everyone in that group had been infected with the nanomachines, would Lucas be able to see inside their heads? Could he read her dad's mind?

The hostages fell silent as Lucas approached, watching him apprehensively. His obsidian eyes looked them over with a stern expression, and Jess wondered how he could stay so calm... until she saw his hands shaking as they hung by his sides.

"I am not your enemy," he said with a steady voice, addressing the group. "I am Lucas Tavera, and I have worked with the United States government in secret for quite some time now. You should know that I have powers like Romana and Liam, the two androids who took you from your homes and gave you to the Rising, but I am not like them. I am here to help."

His voice grew stronger the longer he talked, and his hands became steady. The hostages listened quietly with wide eyes.

"You all have been infected with nanomachines," he continued. "Microscopic devices that inhabit your body and invade your brain. I have them in my body, too. They give me my powers, but you... they've made you susceptible to mind control."

He said this with a broken voice, and a few of the hostages began sobbing loudly again. Most just cried silently.

"Now, please," Lucas said. "Can any of you tell me what happened? Anything that you can remember about what the Rising did?"

"I was sitting at home in my living room!" a man with spiky brown hair shouted. "Then I woke up in a cage! I didn't want any of this - I was kidnapped!"

"I understand," Lucas replied. "None of you wanted to do what you did. Do you remember how they put the nanomachines in you? What it looked like?"

"Lucas," Kowalski spoke up with a serious tone. "You have to get us out of here. We're still vulnerable - they could control us again. We have to be locked up right away."

"Speak for yourself!" another man shrieked. "I had no control over my body, it was like someone else was driving. I could see and hear everything but I couldn't move my own limbs! It was a nightmare!"

Others nodded in agreement.

"We were controlled," a woman said. "It was the white-haired boy!"

"I know that. But -" Lucas said, growing frustrated.

"Lucas," Jess called.

He looked at her, and she beckoned to him. He walked slowly over, glancing back over his shoulder at the hostages. When he was close enough, she leaned in to whisper.

"You can feel their minds, right?" she asked.

"Yes," he admitted, glancing away.

"Can you see what's in their heads?"

"Yes."

"What?" Kenny exclaimed from nearby. Tim was staring at him, too.

"What are you talking about?" he asked seriously.

Lucas looked pleadingly at Jess, who pressed her lips together.

"I can read their minds," Lucas explained, shamefaced. "It's the nanomachines; I can see everything they saw, and hear what they're thinking."

"They're not going to give you a straight story if you just ask them to tell you," Jess told Lucas quickly. "You've got to look into their heads and pull it out of them."

"I don't know what that will do," Lucas protested. "Last time I tried was with a person who was already broken. I don't want to risk causing more damage."

"What do you mean, 'last time'?" Tim demanded. "You've done this before?"

"Yes, with Brick," Lucas said impatiently. "We could communicate telepathically."

"When were you going to tell us this?"

"Probably never, so you wouldn't look at me like you are right now!" Lucas snapped.

"Okay, everyone stop!" Jess broke in. "Look, we need you do it now, okay? We can hash all this out later, after we've dealt with the immediate problem. Got it?"

Tim and Lucas continued to glare at each other, but Lucas slowly nodded. Then he walked back over to the hostages. He stood there silently, his eyes closed, Jess watched, trying to imagine what it all looked like to him, venturing into people's minds. Mostly, she just hoped it would work.

His head bowed to one side, and occasionally his fingers twitched, but other than that he was motionless. The minutes passed by quickly, and no one in the hangar spoke a word. The group of hostages stared up at him with wide, terrified eyes, as if they feared he was going to suddenly call down lightning on them. Then, one person at a time, they each flinched with eyes squeezed tightly shut in discomfort.

"What's happening?" Kenny asked in a whisper, tensing up. "This is taking too long."

"Just give him a chance," Jess replied.

Tim stood by, arms crossed.

"Who's Brick?" Jess asked him. "What were you guys talking about?"

"For twelve years, Lucas was the only person *ever* to come in contact with the nanomachines and live, and that was because of his special genetic code," Tim explained. "He was made to coexist with them. Then a kid named Brick touched them and became infected. Lucas saved his life, but a remnant of nanomachines was left behind in his head. He was mostly paralyzed, and lived out the last year of his life in extreme pain and suffering until Romana killed him. Needless to say, that's not the case with these guys, so what's changed? What do the Rising have now that they didn't before?"

Jess bit her lip, remembering the story that Lucas had told her days before. *Brick… that was Lucas' closest friend, the one who died because of these nanomachines.*

She watched her father, his face scrunched up in obvious pain. She dearly hoped the same wouldn't happen to him.

While the others watched Lucas, EMTs arrived to treat the wounded. Several soldiers were loaded up and taken away in ambulances, while the dead were placed in body bags. Jess spotted the men in dark suits, speaking quietly with some emergency technicians who covered Sangor's body with a yellow tarp. The emergency technicians left, but the two men stayed. They folded their hands behind their backs and stood still, watching the goings-on outside. Jess narrowed her eyes. Were they *guarding* the body? And who are they? CIA? Secret service? It seemed that the government never stopped taking interest in the alien. She wondered what would happen to him now that he was dead. She felt a pang of sympathy in her chest; he may have been a jerk, but she couldn't forget the pain and suffering she'd seen in his eyes. It would be wrong, if he ended up a government lab experiment, opened up on some table. He at least deserved a proper burial.

She clenched her fists with frustration. Apparently, she never really stopped worrying about him either. But what could she do?

Suddenly, Lucas let out a sigh and opened his eyes. He looked at the soldiers standing by and pointed at Kowalski and Arden.

"These two, I need them separated from the group," he ordered. "Take the others to that back room there and watch them."

It took a few minutes of scuffling, getting the hostages on their feet and herded across the hangar to an office in the back before Kowalski and Arden were left alone, seated ten feet apart. Lucas knelt down in front of Arden, who looked absolutely panicked, his eyes were wide open and his jaw slack. Jess squeezed Kenny's hand hard as Lucas, eyes closed, placed a hand on each side of Arden's head at the temples. Arden's face went blank, his eyes staring upward. Lucas' face scrunched up in concentration for nearly a full minute, then he released Arden and straightened up, swaying unsteadily.

"I need to eat," he gasped.

"Somebody get him some food," Tim called loudly.

A couple of agents brought over a sandwich, granola bar, and bag of trail mix. He sat on the ground as everyone, especially Jess, waited anxiously for him to eat.

"Well?" Kenny prompted. "Did you see anything?"

"Too much," Lucas answered tiredly.

"How did the Rising do this?" Tim asked. "How are these people still alive?"

"I don't know that," Lucas replied. "Arden saw a lot of things while he was in that lab, but I don't understand any of it and neither does he. But I do know that they took my arm from the CIA office, and that had to be for a reason. Maybe they were able to do something with that, or learn something they didn't know before. But he saw a lot of other things... like Dr. Lytton."

"Who?" Jess asked.

"The guy who invented the nanomachines inside me," Lucas said. "And inside all of them. They have him; he's alive, but in very bad shape. They also have a lot more androids growing in these… I guess they're like pods."

"Where?" Tim asked.

"Same place they were keeping Kowalski and Arden, and all the other hostages. They took more girls to make them; Arden saw at least five."

"This is awful," Jess said, horrified.

"It is," Tim nodded, grim-faced. "And we will stop it, but first we have to deal with these hostages. How do we keep these people from being controlled by Liam again? Can the nanomachines be removed?"

"Not by me," Lucas replied, fear flashing in his eyes. "The last time I tried, with Brick, it put him through a lot of pain."

Tim seethed. "More secrets?" he hissed. "You're really digging a deep hole for yourself."

Lucas looked away, his expression dark.

"But he lived, didn't he?" Kenny cut in. "He wasn't any *worse* off, right? You have to try again."

Lucas shook his head.

"No, I can't."

"Lucas, you have to try," Jess begged. "Kowalski's right - it's only a matter of time before Liam comes back and makes them do something awful. Please, save my dad. We had a deal!"

Lucas looked at her. She could see the terror behind his stern exterior, but she glared back determinedly. Arden *had* to be saved, and she wouldn't let up until everything possible had been done. Lucas set his jaw, then stood up. Without a word, he walked back over to the middle of the room. He stopped when he was directly between Arden and Kowalski, then took a deep breath and slowly raised one hand. His fingers waved gently, as if to some unheard music, and his hand passed slowly over Arden's head, then drifted to Kowalski. Lucas stepped closer; Kowalski looked like he was nearly asleep, but when Lucas' fingers met his temples, he tensed, then let out a blood-curdling scream.

"Jesus!" Kenny cried, clapping his hand over his ears.

Kowalski shivered, then thrashed, his heels scraping the concrete.

Lucas gripped the sides of his head with both hands and held on, his eyes squeezed shut. Tim ran over and grabbed Lucas' shoulders in an attempt to pull him off.

"Stop! Alright, stop!" he shouted. "It's killing him!"

Lucas pushed him away. He hurled him back with one hand, and Tim gaped with surprise.

"This is what you wanted," Lucas said, his eyes glistening with tears. "This is what it takes to get them out, so he can be free… and safe."

Kowalski continued to scream, and Arden leaned away from him in terror. Jess covered her ears and looked away because she couldn't bear to watch anymore. She began to regret deeply asking Lucas to do this. What if it *did* kill Kowalski? Would it do the same to Arden? If he was torn apart on the inside and paralyzed like Brick, would it be worth it?

Then she realized someone else was yelling. Another voice rang through the doorway of the hangar. Jess stepped around the Jeep and craned to look. There was movement under the tarp. She froze, her heart pounding. That's where the yelling was coming from. The dark-suited guards stared at it in panic, talking urgently into their radios. The body sat up, and Jess couldn't help it. She screamed.

She turned and ran back into the hangar, where Lucas released his hold on Kowalski. He blinked absently while Kowalski flopped to the ground like a landed fish.

"I can't do this," Lucas intoned as Jess grabbed his hands. "They're in his brain, and I don't know how to remove them without killing him."

"We've got other problems now," she said breathlessly. "Look! Look at Sangor!"

Sangor ripped the tarp off, his face streaked with blood. The top of his head was closed up and his hair matted. He gazed around with a desperate, confused look on his face, then clambered ponderously to his feet as Lucas ran forward. The others hung back warily, while Tim helped Kowalski sit up again.

"Sangor?" Lucas gasped. "You're alive?"

Recognition flickered across Sangor's face. He opened his mouth to talk, then coughed violently.

"What happened?" he choked out. "Where am I?"

"Kowalski shot you," Lucas answered. "We thought you were dead."

"Yeah, well, it would take more than that - " Sangor broke off, coughing again, then pressed a hand to his chest. He winced, then swayed unsteadily.

"Are you okay?" Lucas asked. "What's wrong?"

Sangor's expression became fearful; his breath quickened.

"My heart -" he grunted. "I have to calm down... the magic - it's happening."

"Uh oh," Kenny said ominously beside Jess. Her heart began to sink.

*Come on, Sangor,* she pleaded mentally. *Stay calm... don't change... please don't...*

"Okay, just take a few deep breaths," Lucas said. "You're alright; you've healed, and everything is fine."

Sangor gasped, clutching his chest. He fought to take a breath, then collapsed to his knees.

"No... no, no, no, please!" he cried out as he gasped.

"Sangor, you can do it, just breathe!" Lucas shouted at him.

"I won't go!" Sangor yelled in panic, on all fours now. "I can't! Please, no!"

His back shuddered, then his ribs began to expand with a horrible popping noise. Jess couldn't take it anymore. She forced her feet forward and threw herself down beside him. She touched his shoulder, then jerked her hand back. His skin burned like a hot stove, and his sweat began to evaporate in thin clouds of vapor.

"Lucas, remember what Larathel said?" Jess cried, turning to him. "He can't transform again, it could kill him!"

Lucas just stared, his expression hollow. He was at a loss, unsure how to prevent it from happening, now that it had already begun. He stood paralyzed, but Jess refused to give up.

"Sangor, listen to me!" Jess cried. "You can stop this. You're afraid, I know you are, but you can control this. You don't have to let your fear swallow you - you're stronger than that! Don't fight it anymore. This is your power, you can take it back!"

He looked at her as his body shook, and his eyes changed from red to yellow.

"I... can't..." he groaned.

Then his head snapped to the side. His joints popped out of place, and his neck and face stretched. His fingers grew longer and longer, with webs forming between them, and his entire body continued to swell in size.

Kenny grabbed hold of Jess' arm and jerked her out of the way. Sangor was covered in scales now and big enough to fill the doorway of the hangar, and still growing. The pavement cracked under massive claws, and his arms had become wings the size of sails. A snake-like creature now towered over them, its tail whipping through the air. It lowered its diamond-shaped head into the hangar.

"That is a dragon," Kenny gasped with disbelief. "That is a freaking dragon."

The creature's tongue flicked in and out, and a nictitating membrane blinked over yellow eyes the size of the Jeep's tires. Its mouth opened, revealing teeth like daggers.

"Lucas, what do we do?" Tim asked, backing away.

Lucas saw the dragon fix its burning gaze on Kowalski, who still sat looking dazed. As the dragon's tongue flicked over him, he seemed to come alert.

"Jesus Christ!" he yelled, squirming.

The dragon hissed and raised its head, its horned crest scraping the ceiling. Arden yelled in fear, fighting to get up. The dragon opened its mouth, and a glow began at the back of its throat. Lucas leapt in front of Kowalski and Arden and created a wide force-field dome just as a torrent of fire blasted from the dragon's mouth. From inside the dome, the fire was refracted into a kaleidoscope of rainbows. It cascaded over them, and Lucas strained. He was still so tired. As soon as the blast ceased, the dragon let out a terrifying, ghost-like shriek, and Lucas hurled a lightning bolt at it. Thunder crashed through the hangar, and he put on his goggles.

"Tim! Kenny!" he yelled. "Get these guys to safety!"

Lucas knew he had to get the dragon out of the hangar before it brought the place down on top of them; there were still helpless hostages trapped in the back room. Tim and Kenny snatched up Kowalski and Arden, and half-dragged, half-carried them to the back of the hangar. The dragon reared back, its claws raking the concrete and its horned crest rent a gaping hole in the metal siding. With a hiss, it attempted to snake his head around Lucas and bared its teeth at Kowalski. Lucas fired another bolt, forcing it back.

"Sangor, this is really not a good time!" he yelled up at the dragon. "We have bigger problems, okay? You've got to get your shit together, right now!"

The dragon shrieked in response, and the fiery glow ignited in its mouth again.

*Oh no, you don't,* Lucas thought.

He unfurled a force field and wrapped it around the dragon's mouth like a muzzle. The fire was extinguished with a puff of smoke. Then he blasted it with a long, sustained lightning bolt - the biggest one he had ever created. The dragon began to back slowly away from the hangar, scales rustling. Its tail slashed through the helicopters with a screech of metal and a shower of sparks. Lucas staggered, then leaned against the doorway as the dragon's chest smoldered; it arched its back and narrowed its burning yellow eyes at Lucas.

*I can't keep this up,* Lucas thought, gasping for breath. *I'm going to wear out before he does.*

A buzz went off in his skull and he picked up the call.

*Make it quick,* he groaned.

*Lucas!* Jess' voice cried in his head. *The power lines! Use the powerlines!*

Lucas looked up. Thick powerlines fed into one corner of the roof. With his goggles, he could see the high voltage flowing through them. Jess was a genius.

With a breath, he stretched out his hand. His brain called out to the electricity that pumped through the cables overhead. A loud hum sounded, and with an explosion of sparks, crackling power flowed into him. He reached his other hand out toward the snarling dragon. With a thunderous boom, a river of lightning blasted into the dragon. Lucas' suit began to smoke and he felt his skin cooking beneath it, but he didn't stop. He felt like every one of his cells was filled with energy to the point of bursting. The dragon shook itself, then arched its back. It reared up with a piercing wail and spread its wings, and Lucas feared that the lightning wasn't working. Then, to his surprise, it began to shrink.

*It's working, Lucas! Don't stop!* Jess cried.

He gritted his teeth as his muscles began to jump and spasm. Black spots began to appear in his vision and he was certain that his suit was beginning to melt now, but he continued to unleash the full force of his power as the dragon continued to grow smaller, and its wings shrank back into fingers. He let up only when Sangor had returned to the shape of a man, and collapsed onto the ground, gasping.

Lucas dropped his arms, panting heavily. He felt like his lungs were on fire. Sangor lay on the concrete, naked and shivering, and mumbling under his breath. His eyes were wide, yet unseeing, and his skin was white as paper. Pity weighed in Lucas' heart. He walked over and picked up Sangor's coat, then covered him with it. He knelt down beside him, cradling his head with one hand as Sangor flinched and made choking noises. Lucas could feel his pulse racing under his fingers.

*He can't control himself,* he thought. *Maybe he never will; it's just a matter of time before he transforms again, and one more time could kill him. I have to do something… or he will die. And I think I know what that thing is.*

It was a long shot, but if it worked, he could save Sangor's life. One thing was certain: Sangor was out of time and options. He removed the glove from his left hand, then picked up one of the short swords that lay nearby. With the tip, he sliced open his palm.

"Lucas?" Tim asked, approaching warily. Jess was close behind him. "What are you doing?"

"Saving his life," Lucas answered. "There's only one option left; I have the one thing that can save him. It's necessary."

Bright, electric blue liquid began to pool in his hand as the nanomachines poured out of his veins. Tim and Jess gasped.

"Is that - ?" Jess stammered.

"Lucas, no, don't do it!" Tim cried.

Before they could move, Lucas pressed his palm to Sangor's forehead. His body tensed, and he felt like a knife was being twisted in his chest. Then pain spread to his entire body. He felt that terrible, horrible pull as each of his cells responded to the nanomachines' irresistible magnetic force. He gritted his teeth against the pain until he felt a strong hand wrap its fingers around his wrist and pry him off. It was Sangor.

# CHAPTER 20

His fist suddenly collided with Lucas' jaw, sending him flying onto his back. Lucas saw stars as he sat up, head spinning with the shock.

"Sangor?" he mumbled. His jaw felt like rubber.

Sangor was trying to roll over, but his movements were wild and clumsy. He swiped at the air, then glared at Lucas.

"What did you do to me?" he snarled.

Lucas couldn't believe it. He had feared the results would be similar to Brick's experience with the nanomachines, remembering his violent seizure. Sangor struggled to push himself up from the ground, to no avail. His arms shook, then gave out. Lucas bent down and took his hand to pull him up, but Sangor roughly pushed him away.

"I saved your life," Lucas said with earnest. "You were dying, and couldn't control yourself. I can help you now!"

"Lucas, what have you done?" Tim demanded.

"It was the only way," Lucas replied, a knot forming in his throat. "Like Kenny said, he would be no worse off..."

"He was talking about *removing* the nanomachines, not purposely infecting someone with them! You don't know what this could do! What if Romana or Liam gets control of him!?"

Jess suddenly screamed. Tim whirled around and Lucas jumped. He saw her face go white as a black pistol was pressed to her temple and an arm wrapped around her torso. He gasped when he recognized Kowalski's face beside hers as he forced her to walk forward, and she whimpered.

"That distraction was exactly what I needed," Kowalski said in a low voice.

"Seth, what are you doing?" Tim exclaimed.

205

"That's not Seth," Lucas said, clenching his fists.

He could feel Liam's mind inside Kowalski's and hear his thin, rasping voice speaking in unison with his baritone. As soon as he recognized this, a stabbing pain attacked his own mind, forcing him to retreat. Then he felt a change: far away, he sensed the presence of Sangor's mind, a bizarre and wild force. He saw an image of a flagstone courtyard at dusk, the air rosy under a sunset that made the clouds look like they were on fire; gnarled trees with massive trunks grew around it. He knew they were massive because a woman stood beside one of the roots, and it came higher than her waist. She had red eyes like Sangor's, and violet-colored hair down to her waist. A delicate crown sat on her head, and she wore a golden dress with a belt set with diamonds.

Lucas was so stunned by the sight of this woman that he didn't notice right away that there were other people around. Other Bederians - some with black hair, some with red hair and pointed ears, and some with sea-green eyes - stood conversing nearby. One, a young girl with a yellow braid, brought the woman a stemmed crystal cup on a silver tray. She took it with long, slender fingers and brought it daintily to her lips. Over the tops of the trees, glittering towers disappeared into the clouds.

A deep hum echoed in Lucas' mind, and at first he wondered if an earthquake was coming to this beautiful place. Then he realized with dread that it was another mind invading. It came like a frost, the courtyard scene fading away under its touch. *Liam.* The images disappeared altogether, and Lucas found himself in a vast network of lights and sounds. He heard voices speaking in languages he'd never heard of, and saw snippets of pictures - all fragments of thought moving faster than he could see. It was a labyrinth, but Lucas knew instinctively where to go. He settled himself in the back corners of Sangor's mind, then imagined roots planted there. As the foreign mind wound its tendrils inside, Lucas attacked viciously. He blasted it with his lightning, fueled by his rage, while his own mind remained strong and immovable.

The other mind fought back with daggers like icicles, which evaporated on contact with Lucas' heat. Encouraged, he focused his attacks, scorching Liam's presence away. As Liam's mind faded, Lucas gathered strength. When the foreign consciousness was gone, he moved his mind's eye outside. He saw Sangor, kneeling with shoulders bowed, and Kowalski's wickedly grinning face.

"Well done," he chuckled gleefully. "At last, you have learned to play the game."

A sinking feeling grew in Lucas' stomach as he stared down at Sangor's weakened, defeated form and realized with horror what he had done.

"No," he said quickly. "I did it to save his life."

"You *own* him now," Liam said, laughing uproariously through Kowalski's mouth. "You hypocrite! You must feel so awful!"

Lucas saw Tim, Jess, and now Kenny, who walked up slowly with a bleeding wound in his forehead. He felt their horrified gazes, and read the expressions of fear and confusion on their faces.

"No, I will never control him," he said through clenched teeth. "He's sick, that's the only reason this happened. I'm not like you."

"It doesn't matter; you've done it, and you can't back out of the game now. What shall we have our mindless minions do? Fight each other? My Kowalski and your Sangor will fight, and we'll see who lasts longest!"

"Stop!" Lucas roared. "That's not what this is about!"

"That's *exactly* what this is about!" Liam shouted back, his pitch rising. Jess was fighting back sobs, trapped as she was in his arms. Lucas took a deep, steadying breath. Things could not get out of hand, or she could die.

"This is about you and me," he said slowly. "What do you want from me? Why are you doing this?"

"You have never known the suffering that I have," Liam replied. "But now you will. You will know the pain - the *agony* that I feel every day, and then I will kill you."

Kowalski opened his arms and Jess dashed away from him, her cheeks red from crying. Tim placed himself between her and Kowalski, who was now holding the gun to his own head.

"This is the game," Liam said with another chuckle. "*This* is the future of your world."

"Liam, don't," Lucas begged.

"You can't stop me; I own him. I will finish him and then the rest of you!"

*Wanna bet?* Lucas thought.

His heart pounded with rage. Using his own mind like a battering ram, he attacked Kowalski's mind. He was met by painful spear-like resistance from Liam, but he powered through. He *had* to. He had to end this, and free Kowalski. Through the downpour of defensive attacks, he could hear Seth's voice... his real voice, crying out.

*Lucas... I'm sorry. I'm so sorry for this.*

It was as if Lucas had been flipping through the different channels on a radio as he evaded Liam's psychic arrows, and had finally found the right one. There it was: Kowalski's mind, buried deep beneath Liam's deep, poisonous roots. Lucas began to pull them up, one by one, freeing Seth Kowalski's consciousness. It emerged, wary and weak, like someone long trapped under mountains of rubble. Then it shrank back.

*No, listen to me,* Kowalski said weakly. *I don't want to hurt anyone else. I don't want to be used anymore.*

*And you won't be, once I free you,* Lucas beckoned, drawing him back out.

Liam continued to fight, his mind pushing against Lucas' with Herculean power. Lucas rooted himself and unleashed more fire and lightning. More and more of Liam's roots were unearthed and then sliced away with impunity.

*Lucas... your mother, I can't hurt her. I can't bear the thought that they would use me to... do something awful. To hurt her, or you. I can't do it... I can't leave myself vulnerable.*

Just a little more. His voice was stronger now. Liam was forced back even farther though he fought like a rabid cat.

*Seth, I'll protect you. I can do that now.*

*You can't. Not anymore.*

*No, Seth listen,* Lucas begged, his eyes filling with tears. *You're going to be a dad. My mom's pregnant, she told me today... I'm gonna have a little brother or sister, and you're gonna be a part of the family. We can be a real family, all of us. So you can't quit now, okay? We need you.*

Elation traveled across their link. He saw an image that Kowalski's mind had generated of himself holding a dark-haired baby and seeing Leah's happy tears. All of Lucas' anger completely vanished at the sight, replaced by warm happiness. For the first time, he saw what he, Kowalski, Leah, and their unborn baby could be: a real family. Lucas realized, with a deep ache in his heart, how desperately he wanted that.

*I'm going to be a dad?* Kowalski gasped.

*Yes, that's right,* Lucas answered tenderly. *So you've gotta fight, okay? You can't give up. You've got to keep going.*

The elation faded into sadness.

*I am so proud of how far you've come,* Kowalski said. *You are so brave, and strong. You're stronger than me, that's for sure. I want you to know that whatever happens, it's not your fault. You have carried far more than anyone your age ever should, and I don't want you to carry this. It's just that... I'm scared. I'm afraid of what they could make me do to you.*

Liam was cast out completely, and the loud hum vanished. Lucas was fully rooted in Kowalski's mind now, immovable as a mountain. He began to build up sturdy, impenetrable walls around himself. No one else would ever get in; he would make sure of it. It was quiet now, just the two of them. Even the low, deep hum of Romana's mind was gone, to Lucas' surprise and relief.

*What are you talking about?* he asked as he worked. *Seth, what do you mean?*

*You'll be okay. You can do this on your own now; I believe in you. Most of all... remember, this was my choice.*

Lucas got another image of Kowalski, his blond hair a mess and his tie crooked, The sun shone brightly behind his head. They were back in the desert, after Lucas fought Larathel. He heard Kowalski's voice, shouting at Arden: *I love that boy like he's my own son, and I have done everything possible to keep him safe... Everything that I do is for him! Do you understand?* He remembered Kowalski kneeling down in front of him, embracing Lucas tightly, and he felt all the relief and joy that he had felt then flow into him. He felt Kowalski's rock-solid certainty that he was going to be okay. He felt pride swell his chest, and most deeply of all, he felt love cascading across their mental link. He felt it as Kowalski felt it, and it was as real as his own heartbeat.

Then the pistol fired.

Kowalski's hand dropped, and the gun clattered onto the ground. Then he collapsed to the pavement in a heap, blood leaking from the hole in his head. Lucas felt the silence; the space he had been rooted in was now gone, a vacuous hole in his consciousness. Kowalski was gone, his body lying in a quickly-expanding pool of blood.

"No," Lucas gasped, his hands falling open. "No, no, no, no, *NO!*"

He crumpled to the ground, crushed by the sensation that the world was suddenly breaking apart and falling down on top of him. He couldn't breathe. Everything was blurry through his hot tears. His mind was filled with the explosion of light, pain, then deafening silence... repeating... over and over again.

# CHAPTER 21

---·◆·---

Jess stared, dumbfounded, as Tim and Kenny sprang into action. Lucas knelt on the ground, as still as a statue, staring at Kowalski's body.

"Lucas," she whispered. She felt like a sledgehammer had just crashed into her chest.

Then the agents sprang into action. Kenny raised his gun and pointed it at Lucas while Tim forced him onto the ground. He put his knee on his back, pinning Lucas to the ground, then began to cuff his hands.

Jess was stunned. "Wait, what are you doing?" she cried. "Stop! That wasn't his fault!"

"Stay back, Jess!" Kenny yelled. "He's dangerous!"

"No, he's not!" Jess yelled. "Stop! Leave him alone!"

Another agent grabbed her and held her back in a bear hug. Lucas didn't resist as his hands were tightly secured, even has while face was being pressed roughly into the pavement.

"I'm so sorry," Tim's voice said in his ear. "I'm so, so sorry."

Lucas couldn't tear his eyes away from Kowalski's white, emotionless face that lay only a few feet away. Eventually, it was covered by a tarp and he found himself being lifted up, then placed in the back seat of a Jeep. Something sharp stung him in the neck. Then everything went black.

Jess watched him being carried away and fought against the agent's arms. She twisted and kicked. "No, I need him!" she screamed. "I need him to save my dad!"

Only when the Jeep pulled away did she finally stop struggling. Then she stared, tears streaming down her face, long after it disappeared into the distance. The agent let her go, and she felt like she was about to sink into the ground and disappear.

Kenny stood over Kowalski's body, his shoulders slumped.

"We were at Camp Peary together," he said softly. "Bravest guy I ever knew."

Tim covered his mouth, taking a deep breath. He put a hand on Kenny's shoulder. Jess watched the both of them, rage and confusion welling up inside her.

"Lucas didn't do that," she said firmly.

"You want to try and prove it?" Tim snapped, whirling to face her. "The higher-ups will want answers. I don't even know how to begin explaining this!"

"What's going to happen to him?" Jess asked, her voice shaking.

"Whatever chance he had at freedom is gone. He's going to sleep, probably forever."

"That's not fair!" Jess cried. "He didn't do this!"

"Yeah, well," Tim said flatly, shoving past her. "He didn't stop it, either."

# CHAPTER 22

———————◆———————

Location Unknown

*L*ucas woke up in a concrete room. The ceiling and walls were the same dull gray, with rows of tube lights giving off a stale, white glow. He lay on a metal-framed cot, still wearing his suit, though his gloves and boots were missing. At the foot of the bed sat a stack of white cotton clothes. Adrenaline shot through his veins as panic set in. He struggled to sit up, casting his mind outward to get his bearings.

*No, no… not another underground room,* he thought, his heart racing. *Not again.*

Yet that was indeed where he seemed to be. He couldn't feel anything except the electricity that powered the lights and door to his room. A thick, green metal door stood to his left, with a camera mounted in the corner above him. Everything looked… old. Decades old. It smelled like dust and mildew, and the air pumping through the overhead vent was cold and damp. He angrily shut off the camera, then the rest of the power. The result was inky darkness and oppressive silence. Lucas wondered if this was what it was like at the bottom of the ocean. Even in his thickly woven suit, he was cold, and hugged himself for warmth. Then, just to be rid of the eerie blackness, he willed the lights back on.

"Hello!?" he yelled, pacing the perimeter of the room. "Anybody out there?"

He almost called for Kowalski before the weight of grief found him again and he felt suddenly sick. Kowalski was gone. Dead. That reality was like a lead blanket on his shoulders.

But there was something else out there. A flicker of light and electrical force that his mind reeled in like a fishing line. He bridged the connection, then felt around with his thoughts. Whatever this was, it was familiar, yet chaotic. A million lights and sounds floated haphazardly through a vast maze. Lucas dove further, then recognized his surroundings.

*Sangor?*

The response was immediate. A loud flash, like a firecracker, blew up in his mind.

*Get out!* Sangor's voice shouted.

The attack wasn't enough to force him out. He was already rooted like a tree in Sangor's consciousness. He wormed his way through the maze, then found himself looking out through Sangor's eyes. From what he could see, Sangor was lying on his side on a cot, in a similar room. In fact, he was right next door. He was wearing plain cotton clothes, too.

*Look, I'm sorry,* Lucas said gently.

*You had no right,* came a snarling reply.

*I promise, I only did it to save your life. You were going to die. But now that I'm in your head, I can help you. You won't be able to transform accidentally because I can stop it. We can learn to control your magic together!*

*You said yourself that you wouldn't control me; I heard you say it. Did you lie?*

*No,* Lucas said firmly. *I will interfere only as much as it takes to save your life. I swear it.*

Doubt still carried across their mental link, but also sickness. Lucas sensed pain; Sangor was in physical anguish. He lay curled on the bed with his knees pulled to his chest. His hands shook like leaves.

*If it's any consolation,* Lucas said. *I know how it feels to have someone else in your head and to feel out of control. I don't want to do that to you.*

Instead of answering, Sangor set off another explosive mental flare. It was just as feeble as the last one, but it made Lucas wonder where he had learned to do that. Were psychic attacks common where he came from? Or was it just another one of those forms of magic that all Bederians knew? He backed off anyway, allowing Sangor some space to gather his thoughts. Placing his hand against the concrete wall that separated them, he took a deep breath. The wall felt damp under his fingers, but he sat down with his back against it, then rested his head on his knees and closed his eyes. He was a prisoner again, and it was probably all his fault.

*Please, I don't want to be alone here,* Lucas begged. The emptiness inside him, that hollow ache, felt like a black hole about to swallow him up, and he was terrified of it.

*I have no obligation to make you feel better,* Sangor replied.

*I know that. You must hate me.*

Sangor said nothing, but Lucas could feel the venom in his anger.

*In your head earlier, I think I saw your homeworld,* Lucas ventured. *There was a woman there, with purple hair and a crown, and a golden dress. Who was she?*

The anger lessened by a small degree. It was replaced by a sense of longing. Lucas was surprised. Could the woman have been Sangor's wife, maybe? Or girlfriend? But the memory couldn't have been Sangor's, because he didn't have any of his own left.

*You saw my queen, Anthea,* he said. *One of the few times Larathel ever saw her. We were engaged to be married.*

Lucas was taken aback. He said it so simply, like the words had no weight to them. It was just a fact.

*You had a fiancee? Why haven't you said anything about her until now?*

*Because I don't miss her,* Sangor replied. *I should, and I want to, but how can I pine over someone I barely remember? One of the worst parts of all this is knowing that one day I might see her again, and how much it will hurt her. How could I do that to her? What would I say?*

*Jesus, man, I won't even pretend to have an answer for that one,* Lucas admitted. He had no idea what to say. *I'm so sorry.*

The anger lessened a bit more, but the crushing sadness remained. Lucas decided to change the subject.

*Do you have any idea where we are?* he asked.

*We traveled south,* Sangor answered with a tone of resignation. *That's all I could tell before they put me to sleep.*

*I can't believe all of this happened,* Lucas sighed. *It all went so wrong. And what's going to happen now? They have the President, so the country is probably in chaos, but what I don't get is why they waited. Romana and Liam could've taken him at any time, if they wanted to. Why the fight? Why did they wait?*

*Isn't it obvious?* Sangor replied. *It was all planned. The battle wasn't necessary at all, except as a show of power. That's really what it was all about. A demonstration. It was about gaining attention, then making a show of defeating you and taking your leader. I have been used in the same way, when Morlann cast me out. There's something about seeing a leader fall - not just lose, but fall the farthest that they possibly can - that incites a feeling of defeat in his people. And that's how the enemy wins.*

*Well, the Vice President has likely been sworn in by now, so that -*

*I'm not talking about your President,* Sangor interrupted. *I'm talking about you. You are the leader of the resistance; it is time you saw that. And you are the one that has fallen.*

Lucas rubbed his eyes.

*I don't think I'm ready... I can't lead anyone. Like you said, I've already fallen.*

*Then you must get back up.*

*How?* Lucas pleaded.

A fire seemed to ignite somewhere in Sangor's consciousness: Determination. It traveled into Lucas' mind and burned away tiny bits of the fear and defeat that weighed down upon him. He felt warmer. Sangor coughed, then sat up shakily. He tried to stand, leaning heavily against the bed frame. He was still weak, but stayed upright.

*Well, it seems that we are in a similar predicament,* he said wearily. *But if indeed you can help me get better, then I will help you get your revenge. I did swear to serve you, and I will keep my word. We will escape from this place, Lucas Tavera, then end the Rising once and for all.*

*Thank you,* Lucas replied. *And thanks for not giving up on me.*

*The same to you,* Sangor answered.

A loud clang echoed through the room, and the door shuddered. Lucas jumped to his feet, his fists tightly clenched and raised to fight.

*Someone's coming,* he said.

The door opened, its rusted hinges creaking under its weight. A man in a pinstriped suit stepped inside, and Lucas dropped his hands.

*Who is it?* Sangor asked.

Lucas glared at the man, bile rising in his throat.

"Hello, Lucas," the man said. "I'm Jensen Dunn, director of the CIA, though I'm sure you remember me. Welcome to the Cave."

# EPILOGUE

Austin, Texas

Machines beeped. A rasping, sucking sound emanated from the respirator. Jess sat by the bed, her head in her hands. Arden lay with a tube in his nose and tiny metal disks attached to his forehead and temples. The doctors had shaved his head, and his pale, bare scalp made him look older.

Besides the ECG machine and the respirator, Jess didn't recognize any of the equipment gathered around her father, and she had seen more than her fair share. Monitors displayed colorful graphs and scrolling lists of numbers, and dials swung back and forth. Jess had studied it all for hours before finally giving up. What did it all mean? What was happening to her dad? She didn't know. Did anyone? Did any books or medical charts exist that explained the proper treatment for mind-controlling nanomachines? Arden's barrel chest rose and fell slowly, his eyes rolling back and forth under their lids. People in white coats came and went, intermittently checking the strange machines. They gave her pitying looks over the tops of their clipboards, and it took everything she had to maintain her composure.

"Hey."

Jess turned in her chair, wiping her eyes. Through blurred vision, she saw Kenny standing in the doorway. A thick bandage covered the left side of his forehead, and he held a steaming cup in each hand.

"Here's that coffee you asked for," he said, offering one to her. "Sugar, no cream - right?"

"Right," she said, taking the cup.

"You might want to give it a minute," Kenny told her. "It's real hot. Damn near burned my tongue off."

"It's not for me," Jess answered.

She wrapped her fingers around the styrofoam cup and rested it on her knees. She breathed in the aroma as she watched Arden. Some tiny part of her hoped he could smell it, too.

"You should sleep," Kenny said, studying her.

Jess shook her head. "I can't sleep in hospitals."

Kenny cocked his head to the side, but said nothing. He took a small sip of his coffee.

"He was halfway through his book," she said, her voice tight. "It took him months."

"Reading or writing?" Kenny asked, leaning against the door jamb.

"Writing."

"What was it about?"

"I don't know," Jess replied with a hollow laugh. "I never read any of it. He wouldn't let me, but I didn't really try that hard, you know? I'm not sure he even knew what it was about. He was doing it for her... for Mom. She loved books."

She sniffed, wiping her eyes again. "You guys have his computer," she said. "Maybe you could read it and tell me."

"He'll get better," Kenny said after a moment. "He will, then you can ask him yourself."

"How can you say that?" Jess said, her tone rising. "Nobody here knows what's happening - how can anyone honestly say that? The only person who *knows* for sure is -"

"Shhh," Kenny hissed, stepping forward with a finger to his lips.

Jess glared at him, her breath coming fast, but fell silent. In this room and throughout the corridor, machines continued to beep and hushed, clipped chatter continued.

"You're right," Kenny said in a low voice, his eyes flinty. "Nobody here knows what's going on. And it has to stay that way."

There were so many things that Jess wanted to say, all of it like lead weights on the tip of her tongue. She took a deep breath and opened her mouth.

"Jess," another voice whispered, and she froze. Kenny gaped, staring past her.

She whirled around and saw Arden's head turn her direction, his gray eyes blinking. His face looked Ashen, and his skin papery.

"Daddy?" she squeaked out, practically falling at his side. She felt weak with relief. "How are you? How do you feel?"

"Sick," he grunted, wincing. "The room's spinning."

"It's just the sedatives, Dad," she assured him. Through the corner of her eye, she saw Kenny slip out of the room.

Her fingers wrapped around Arden's, but he didn't hold her hand back. His hand lay limply on the bed.

"I felt him, Jess," he said. "He was in my head. I felt it, and saw it - it was like a movie, everything he was thinking. My thoughts weren't my thoughts anymore… my emotions… whatever he wanted, it happened."

More tears of fury leaked down Jess' cheeks. *Liam.* He truly was a demon.

"I'm so sorry that happened to you," she whispered. "But everything's going to be okay now. We're going to figure out how to fix you, I promise."

His eyes widened, staring. He wasn't looking at her, though, but seemed to be gazing straight through her. The whites were visible all around.

"Kowalski - where is he?" he gasped.

"Um, he's… gone," Jess answered.

"Did Liam get him? He said he was going to."

Jess didn't understand what that meant. "No, he shot himself in the head," she said heavily. "He killed himself."

Arden's lips parted, then his head turned up to the ceiling as he mumbled under his breath. His eyes continued to stare, but remained unfocused, like he wasn't really seeing anything. Jess glanced back over her shoulder and saw Kenny, Tim, and one of the white-coated people watching from the doorway. Suddenly Arden's fingers locked around hers.

"Listen to me," he said hoarsely. "Lucas - you've got to help him. He's got to fight Liam, but he won't win without your help. It's what Liam wants - it's what he's always wanted, more than anything else. Lucas has to win; you've got to make sure of it, or we're all lost."

He looked delirious. Jess didn't know if it was the sedatives or the nanomachines in his mind, but something was definitely off about him. His eyes were wild, and there was spittle in his beard.

"Lucas is good at heart, Jess," he insisted, as if she were arguing with him. "I've seen it, and I've felt it. He is good, and the only thing standing between us and despair. He has to win, do you understand? He has to win!"

Jess swallowed down her sobs. Strong hands took her by the shoulders, and she stood up.

"Come on, Jess," Kenny said gently. "Let's get you home."

Arden's hand slipped away as Jess was guided out of the room. She hid her face, unwilling to look back at him. She trembled until Kenny drew her in close. She took a deep breath, her head on his shoulder and her tears soaking his shirt. Finally, she pulled away.

"Are you okay?" he asked her.

"No," she answered. "But I can do this. I've been here before."

"I'm supposed to take you to your grandparents' house in Odessa."

Jess lowered her brows. "I'm supposed to just go home? Just like that?"

He stood back, crossing his arms.

"That's what you're supposed to do, yes."

There was something in his tone, something he wasn't saying. He raised an eyebrow, and she bit her lip. Twenty feet away, inside a glass-walled hospital room, her father lay broken. People stood around him, talking and writing things down. It all seemed so futile. So meaningless. None of the answers were here.

She lifted her head, standing straighter.

"Are you going to stop me?" she asked.

"If I have to," Kenny replied.

"Are you going to follow me?"

"Depends on where you're going."

She turned on her heel and strode up the hall, without looking back to see if Kenny was coming along. She reached the door and pushed through it without pausing, and his boots echoed behind her.

There was work to be done.

Printed in the United States
By Bookmasters